BAD APPLE

BAD APPLE

BAD APPLE

A NOVEL OF THE ALAMO

LANCASTER HILL

WHEELER PUBLISHING
A part of Gale, a Cengage Company

GALE
A Cengage Company

LIBRARY OF CONGRESS CIP DATA ON FILE.
CATALOGUING IN PUBLICATION FOR THIS BOOK
IS AVAILABLE FROM THE LIBRARY OF CONGRESS

ISBN-13: 978-1-4328-8014-9 (softcover alk. paper)

Published in 2020 by arrangement with Pinnacle Books, an imprint of Kensington Publishing Corp.

Printed in Mexico
Print Number: 01   Print Year: 2020

BAD APPLE

PROLOGUE

Fort Gibson, Oklahoma, May 1836
Ned's Story
Save for the steady *plick, plock, plick* of the longcase clock across the room, it was another cemetery-quiet night at the Hickory Bar. That was the saloon I established two years ago, shortly after graduating from school back east, coming west, losing my wife Lidyann and child in childbirth, and finding just enough silver in a sandstone deposit to buy out the barbershop and the cooper's place. I knocked down the wall between them and used the barrels the cask-maker left behind to start distilling my own brands. One day, I hoped to sell them. First, I had to keep from going broke.

The Hick, as she's called by those who love her, is just a big jump past Fort Gibson, whence came most of my legal clientele. The illegals — Creeks mostly — had a special knock they used at the back door in the small hours of the night to make their own private, illegal purchases. As of this evening, the Indians were my only regular customers, sometimes paying in gold dust; I hadn't much use right now for the animals they also brought in exchange for alcohol, since there was no one around to enjoy my celebrated Three Hare and a Frog Stew.

The Hick was a very private place. The entrance was not at the front but on the side, on a broad alley. That kept the dust and the sound to a minimum. It also allowed me to focus on my job tending bar, not listen for every potential new customer. But there's private . . . and there's dead.

Right now, we were dead.

I take the liberty of sharing this little bit about myself and my place of business because, frankly, this is all the time I get in the footlights. Hereafter, the stage belongs to another. Another who is unlike any man who ever passed through my swinging doors. A man who would become a legend different from the legends he would talk to me about.

This night — the sixth in a row, by my mournful reckoning — the Hick lay as hollow and silent as the Liberty Bell. The chalkboard hanging behind me had the same scant menu it had a week ago. There was a section of the wall across from the door where I hung pictures drawn by customers of the strange things they had seen on their journeys, from man-bears to contraptions that flew. One of my regulars from the fort, a Frenchman, was an expert with the rapier and had given me such a relic to hang there. I looked at it often, thinking about the weapon that helped to conquer an old world compared to the new and better firearms that were spreading us west and south.

I had not added anything new to the wall for weeks. Things had been that way since the troops and harder-drinking officers of Fort Gibson had been sent south to babysit the war. Old Hickory, the president of the United States — for whom this institution was respectfully named — the great Andy Jackson had drug every man in uniform, and some who weren't, from the garrison and sent them to the Texas border in case any Mexicans tried to enter the territory in pursuit of rebels. I didn't know how that struggle for Texian independence was going, save that everyone was upset about the massacre at the Alamo. But I kept a flintlock musket under the bar in case any of Santa Anna's weasels tried to enter the Hick. The only ones who liked those kill-minded loons were the Indians, only because the Mexicans were hated more.

I did have one customer at the moment, though. I'm pretty good at reading my customers, but this was a puzzle of a man.

The oil lamps nailed to the wall behind me, athwart the big mirror, cast just our two shadows across the half-dozen empty tables, the unlit lamps on them, and wooden floors, planks that were scuffed from boots on the bar side, scarred with barrels being rolled and tugged across the other.

The man at my bar was about sixty. He might've been younger; it was tough to say with a face so cracked and lined it looked like sunbaked clay. He wore a beard, though that might be from inattention rather than choice. It was careless and naturally uneven. My customer hadn't bothered to take off his hat, so I couldn't see anything above the middle of his nose. But the tilt of his head said he was looking down. Remembering, from the stillness of him; tired men don't sit still, they pass out. I couldn't tell the man's trade, either. He didn't stink like a trapper or a ranch hand, which was most of my trade that weren't soldiers or Indians. There was a faint smell of gunpowder about him, possibly from the two Colt revolvers I saw him wearing when he walked in. The firearms were new but these did not gleam in the light. They looked as toughened as their owner. There was also a long, sheathed knife tied to his right leg.

The man's clothes looked as weathered as the man who wore them. He had on a sheepskin vest, dirtier I'm sure than the sheep who once wore it. His slouch hat was probably gray under its uneven, dusty coat. His beard and moustache were as un-groomed and woolly as his vest, though they were definitely gray. He had likely washed his face in the horse trough after riding in from wherever he'd come. The mouth tucked amongst the whiskers was pencil straight and only moved for the intake of liquor.

This gentleman's tall, lean frame was bent over slightly, like there was a slow-leaking sack of grain on his shoulders; they had risen just a little since he sat down. He was leaning mostly on his left hand, which was flat-open on the bar. The other hand did not release the glass. I'll get to those hands in a moment.

He was drinking the house whiskey — Wildnut by name, on account of the bit of walnut I brewed in with the alcohol, sugar, and chewing tobacco. He had sat there for maybe ten, fifteen minutes before gulping the glass down. Then he sat there some more, not moving, not saying anything. I gave him a shot on the house, not even sure he could pay for the first one, but what the hell. Another one might open him up, help me pass the night. The man acknowledged by raising a finger. He didn't look up, he didn't say thanks, he just lifted that finger — which, like the rest of him, looked like it had seen better days. Now I've seen stranger fingers since I draped that big OPEN FOR BUSINESS sign outdoors that got blown away the first day. I saw one that got flattened by a cow and looked like a spoon; one that got shot off by an arrow at the knuckle, leaving little notches in the adjoining fingers; one with a tattoo of a naked squaw who danced when it moved. There's a lot of uncommonness comes through my swinging doors.

But these fingers were not simply grotesque, they were — I once heard a traveling salesman describe a brass nutcracker as "utile," and I would use that word to describe eight of these fingers. They were straight and they were filed or stropped sharp, except for the trigger fingers. Those nails were sawed-off at the tip. The skin was also utile — rough-looking, almost like tree bark. Taken as a whole, each hand had four sturdy little knives like some beastie from the English penny awfuls I read when I attended the Philadelphia College of Apothecaries. The creatures and unnatural beasts of those stories gave me the shivers, and so did these devilish little fingers. And they hadn't even done anything, except one of them coming briefly to attention.

That was the thing about this man. Based on absolutely nothing that he had done, he seemed like a coiled snake, just waiting for the wrong thing to make him strike. I didn't want any question of mine to be that wrong thing, so after pouring the second drink I walked away to blow dust from the bottles that lined the wall under the mirror.

But I glanced at him again, though, at his reflection. And I saw something I did not expect to see.

A single lamplit tear on his left cheek.

There being no minted money in these parts, not yet, I was always curious to see what my customers would offer for payment. This man had a pouch under a kerchief and used a long nail to hook out a lump of gold. He dropped it like a shovel emptying dirt. I swept it up, put it in the till behind me, and turned back to him. "Do you have a place to stay?"

After dusting and polishing and stepping

13

outside to look at the full moon, I risked asking that question because it was not personal, it showed polite concern, my voice was quiet like I was talking to a spooked mustang, and it was the kind of thing any barkeep would hospitably be expected to inquire about.

It was the first time I heard or saw the man breathe. He drew air through his nose, the mouth still not moving — though, while I was distracted by my busywork, he had managed to empty the second glass.

"The question I have been pondering, sir," he replied in a deep, quiet voice, "is do I have a place to go?"

He obviously did not mean for the night. His searching question — though directed more at the surface of the bar than at me — prompted me to ask, "May I inquire where you have come from?"

I thought he had gone dumb on me again when he finally answered in a voice barely more than a whisper, *"El degüello."*

That was Mexican death music. It signified the slitting of the throat, murder without quarter. I had heard it discussed by the soldiers, in particular a bugler who played the damn thing and brought the kind of silence to the Hick that is reserved for churches and piano recitals.

14

The man's dull, mournful reply suggested one answer to all the questions I had.

"You were there," I said.

I didn't have to say where "there" was. His silence was my answer.

He had come from the Alamo.

I moved away slowly, respectfully giving him room to reflect without distraction. But he did not seem to need — or want — privacy. He looked up for the first time, that single streak now dry on his cheek. The face was like something on a Creek totem, stiff and grim. But the eyes were bright and green, almost like emeralds with a touch of mint.

"I was there but I was not," he said. "God Almighty, I was unable to help my brethren."

As he spoke, and probably without realizing it, he used the sharp middle finger of his left hand to cut what looked like a small cross in the drink-stained surface of my oak bar.

"What's your name, if you don't mind my asking?" I asked anyway.

"John," he replied wearily, as if he were falling asleep and already had one foot in a dream.

"I'm Nedrick," I told him, a little more sprightly. "Nedrick Bundy."

If he heard, he made no indication. "The *degüello,*" he said again.

"What about it?" I asked.

A pained squint slowly closed in around John's eyes. "They needed guns. Men. You know what I had?"

"Tell me," I said.

He was still looking through me with those narrowed eyes. A second tear followed the first. It was not a dream but a nightmare he was in.

John uttered a single word with such sadness, such longing, that it uncorked a bottle of hurt that just flowed . . .

CHAPTER ONE

Mansfield, Ohio, December 1834
John's Story
For half the year, the hills and the farms are easy. The two fingers of the Mohican River were touched by God with fertility, as surely and whole hog as the rambunctious Adam and Eve. The town that grew there was just as fecund, producing farms and businesses and population with rapidity that at first intrigued the local red men, then perplexed and alarmed them.

I got there in 1832. I was in my fifties, then, and a little less patient than I had been in my youth. No, maybe that's not the word. I was patient to watch things grow. I was unforgiving — that's a better word — unforgiving for things that grew bad. I could nurse blight or bugs from my plants but that was a natural, God-created competition. What people do is rarely that.

Where I lived before, in Warren, Pennsylvania, was showing signs of smoky, noisy blight. Too many forges, too many mills, too much hammering, too many people hollering to be heard, too many horses complaining, too many cartwheels turning, too many youngsters shouting and crying and getting yelled at.

Too much civilization.

I worked on a sheep and goat farm nigh the Allegheny River and wasn't attached to a thing but the earth. I would always stay out until sunset and took that moment to look west and admire what remained of the uncorrupted work of God. I would go to my shack, then, and read the Good Book by the failing light before joining my employers, the elderly Brandons, for supper in the main house. It was over apple pie one night that I announced my intention to leave. I hadn't planned to say that, hadn't even planned to go; it just, suddenly, felt right. I waited till a replacement could be found and set out on a spring morning, at dawn, with just a rifle, my Bible, and a grain sack generously filled with produce I had grown.

It took me about six months to arrive at where I didn't even know I was headed. I was meandering west and Mansfield got in the way. I planted myself there for two reasons. First: the soil was so rich I wept when I touched it. I swear, if there were seeds, those tears would have grown them. It was like God had sent me a vision instructing me to work this land. Second: that good earth was the only sign of God in the region. Oh, people had dutifully built two churches, but few parishioners passed through their doors and the parsons lacked enthusiasm. One of them told me he had agreed to this sinecure just to be close to Pittsburgh for when some aged clergyman there hung up his frock.

"I want to be in a real city," he told me, "with real sin."

I was not sure how the padre meant that, but I decided to trust the calling and not the man.

With more faith than planning, I elected to use what money I'd saved to buy a small plot, plant my own fruits and vegetables, and use the unsteady old barn for Bible meetings.

I did not grow up prayerful. I was born and raised on a small farm in Massachusetts before, during, and after the War for Independence. We were the people who constantly broke the king's peace, and we suffered the first and enduring wrath of the Redcoats. Floggings, hangings, deprivation of goods and services. I learned to shoot at a young age — at game, since my pa was off fighting. I learned to work the land. When the war ended and pa didn't come back, me and my younger brother Nathaniel stayed on till my ma went too. From sadness, I believe. She was the one who had turned to the Holy Book and found solace in its lessons. I often sat by her as she read, more for her comfort than mine. She taught me reading and soon I was reading to her — right up till the end.

Nathaniel apprenticed with a granite-carver — he had the stocky build and arms for it — but I did not want to stay. The spirit of freedom smelled too much like blood. It still does, only then — well, then I was younger and thought a new place would clean it from my nostrils. I picked and hunted my way through New York and into Pennsylvania. I read verse by the light of many a campfire. I felt the presence of God Himself under the million eyes of night — the stars above and the lesser ones lurking in the shadows, "all kinds of living creatures" that were created amidst the innocent coming of the world. I stopped in Warren, partly to share my faith but also to put my hands in soil again, to make things grow. When the choke of man became too great, I departed.

You know of my reaching Mansfield, about me growing food outside the barn and over the next two years, one by one, then two by two, and eventually in groups of ten or twelve growing souls inside the barn. They grew me too, a community of loving souls as surely my God had intended. Eventually, I fell hard in love with a member of the flock: Mrs. Astoria Laveau, a New Orleans–born widow who used her inheritance to found and run a library.

I knew how to read, but it was there, from her, that I learned how to *read*. How to understand what was in the mind of the writer, why words were chosen just so, why some writers described everything in detail and while others did not. Why some stories were told by narrators and others were not. A world opened for me, and with it, my heart opened, too.

Everyone, if they're lucky, has love. She was deeply mine. She was spiritual. She had all those many books — not a day went by that I did not learn from her. She was worldly and desirable, yet we did not cross into sin. Not that I did not desire it. I went to kiss her, one time after a springtime walk, but she bowed her forehead to me. It was love-made-chaste . . . at least, for me. Alas, when I finally summoned the gumption to propose an official courtship, I was spurned. Astoria said she loved me as a preacher, as a friend, as that accursed word "brother," but not as a man. I learned that at the same time I was considering betrothal she had feelings for another man, a blacksmith. It was just gossip, whispers, until they came to a dance together and I saw how affectionate she could be within the bounds of public decency. My heart stopped beating for anything but getting away.

I left carrying what I had left Massachusetts with. It was nearly winter, last winter, and at my age and lack of girth, it meant the only direction I could plausibly head was south.

CHAPTER TWO

Fort Gibson, Oklahoma, May 1836
Ned's Story

"So you got away to Texas," I said. "Love broke your heart. Did Texas heal it?"

"In . . . in a manner of speaking," he replied.

John was still looking ahead. He had told the story without stopping, without hesitation, and without emotion. Just like he was reading from the Bible, but to himself.

When John didn't answer, didn't nod, didn't even blink, I approached the bar with a cloth and pretended to wipe it. I had already done that before he'd arrived, and it was spotless.

"You got to Texas a year ago," I coaxed. "That was before things boiled over."

His eyes shifted to the mirror. If he saw his own reflection, he did not react.

"So few people . . . so much anger," John said. Then said no more.

"I heard people talking here how Santa Anna upset his own people when he threw out the Constitution," I said. "Do you remember that?"

"Central government, more power to him, less to the states," John replied, nodding. "I remember that. And the revolts. We heard about the revolts in Oaxaca, Zacatecas, others."

"We?"

"Colonel Fannin. Colonel Bowie."

"Jim Bowie? It must have been exciting to know him," I said. I took a second look at the knife visible on his hip. It was as sure a *carte-de-visite* as any.

"It was — a time," he said vaguely with the first hint of a smile. "I learned that Bible, fist, and gun were connected. Knit. Security, life, and salvation did not exist separately."

He was becoming talkative and I went to pour him another drink. The hand uncurled from the glass and settled on top.

"Thank you, no," he said. "Any more would be vulgar."

I had no idea what that meant, except that he didn't want any. I set the bottle down. "I have bread . . . some rabbit in the back."

He did not respond. I shouldn't have led him down another road. His story interested

24

me and I wanted to hear it.

"Where did you meet Colonel Bowie?" I asked.

He replied, "Just outside a war, in Mexico."

CHAPTER THREE

Gonzales, Texas, September 1835
John's Story

Working so much in gardens, I had taken to not wearing shoes much. Even when I went south, I preferred to toughen my soles with pinecones and walk like God made His animals to walk, feeling the earth beneath them. As a result, I could feel rocks and sticks and adjust my balance quickly before they knocked or cracked. I made a very, very quiet scout.

I reached Texas in April, intending to make my way to the Gulf. I knew nothing about life on the sea, or boats, and that experience seemed worth having. I had heard there was arable land year-round and that appealed to me. I came to a saloon like this one morning only to discover that I had strayed a little west. I was in San Antonio de Béxar. On the way into the establishment I had stepped over a body on the wooden sidewalk. On the way out, after assuring myself he was alive, I picked him up and put him on a bench nearby. His arms fussed and fluttered about and his hand landed on the white bone hilt of a long, sharp blade. He slashed blindly in front of him, forcing me to stumble back off the walk.

He was a foul and inhuman sight, grizzled and unkempt like a starving bear that had pawed down the clothes of a scarecrow and crawled in. The clothes were a soiled double-breasted blue coat, presently unbuttoned; a white shirt, also soiled; gray trousers, likewise stained; and riding boots with the spurs still affixed. They jangled, like little fits of laughter, each time he swung the blade.

The man stopped slashing when he ran out of startlement. He opened his eyes and found himself blinded by the sun. He slapped his free hand over his face and slumped back. The knife hand flopped to his knee, stabbing the wooden bench.

"Where am I?" he asked from under his palm.

I looked up at the name of the place. "The Friendly Ace," I said. I guessed, at night, there was gaming in addition to drink.

"Good," the man said. "I got a meeting here in the morning." He hesitated. "It's still morning, yeah?" Then he answered his own question by cracking his fingers. "Sun says about ten."

"It's ten," I informed him.

"Did — did I just attack you?" the man asked.

"You swung your blade around a bit," I told him.

"Just the flight of a startled hornet," he said. From his subdued tone that was apparently supposed to be an apology.

The man lowered his hand, slumped back, exhaled. "Christ, I hate this life."

He could have meant drink or his personal existence in general. I wasn't curious enough to find out. I turned to go back to the large mule I'd bought in Oklahoma. Even with shoe leather, which I had on now, a man was at risk in these lowlands from rattlers and scorpions.

"Mister!" the man on the bench called after me.

I turned back. "Sir?"

"Can I buy you breakfast?"

That was how I met Jim Bowie and also James Fannin, who the meeting after breakfast was with. I was invited by Bowie to remain. He was just two years younger than me, and we had gotten along like old dogs. We had a lot of the same kinds of experience only in different places — him living off the land in Kentucky and Louisiana, before he veered off into fighting for a living. I learned that passing out drunk was a practice of two years standing. In 1833, he had moved his family from San Antonio de Béxar to distant Monclova, Mexico, to escape a spreading cholera epidemic. But Monclova was where the disease hit, resulting in his pregnant wife Maria, their daughter, and Maria's parents all dying.

The way he told the story was a form of penance, it seemed, or maybe self-flagellation, making himself hear, again, what his actions had cost. I didn't try to console him with Scripture, I didn't share my own pale story of lost love, and I assuredly did not judge him. I just folded my hands under my chin and prayed in silence. He must have known I was praying for the Bowie ladies. When I finished, he thanked me. Some of the cloud from his storytelling seemed to pass. Maybe for good, I hoped.

Then Fannin strode down the stairs of the three-story hotel-eatery. The officer had arrived the night before, by boat and horse from New Orleans. That was where Stephen Austin was living. He had gone there to escape the reach of the Mexican government, which had already arrested him for inciting violence.

I had heard of Bowie but not the others. Austin, I learned, was right betwixt Bowie and me age-wise. But this Fannin — he was a peach-faced boy of barely thirty. He talked like a man, but he walked and dressed and ate as proper as a cadet. Which he had been, I discovered, at West Point, so maybe that explained it.

After Bowie assured the pup that I was "a saintly square fellah," I learned that the short of things was, Austin wanted firsthand reports from Nuevo Mexico. He wanted to know which side the Mexicans there would fall if Texas revolted. All he was getting were second- and thirdhand stories from Mexicans and Indians, relayed by Texians, that the locals would side with anyone who opposed Santa Anna.

"We've heard that the *generalissimo* is attacking his own people, conducting executions without trial," Fannin said. "We need trained personnel to infiltrate and ascertain the facts of the matter."

To which Bowie replied, "If you mean you want to go down and find out the truth, Fannin, just plain say so."

"He did," I told Bowie, seeing a means to endear myself to one who still seemed wary of one "spiritually square."

That was how I got invited to go south with the Jim and the James.

I swapped my trusted mule for a less sturdy horse, which Bowie traded for a more endurance-minded one. He was canny. He knew the horse trader and, more important, the horse trader knew Jim Bowie. The man made the exchange without even being asked — he was just looked at a little dark-eyed.

Texas had not been what I imagined from books and newspapers. Yes, it was flat and scrubby lowland in many spots, but there were also green hills and active, clean rivers, all manner of bird and plant, and some of the bluest skies I have ever been under. I was sorry to be pulled off my course, since I really wanted to feel the misty cool of a gulf morning on that shore, something I'd read about in a diary donated to my widow-lady's library. If I could've managed the extra encumbrance, I would've stolen it from her shelf. The script was legible and the words were written by a man of quality. That realization grew as the three of us set out to reconnoiter for Mr. Austin. It's a good thing Bowie was with us, because there were times when my mind went roving among the beauty. Not him. He didn't *look* alert, but he had a sense about things.

That's why he rode point. Fannin was a few paces behind, listening to whatever might come from the rear.

Fannin was a bit of a fop, but he wasn't a slouch. Along the early evening of the first day, he stopped, doubled back a little, and listened. He reported to Bowie that he heard something on our tail. He said he couldn't see anything but a rolling dust cloud — which, to him, meant one of two things.

"It's a dust storm or a complement of horses," Fannin said.

"Wild herd?" Bowie asked.

"Not in that kind of straight line south," Fannin answered.

We rode all through the night to put distance between it and us. Bowie knew the country well, kept us on flat land where neither Indians nor cats were likely to find us.

The second day out there was no longer a cloud. Either the storm had died or the horses had cut off in another direction. We rested, partly from being tired, partly because the sun was hot as an oven. It was late afternoon when we started up again, and quickly got the firsthand evidence that Austin wanted.

There was a party of six or seven families

moving west, most on foot, some of the
ladies on burros. They were worn out and,
through Bowie, they explained that they
were fleeing *soldados* who were going village to village in search of folks who weren't
happy with Santa Anna. That would've cut
a pretty wide swath through the population,
since if you were hungry or poor or sick or
infested with bugs inside and out — and
most of them were all of these — the
soldiers took that as meaning they dis-
approved of the generalissimo. Just being
discontented got them whipped, jailed, or
hanged. These particular families, along
with others, went north, south, or east from
Gonzales, which Bowie told us was about
two days' ride east.

"Could be where those horses headed,"
Fannin said.

According to these haggard few, that left
the town populated by eighteen men and a
cannon. That was it.

Wishing the families *buenas tardes* — and
meaning it — Bowie headed us off in the
direction of the city. We didn't know it then,
but we were about to stumble into the start
of the Texian Revolution. All I did know, for
sure, was at least I was going in the right
direction if I still wanted to get to the gulf.

We got there to find a nasty little mess in

the making. The hour was near sundown and we saw campfires on the horizon, so we slowed. Bowie left us behind with his horse and stalked up close. He came back pretty quick.

"At least a hundred *federales*," he said, using what I later learned was a term of disparagement for Mexican officers who killed to enforce Santa Anna's peace. "They're camped about a half-mile outside the town."

Now, Gonzales wasn't very big and it wasn't very old. You probably know that. The town moved around a bit to stay out of the way of hostile Indians but finally got surveyed and planted in 1827. Those redskins were the reason the Texians possessed what the Mexican dragoons had been sent to recover: a small, bronze swivel cannon that had been given to them for protection. If the locals were going to be in rebellion, the man in charge of the Mexican military thereabout did not want them to continue possessing it.

First, Colonel Domingo de Ugartechea had asked nicely. The answer he got back was what the ancient Spartans told the oppressor Xerxes: *molòn labé.*

Come and take it.

"So that's what the soldier men from the

34

south plan to do," Bowie finished his recitation.

"Let's go wide around," Fannin suggested. "Those defenders can probably use three more able bodies."

We didn't rest that night. Instead, we picked our way through grassy lowlands that lay between a pair of wooded regions. Bowie was once again in the lead. How he knew where to step, I don't know. He seemed to sense where there were furrows and toppled trees and predators; I couldn't see past the mane of my fine mount, nor smell anything but its sweat. Until, that is, we had gone some distance. Exactly how much distance I couldn't tell you, because it wasn't a straight line. But after a time there was a strong odor of defiance. That has a smell, you better believe. It's partly men, it's partly a wild mix of fur or cotton or whatever they've been wearing for weeks, it's partly cooked food and human waste hanging in the dark of that spot where defiance is rooted.

There were no torches, just in case Mexican shooters had it in mind to pick men off. So we dismounted and set a good distance away so *we* wouldn't be shot at by either side. Come dawn, which shined its full light on our eastward-facing selves, we rode into a sack of men and their cannon.

The gun was a sight. Two big wooden wheels and a tiny tube stuck between them, like a chipmunk peeking between two boulders. It was pointed backward, toward the encampment, for reasons that were not then evident to me. The men around them seemed built of stronger metals — tall, upright, armed, and watching the west. We saw them see us, but they were watching somewhere else: ahead. A man was running hell-bent toward them.

"They're mounting!" he yelled when he was close enough to be heard. " 'Bout thirty of 'em!"

One man in the front of the group gave orders to what looked like seventy, eighty men to his rear.

"Do not shoot unless shot at!" he yelled.

Then, turning in our direction, he motioned us over.

"You with us?" he put it to us bluntly.

"Jim Bowie is with you," our companion said.

"And James Fannin," added the other, though it wasn't needed.

The leader was not impolite to Fannin but he had his mind full of something else. He saluted the man with the big knife sheathed to his hip and nodded at us but gave us no orders. He must've known Bowie would know what to do. He left to see to the deployment.

We rode around the back of the line so as not to interfere and, I figured, so we could see where we'd best fit in. There were women and children well to the rear, those who didn't leave — as Texian women are not ones to stand down in the face of anything that isn't nature-sent. And even then, it has to be a helluva blow. We dismounted, tied our horses to a tree since there wasn't time to lead them to the corral way back. The leader did not seem to want a cavalry charge. Maybe they hadn't drilled enough together. Men were apparently coming in daily to support the cause of defying Mexico.

Bowie took us to a spot behind what was turning out to be two lines of men, twenty or so each. The rest dropped back into reserve. He was closer to the fighting men than the reinforcements, signaling his preference. He got it. The leader put us at the end, Bowie up front, Fannin and me behind.

I later learned that this striding, restless man was Captain Mathew Caldwell, "Old Paint" as he was called by those who knew him. I put him at about forty plus a whisker. Turns out he had a nice house back in town

37

— which was some ways away — and a wife, Miss Hannah, who was somewhere at the tent that had been set up as a hospital in case things got ugly. And since, just days before, the men of Gonzales had voted to go to war against the dragoons and the nation they served, no one was expecting a sudden breakout of peace. Behind him, always at the ready, was his backwoods right arm, a crack shot by the name of Willie Miller.

Then the thirty men appeared. They just waited in a column, not a line. The new sun glinting off the buttons of the man at point, they waited a lot of time until a spread of dust rose behind them —

The rest of the Mexican troops.

CHAPTER FOUR

Fort Gibson, May 1836
Ned's Story
John's long fingernail had drawn a straight line on my bar top. Closer to him he drew another straight line going the other way. To me, it looked like a "T." Those were meant to represent, I suspected, the two facing armies. To the generals in Mexico and probably to Steve Austin, this was also how it would have looked. But to John they were lines of men, some of whom would soon be mulch for plants and trees.

"You know what war is?"

The man's question was a sudden stop in his narrative. Once again, the swinging pendulum of the clock was the only sound. Funny thing. I had come west because, growing up on the port of New York City with its constant noise, I wanted — not quiet, exactly, because I'd buried too many relatives in my big Lithuanian family, been in too many silent graveyards. Both parents died during the uprisings against the Russian Empire, and that was from heart failure. They were upset having come to America when their friends and other family members were dying back there.

So I didn't want quiet, just different kinds of noise. The fort and the small settlement around it provided that. And — this may sound strange — it also provided scope. Oh, I could occasionally hear a bell or a cannon on the harbor of New York. But they had to be pretty big noises to hear them. Out west, horses' hooves could be heard a great distance across the plain, getting closer and closer. Gunfire rolled in from hunting or drunkards or soldiers target practicing. Dogs barked like in New York, but with a different kind of agitation. Here, it was about hares or other dogs and not someone whipping them to shut up or asking them stupidly what they were barking at, as if they could tell you it was a burglar or someone passing water in an alley.

The last few days, this cemetery quiet was something that was new. I might just as well be a mountain man as a barkeep, except for the clock. And not being frostbit, as I've seen in some of those crazy hermits.

"I've never been in a war, thank God," I

answered. "I know what others say it is. What the books have written."

"I don't mean combat," John replied, his eyes still on the past. "That's just blood and fear and chaos. That's physical and animal. Kill, shoot, slash, step on, stab. Set fires to brush or bridges or corrals. For the women, put fires out. Retch, shit, sometimes both while you're charging or ducking. Fire a cannon and hope it doesn't blow up on you — then grease, ignite, fire, repeat. It's mechanical, almost. No," he said. "War is also — maybe mostly — planning and spying and deception. Knowing that someone would be watching them from concealment, the Mexicans had showed us a small force preparing. When that had deployed, a spy would've run off to give his intelligence to the commander. With no one watching, the Mexican leader would execute the second part of his plan. Which was to send everyone else."

John paused. He seemed to be wrestling with something behind the eyes.

"Still," he said, "the intention of the Mexican leader may not even have been to fight. I've been wondering, since that day, if his goal was to use bigger numbers of men to collect the cannon, fulfill his mission, and take his troopers home. Because saving lives

41

is war, too. Soldiers' lives, civilians' lives, your own life. The gratitude of the folks back home, the families — that's war, too. If you're a leader you want them to thank you, not hate you. No one but a glory-seeker or a butcher or someone who is safe in a rear-line tent or government office wants the shooting to start."

"You — or rather, Captain Caldwell — were surprised by the large numbers?" I asked. I inquired not so much to get him to resume the story but to get out of the misery his brain was working through. I could see that, raw, in his dampening eyes, his softening voice.

"Maybe he was," John replied, returning a little to the present. "Colonel Bowie was not. From where I stood I could see him half-smile, like he was expecting a subterfuge."

"You mean, let the spy see one thing, report back, then do something else."

"That's right," John answered. He grinned himself, then. "If that was the case, the Mexicans underestimated not just Caldwell but the men serving under him. I can tell you that the Mexicans were not expecting what they got."

"What did they get?"

"I didn't know the names and numbers,

then," John said. "Fannin told me later. We had .41 caliber rifles. Couple of Kentucky long rifles — which, like me, actually came from Ohio. There were .50 caliber hunting rifles, some pretty fancy with silver inlays."

"Surely they knew that," I said. "Your position was — how far away?"

"Maybe three hundred yards from Mr. Shiny Buttons on his well-fed, well-groomed animal."

"So they would have seen the guns."

"Sure," John said. He was silent as he cut a little apostrophe on either side of the Mexican line. "But the enemy also got something he saw not."

CHAPTER FIVE

Gonzales, October 1835
John's Story

Captain Caldwell stood in the middle of our line — a step or two out front, in fact — watching the dust cloud like the rest of us. He did not hold a rifle but gripped a saber, from the aged look of it a piece that dated to the last War of Independence. Somewhere in there we heard a drum. Couple folks laughed when they heard that.

"Must be nice to have extra men," someone in front of me said.

"Prob'ly a boy," someone else replied.

"Maybe Mingo's giving him a taste for conquest," the first suggested. He was referring to Colonel Domingo de Ugartechea.

That sobered everyone a little. Many of the Texians had sons, some of them here. What would befall a boy of nine or ten if his pa got leg-shot or lost an arm or died here? Well, we also knew what would befall

44

any family that had to live as serfs to Santa Anna? That idea was viler than death and, more important, was viler than pain or death to loved ones.

Wherever I lived there had always been a sense of people more or less pulling together. You have to. Otherwise, you don't have civilization. But this was something new. It was different cloths, put shoulder to shoulder, somehow forging a quilt that no man, no invader, no foreign land would ever tear asunder. I suspect the word "republic" was made up to describe just such a thing.

So the Mexicans gathered, and the colonel himself emerged from the dust and rode to the front and shined even brighter in the new sun than any of his men. A man with a Mexican flag rode beside but behind him. Caldwell said something to a pair of men on his right and they unfolded their crude banner, black writing on white:

Come and take it

Above it was a silhouette profile of the cannon and above that, also in black, a lone star.

A little cheer quick grew into a big cheer as that flag, backlit by sun, threw its shadow on the dry, bent grass between the two armies. It was as if God Himself had added his voice to the proceedings.

The general reached his position and halted. I did not yet understand a word of Mexican but I understood the tone of the man who had been waiting patiently in front for the colonel to arrive. He did not approach under a flag of truce and deliver a written order, as was customary, I later learned. Such had already been sent, torn up, stomped on, and burned. I once saw a lady back in Warren do that to a proposal of marriage, but that was anger. This, as I said, was something bigger.

The orator orated, in not-so-bad English, demanding the return of the cannon, I presumed. Instead, at a nod from Caldwell, the cannon barrel was swung from back to front so it was pointing toward the field of combat. Now I understood. The Texians hadn't wanted to be intimidating at first. Swinging it out showed they meant business. If it had already been facing the Mexicans, the only next step left would have been to fire it.

The message "no" had been delivered in a more universal lingo. The next move was up to the colonel. If he charged, he would overwhelm the defenders — but it would have cost him a lot of men and horses. If he turned, it would have cost him his honor. Caldwell had not really left him a choice, which was kind of the point, I guessed.

Mingo did not retreat to safety. He drew and raised his saber. From behind, his men arrayed like a lady of quality spreading her fan right in our faces. There were layers and layers of mounted Mexicans, and it was clear that they would be spreading left and right, north and south, drawing our fire off to the sides so that a central column could bear down on us like a lance.

That was Mingo letting us know that he, too, was ready to commit. It was like checkers but everything stopped then. No one got kinged. Next move was up to Caldwell, and he was in a mood to just let the rising breeze blow through everyone's coat sleeves. After all, he had to reason, they had already announced their intention: come and get it. He was standing by that.

Couple of minutes passed and then — well, I figured Mingo had just one course of action. He didn't have enough men to surround us and lay siege, so that was out. I doubted his orders included going wide around us and burning down the town. It would have been kind of stupid to do what they'd given us the cannon in the first place to prevent. Which meant he had to either charge us or shoot at us. He had made a show of deploying for a charge, and he was sort of married to that.

So he ordered a fanning charge, which he probably hoped would cause the defenders of the cannon to scatter. It got off to a bolting, slightly disorderly start and got worse when sniper fire erupted from both sides of the woods. The men on the outside were knocked against the men beside them, then some of those men were shot as well. Their horses reared or twisted or ran into other horses, and the charge quickly became a mess of a standstill, a churning mass of steed and rider.

Mingo and his flag carrier had ridden out ahead. They came to an urgent stop when they realized they were alone at the front. It wasn't cowardice but practicality that caused him to order a full retreat: after the first two volleys, though the snipers had stopped firing, he had no idea how many men he'd lost.

The answer was seven — physically. How many more he had lost to suddenly plucked overconfidence it was not possible to say. But a courageous few quickly, ducking, gathered the dead and draped them on their skittish horses, and they were off, and when the men began to cheer, Caldwell silenced them by extending his arms. He turned to face them, his arms still outstretched.

"With a silent cannon, we have declared ourselves in revolt!" he cried. "Who goes to send these lads back across the Rio Grande?"

Every rifle was raised and a few hats flew toward the bluing sky. The men did not go to the corral but after taking pouches of ammunition and water, as well as hugs from their women, set out on foot behind Caldwell. They were like the Children of Egypt following Moses, with no purpose more alive or precious than freedom for their people.

All were caught up in the moment, no doubt. I went with them because the two Jameses had obviously just signed up — each for his own reason. Fannin because he was a patriot and Bowie because he was a landowner and a Texian. As I've said, there wasn't any other place I had to be — and this passion of the Texians excited me. Even when I was standing in that line, facing the Mexican soldiers, I hadn't considered that I might be killed. I didn't think that now. There was just this sense of purpose that trampled every other consideration. And it was contagious. Folks from nearby towns arrived even as we were setting out. They

49

did not have to hear anything other than that we were intent on making Texas for Texians. With a whoop and a smile, and a quick refill of water from our cisterns, they fell in. As we were going, a couple of women ran over with canvas sacks full of apples for us to eat on our journey. Not having eaten since the previous night, I accepted one and chewed it as we set out.

The cannon remained where it was, its care and feeding taken over by the women. If Mingo had it in mind to draw us out and circle back, he would be blasted for his efforts — and then run down by steeds who were being tied together like a big, ungainly clothesline of horseflesh. In motion, though, it would turn back anyone coming east.

We did not give chase as such. For a day and night, we were more like a biblical swarm that rolled after them right to their lair. And we collected people as we headed west, a man here, two there, who were on their way to join us. By the time the Mexican camp was in sight we were well over one hundred men strong,

It was, I have to remark, a sad-looking encampment. Proud and upright, the tents looked fitter than the men. We made no secret of our coming; many of the complement were singing "Turkey in the Straw" only now it was "Mingo in the Creek" with all new lyrics.

Caldwell stopped the "bearded deerskin choir," as he called them, just out of range of the nearest picket — which wasn't much of a line, just a handful of dragoons behind a few supply carts that had been rolled over and upended. Apparently, until now, they had never entertained the thought that we might attack them. The Mexicans shouldered their rifles as Mingo came galloping over. He stood behind them, tightly reining his horse. That meant he intended for them to fire. Caldwell stepped out a few paces to give them a target. Four rounds were discharged. One of them landed on the toe of his boot, a tired little bird falling to earth. It scuffed the leather. The others punched up dirt a few yards in front of him.

The Texians cheered. I didn't think it was because the Mexicans had missed; we pretty much knew they would. The hoots were because they had fired — which meant that battle number two was officially begun.

CHAPTER SIX

Fort Gibson, May 1836
Ned's Story

John's story paused for two reasons. The first was that he just stopped. The second was that something quite unexpected had occurred: a second customer had passed through my swinging door.

He was a tall man, a half-head taller even than John, and his long, fortyish face and high beaver hat made him taller still. He was pulling off calfskin gloves and tucking them in his wide leather belt. He was dressed in a blue wool tailcoat, double-breasted, over a white linen pullover shirt. His pants were the slim-leg variety of broadfalls, with wide flaps over the pockets. He wore a black cravat but no vest; it was a hot night and, out here, no one gave much of a damn about style. But he was a borderline dandy or, at least, from someplace that was more town than outpost.

"Good evening," he said with a voice that started somewhere around his kneecaps. After listening close to John, who spoke in a voice that was more cracked whisper than talk, the new man sounded like he was shouting.

"Evening," I replied generously loud, stepping past John so as not to deafen him or rouse him from his reflection. "I know you?"

"I've been here before, consuming ale with the locals," the red-cheeked man replied. "But we've not been introduced." The gentleman walked forward with his bare, soft hand extended. "Deems Pompey Hulbert of *The Brazoria Advocate,*" he said. "Or more accurately, *The Brazoria Advocate of the People's Rights.*"

"A newspaperman," I said. "Should've guessed from the bulge in your left pocket. Notebook?"

"And pencil, both ever ready." He placed his hat on the bar with one hand, patted that pocket with his other.

"You're welcome here, of course," I replied. "Though as you can see, I won't be needing to advertise —"

"I am not a salesman, I am a reporter Mr. — ?"

"Nedrick Bundy," I replied. "Proprietor of the Hick. My other guest is John, who has had a wearisome time." I added that in the hopes that it would protect John from inquisition by this man of the presses.

"My condolences, John, for your personal misfortunes," said the new arrival as he settled two stools away to his right, myself betwixt. He gestured around the empty room. "These are changing times for all." He looked at my other guest. "And you, sir, I presume, are the owner of that chestnut with the Mexican saddle?"

At first, John did not answer. The man looked at me as if to ask if he were drunk. I shook my head. The newspaperman said, "You look to have come quite a distance."

"I've read your publication," John said.

And there, right then, that coiled-snake quality I felt earlier came hissing back. I had dealt with drunk soldiers, angry indigents, and aggrieved women, but the way John spoke was the single most chilling sensation I had ever had in my little tavern.

"You honor me," replied Hulbert, removing his hat with an extra flourish and setting it beside him.

"I do not honor you," John remarked without looking at the man.

"Sir?"

"I said 'I do not honor you,' nor your regrettable publication," John said. "You

54

have written unkindly of Mr. Austin."

It was the liveliest John had been since arriving. As much as I wanted to intercede on his behalf — he being tortured and worn, Mr. Hulbert being well-dressed and frothy — I decided to wait a spell. I poured the reporter his drink.

"If you know that, sir, then you know the reason."

"You're missing a letter," John replied, still looking ahead.

Hulbert frowned. "I don't understand."

"The word is 'treason.' "

With that, we had fast-leapt into affair-of-honor territory. So before the openly aggrieved newsman could think to draw a glove and strike my — so far — only paying customer, I said, "Your pleasure, Mr. Hulbert?"

Hulbert had tensed, raising his shoulders even higher than normal, and it seemed like an effort to turn that lean face from John to me. He finally did, it taking a moment more for his brown eyes to follow.

"Do you serve cactus wine, Proprietor Bundy?"

"I can give you tequila without the peyote," I replied. "That's closest I got."

"Then tequila it will be," Hulbert said. He looked back at John. "That is, if your

55

other customer does not mind my drinking here."

"My minding is of no consequence," John said. "With the blessings of the Lord God Almighty and the help of Mr. Steve Austin and other patriots, Texas is a free country."

Mr. Hulbert did not indicate whether he agreed or disagreed with that sentiment. He simply leaned forward, relaxing a little.

"Are you staying long, Mr. Hulbert?" I asked.

The newsman took a swallow, stretched his mouth to the sides with contentment, exhaled. "Only until the morning — I am bivouacking at the fort and then moving on toward San Antonio."

"Were you a soldier in any war?" John asked.

"I personally was not but I have felt its ravages," the man replied, his chest inflating. "My father died in the conflict of 1812 between the United Kingdom of Great Britain and Ireland."

"I salute your father," John replied. "The question was posed to you."

"I have not," Hulbert answered — still puffed, but now with just air. He started, just seeming to notice the clawlike hand poking from John's sleeve.

"When a man and his fellows shield an

idea from bullets," John said, "when he protects the continuance of that idea with his body, his life, and the lives of his beloveds, he does not care for the drumbeat of linotype that is opposed to his actions. You wrote about the 'interminable difficulties' that would be inflicted on the population of Texas. You cheered the exile of Mr. Austin." He finally turned toward the newspaperman. "You called us 'few and weak.' Few we were, but weak?" John looked away. "It is only my respect for the idea of unfettered speech, however stupid, that keeps me from replacing this glass with your pale throat."

Hulbert saw John's fingers shaking and red as they clutched the glass. He finally deflated. He did not turn from John — that would have been an admission of defeat or, worse, the very cowardice of which, if I heard correctly, he'd just been accused. He took the rest of his tequila in a gulp, put the glass down, and firmly tapped the rim for another — as if to show he was a man who could hold his liquor.

The reigning silence was not exactly an invitation for me to redirect the conversation, but I did so just the same.

"John was telling me what it was like at Gonzales," I said.

"Gonzales!" Hulbert exclaimed. The man raised his freshly filled glass toward the man. "Our differences aside, I salute your bravery and ideals."

John ignored him. He was no longer engaged with the newsman or even, apparently, aware of him. My guess was that he had gone back to the battle.

CHAPTER SEVEN

Gonzales, October 1835
John's Story

It was more than the second part of the battle that started on that morning of October 1st. It was the revolution, that is now in full flower. We knew it, all of us, and most were downright moon-loony about it, like uncaged animals. Fannin, for one. He was no longer a proper product of military training but a zealot with the eyes and grin and sometimes even the bark of a mad dog. Bowie was more like a stallion, eager to be released from the corral. The others ranged from wolves in a pack to eagles soaring, watching, waiting to strike. I was an outsider, not even a Texian really — though Bowie said I had become one just by being there and taking up arms.

He was right. Up till we stood up to Mingo, then chased him here, I'd felt like I was just visiting. Then, suddenly, I was a soldier in the Republic.

So the first volley flew, scratched Caldwell's toe, and earned the Mexicans a return volley that targeted the facing floorboards of the wagon. At his order pops and bangs rang out along the line, splinters flew, and Mexicans ducked. They not only ducked, they crawled away from the wagons because those first rounds had gone clear through in spots, sending shafts of sunlight on their white-trousered bottoms. We could see Mingo standing outside his command tent, mortified by the conduct of his men but not ordering them back. See, he had not planned to fight a defensive war. He really thought he would reclaim the cannon and be packing up for home about now.

"You're going in the right direction!" Caldwell shouted after the retreating sentries. "Another 150 miles should do it!

Once again, a cheer and hats went up, but Caldwell did not allow the men to get cocky in their celebratory mood. There was still an army of the enemy out there and he immediately turned and decentralized the fighters, sending pockets to trees that were within range. Some men climbed, some stood behind, and soon there was a forest of some thirty Texians overlooking or within shooting range of the Mexican position. The remaining men he sent wide around, some to lie flat up close, others to provide cover from behind them. All of this happened while Mingo was still yelling at subordinates to secure the perimeter. I am pretty sure we could've rushed them, but that wasn't what Caldwell wanted.

"There's a smart man," Jim Bowie said.

Fannin was looking around from our own position behind a boulder. "It's a good array of —"

"I don't mean the troopers," Bowie said, with more than a whisper of impatience. "The tactic. He don't want dead soldiers, heroes. He wants live troopers, going home shamed and beaten."

"Where's the sense in that?" Fannin asked. "Santa Anna will only send more.

"Yeah," Bowie said. "A lot more. Everything he has."

"To overwhelm us," Fannin said. "He has the numbers."

"But not the heart," Bowie replied. "While they're here, Mexicans get uppity at home. He has to start sending men back. More and more of them. The longer we fight, the weaker he becomes."

Now Fannin was a military man and I could see in his dubious eyes a question about how many men Steve Austin could find and field. Just getting these men to Gonzales had taken weeks . . . and we still had well under two hundred. It was a dangerous game to play with a dictator who did not want to lose his lands to the north.

That was still just talk among us three, though. Not only wasn't it a known policy, there probably wasn't a known policy — otherwise Fannin should know it. And I could see, in those eyes, wagon wheels turning: a war had started and we weren't quite ready for it.

It's been called a battle, but Gonzales was barely that. The Mexicans settled in, not venturing from their camp much that first day, and when they did they were sent back with precise gunfire — the kind from men who were used to hitting hares and wild turkeys from a considerable distance. Some Mexicans were shot, a handful killed, and they stopped testing both our will and our aim.

Caldwell was forced to send men back to town in shifts to form a supply line and it wasn't long before hours were passing without a single shot being fired. That first night in the field was real quiet — no songs, no campfires — because our commander did not want us to be taken by surprise by belly-crawling intruders with knives. All it would take to fire up the Mexicans was a successful incursion. It must not happen, and Caldwell walked from group to group to group until dawn.

The second day there was a skirmish as Mingo sought to show some teeth. The Mexicans started firing from behind trees and carts, firing in all directions; they were turned back by the snipers in the trees, losing several men in the process. The firing resumed after an hour or so when two columns of Mexicans formed and marched toward either side of us, drawing some blood. But we drew more and they retreated. A couple of dragoons with sabers tried one last time to break our resolve. They came around wide on horseback and get behind us, but they ended up being captured. One of them did manage to inflict a slashing wound on one of our men when his gun failed to discharge. The blade cost him an eye and part of his face.

Bowie flung his knife into the ground to clean off the blood of a Mexican.

"My girl never misfires," he remarked as he drew it back and wiped the clinging dirt on the pale grass.

On the afternoon of the second day, without any further fighting, the Mexicans started to pull out. There was no parlay, no pomp, just an orderly departure. Caldwell gave them their retreat by forbidding any show of joy or contempt.

"They are soldiers, after all, away from home," he said. "Let them leave with the memory of a gracious host."

"A gracious host," I thought.

How quickly the minds had turned from colonists and Tejanos, from Americans and Mexicans, to the builders and sole masters of a republic. When Mingo and his men had departed, most of the men from Gonzales and elsewhere returned to those places. Fannin and Bowie went with them.

I remained.

"What do you plan to do?" Bowie asked me as the others headed east.

"I'll follow, I suspect," I told him. "But not just yet."

"Why?

"There's something I want to think about," I said. "And here's the place for it.

Bowie didn't understand but neither did he argue. He left me my new horse and my ration of food and took off to catch up to Fannin and the others.

It was quiet once all the combatants had gone. Quieter, I'm sure, than when everyone had arrived. That was because of something I saw the Mexicans do.

They had left their dead, planted them in the soil where they fell. I suppose there was a little bit of defiance in that. A man, the family of a man, would want him to be buried in his home soil. To Mingo, even in the departing, this was still Mexico.

To be alive is to be around death. We bury loved ones in the course of our days. That is the way of God's world. Save for the times when little Pansy Small drowned in a water barrel in Warren, and old David Drye was run down by a feed cart in Mansfield, I had only been around natural death. Never slayings.

I walked over to where the Mexican camp had been and where the dead still were. Crosses made of wood from the shot-up wagon marked the nine graves. I prayed over them. I didn't know the men, but it seemed the right thing to do. It also seemed to me a cleansing thing. To this otherwise pleasant if not idyllic spot something gray and unsavory had been added. Getting on one's knees and talking to the Lord Almighty had a way of cleaning that tarnish. I happened to notice, then, seeds stuck on my clothes. They were apple seeds from my lunch. I absently brushed them away while standing at the northern end of the row of graves.

They landed on the first plot, by the cross.

I thought, suddenly, of seeds my mother had planted by a wooden trellis on our farm in Massachusetts. I thought of my own livelihood in Mansfield, growing things. I instinctively knelt to do what I had always done, till the soil to hide the plantings from the birds.

"But this is a grave," I said to myself.

And yet, I resumed in words respectfully unspoken, *what place merits new life more than a grave?*

I searched my clothing for additional seeds, found two, planted them atop the adjoining mound. Then, still in genuflection, I ate one of the two apples Bowie had left me and, snapping the core in two, I put the entire one-half each beneath the soil of the third and fourth graves.

I rose, deeply satisfied with this action. I looked toward the setting sun, whence I assumed God to be watching. *Was He satisfied?* I asked. Had I profaned or sanctified this burial ground?

The answer was a sudden breeze where none had been moments before. It moved across my face and open hands like goose feathers, gentle and consoling. I felt as if my feet were suddenly gripped by Mother Earth — not snared, like my foot had snagged on a root, but held as if I was a tree myself, an extension of her bounty.

The breeze, the sense of rooting, all were gone in a moment. What remained was the feeling that I had done something *right*. I walked from the graves to give the occupants their peace. But I did not leave that place. I went and got my horse and walked him to where the Mexicans had lately camped.

How strange was time. Had I come to this spot three hours before, I should have been shot. Now, all that remained of the Mexican camp were the tracks in the ground . . . and the bodies beneath them.

I made a fire and sat beside it. Embers popped skyward now and then, before quickly perishing. *Time.* Perhaps we were like that, burning out slower but burning out nonetheless. My mother had once said that the stars above were souls. I had no reason to give credence to her belief, since she offered no evidence other than it was what *her* mother had said. That is the way of mothers.

If human beings are like campfires, burning then rising, then it might be so. But, I thought, if they are not then the way to ascend and endure was through the trunk and limbs of a tree.

I knew, then, what I would do . . . and where.

CHAPTER EIGHT

Fort Gibson, May 1836
Ned's Story

Deems Pompey Hulbert looked as if he had dropped through a hole in the earth and found the bejeweled treasure cave of some ancient chieftain. In fact, his mouth looked very much like such an opening. It hung there at the conclusion of the narrative, but only briefly.

"I had come here hoping to secure first-hand reportage," the newsman said with a carnivorous smile. "Sir, you have given that to me. Would you mind if I made a few notes?"

I didn't expect John to grant or deny permission, and as the other man was already reaching for his pocket, the query was respectful but moot. Hulbert adeptly removed pad and pencil like a gunfighter drawing. With a flourish, it was open in his left palm, his right hand writing.

"Might I further impose to ask your surname, friend John?" Hulbert said.

I had anticipated my first guest to ignore this question too. He did not disappoint.

"Mr. Bundy —" John began.

"Nedrick," I interrupted. "Make it Ned, please."

"Ned, I am tired and —"

He stopped abruptly. His eyes had been roving the bar top and stopped on the carving he had made.

"Did I do that?" he asked.

"You did."

"My apologies," he said. "I will pay for the damage."

"That's not damage," I said, "it's story art, like the painted caves I've seen red men leave behind."

His sad eyes found mine. "Thank you. For that, and for your hospitality. I am tired. Where does one sleep in this town?"

"If I may," Hulbert intruded, "I have secured a room at the fort through an acquaintance in Washington. You are welcome to share it."

"I have a drunk bunk in the storeroom," I said, both of us ignoring Hulbert's offer. It may have been Christian charity, but John and I both knew it would be rebuffed. "I keep it for those who from time to time overestimate the amount they can drink."

"I gratefully accept your hospitality," John said. "I am . . . so tired."

Hulbert looked as if he wanted to ask "Why?" but either thought better of it or was interrupted by the arrival of a third visitor. He was short, stocky, and swarthy and draped in a sun-blanched serape. He had a head of dark, tousled hair plopped atop a round face. There was a whip in one hand and a Colt revolver holstered not far from the other; the man was alert, looking about the Hick before entering entirely, though a draw did not seem imminent.

Hulbert apparently reached the same conclusion. "You really ought to move the entrance to the front," he suggested. "Surprises aren't good for the digestion."

The man entered, the bar lights throwing his shadow around behind him like the fat hand of a clock. He did not come directly to the bar but faced it — faced John.

"You are a coward, John Apple," he said with a heavy Mexican accent. "One who has run far enough."

John did not move, not even a twitch. I did, but only my insides. Bar fights were rare here, robbers had come but once — come, but not left, my customers having undone them — and even drunk troopers

71

managed to remember that they were soldiers. This was new and reeked of uncommon danger. I did not even realize until after it was all done that the stranger had given us John's full name.

The Mexican's whip hand quickly grew restless and he shook out the lash.

He took a step but that was more to widen his stance than to come any closer. He didn't need to approach: his whip would reach.

I did not move. My hands were on the bar and I left them there. I kept a pistol of my own under the counter, right across from the cash register, but if I made a move for it the Mexican would see it. I did not want to learn, in my dying moments, that he was fast on the draw. I also didn't know what Hulbert would do. He was turned halfway round, away from me, looking at the man. If I made a move, he might lean or step or jump right into my line of fire. For now, though the property was mine, the fight was John's.

John turned the stool toward the man. Now Hulbert moved; or rather he slinked, oozing from the stool that put him directly betwixt the two facing men. He went to one of the empty tables, hiding his notepad along his John-facing thigh just in case the

Mexican had a grievance with the press. Many did. It was something that often, here, caused disparate souls to bond.

John's hands were palm down on his thighs, fingers splayed, those sharpened nails extending each one unnaturally. He sat there a moment, the Mexican stood still for that same moment, and then John rose slowly. Before John was fully off the stool the whip uncoiled fast, bit the air less than two inches from his face. John froze, blinked, but he did not flinch.

"Take care, *amigo*," the Mexican warned. He raised the whip handle menacingly. "I would be just as happy to flay you here as to shoot you in the street."

"I will go with you," John said softly.

"Come to me with your hands out, away from the guns and from that pig-sticker," the Mexican said, stepping back. He motioned with the whip for John to proceed. John's hands floated away from his hips like weeds in a river, light and delicate . . . but with those odd thistles on the end. John's eyes remained on the Mexican as he approached.

The old man's movements were not quick but they were precise. As he passed one of the chairs by one of the tables, his floating right hand hooked it up, swung it in a fluid movement, and the legs hit the Mexican across the side of the head. The blow sent the man stumbling to his right, caused the whip to shudder, and left the gun hanging mute and useless and pointed at the floor. The Mexican's head had stopped the chair but it did not stop John. Turning, the older man grabbed the still moving chair with both hands and pushed the bottoms of the legs into the Mexican's chest. The chair was like the maw of a great beast that had suddenly swallowed a human torso and head. John pushed him back and back again, pinning him against a post that helped support the second floor of the establishment. Immobilized with his arms pointing down, the Mexican could not raise whip or gun. He could not prevent John from holding him there with one hand pressed against the underside of the chair while, with the other hand, the angry Texian plucked a small lamp from the nearest table and swung it too, smashing the glass bulb into the man's hairy knuckles. The man's gun hit the floor.

At this point, I scooted around the bar and snatched the weapon. I held it on the Mexican so John could back away with my chair. He did so with rage in his expression — and in his voice.

"You do not come to *my* home and dictate

terms of surrender!" John shouted.

He put the chair down, grabbed the Mexican by the hair with both hands, and thrust him back against the pole, hard. The whip dropped. Hulbert ran over to grab it but John stomped a foot on the handle. The newsman did not argue about it. He stepped back two paces.

"The somnambulist turns pugilist," the reporter muttered as though composing a headline. Maybe he was, though the only part I understood was the silver-dollar word for fist-fighter.

The two blows had left the Mexican dazed, but he was still conscious when John dropped him to the floor. The bearded man bent and retrieved the whip. Then he straddled the man's legs, tied them together, and dragged the man into the night.

"You have any law in this town?" Hulbert asked.

"Not presently," I replied.

Having no idea of John's further intentions, I followed him into the alley and, from there, into the street. Except for the glow from the window, which cut a crescent in the main road, it was dark as a well. I could only faintly see John tying the handle of the whip to the tail of a horse.

Hulbert and I stood a few yards away, at

the corner of the alley and the street.

"Not yours, I'm guessing," I said to the other.

"I parked my horse and buggy at the fort," Hulbert said. "Dear God, he can't be intending what I think."

"Our Mr. John Apple is clearly a fella of extremes," I said.

John untied the reins from the hitching post and turned the horse generally in the direction of Mexico. Then I dimly saw him spread his fingers wide, so wide they bent back like a cat's paw, and dig those claws into the horse's right rump. The animal whinnied and kicked and then bolted down the street dragging the Mexican behind. The more the animal ran, the more the dead-weight on his tail caused him pain, the more frenzied and fleet he became.

"You're not making notes," I remarked.

"I believe I will remember this," Hulbert replied.

The neighs and the clop of hoofs diminished in the dark, like a half-forgotten nightmare. Only one piece of the vignette remained, staring into the night: the gaunt, suddenly deathlike figure of John Apple.

Hulbert and I returned to the Hick, where I checked my chair — it was scratched but otherwise undamaged — then gathered the shards of glass from the lamp. I went back to the bar and refreshed the newsman's tequila. I generally did not drink on the job but took a swallow from the bottle. I felt deflated by what we'd just witnessed; my now-only patron was just the opposite. His chest was puffed, his eyes bright, his attitude uplifted.

He leaned forward so his naturally loud voice would carry a little less. "Do you realize that the story John Apple was telling — is not over?"

"That now seems apparent," I observed.

"No, what I mean is a newsman usually arrives after the fact, whatever that 'fact' is," he said. "Rarely in the middle. Something that began after Gonzales, perhaps after the Alamo, is still going on."

I leaned on the bar, on an elbow, and jerked a thumb toward the south. "It may have just ended."

Hulbert shook his head and had a swallow of tequila. "There is no chance of that. He just executed a man."

"Who had threatened him," I pointed out.

"In which case he should have been jailed at the fort to await a trial or tribunal," Hulbert said. "In his earlier recitation, did John mention anything about fighting skills or a murderous temper?"

"He did not. He talked about farming and preaching."

"Farming and preaching," Hulbert repeated. "Nothing about combat with furniture, Hector being dragged behind the chariot of Achilles, fingers that gouge like talons."

My eyes drifted to the etching John had made in the bar. "Not the first two."

Hulbert saw my gaze shift. "He did that? With one of those fingernails?"

I nodded.

The newsman studied the carving. "It looks like a crucifix with bells strung from the crossbar —"

John walked in then and we both shot upright like guilty schoolboys around a French etching. The man appeared little different from before the encounter, his movements stiff, slow, weighted at the shoulders. He returned to the barstool but did not sit. His eyes fell on the broken lamp I had set on a stool.

"I will pay for the damage," he said.

"What you gave me before covers it," I informed him.

He nodded graciously.

"You, uh — you had some previous business with that fella?" I asked.

"In passing," John said. "If your kind offer

78

remains open to me — if I have not blighted my welcome — might I trouble you for the bed?"

Curious word for him to have used, I thought. "Blighted."

"My offer stands," I answered, "though I am obligated to ask — am I to expect any more like what you just . . . just, uh, sent home?"

Hulbert scowled at my genteel phrasing.

John looked out the door. Again, it was like he was seeing something other than what was in front of him.

"In all truthfulness, it is possible," he confessed.

CHAPTER NINE

Gonzales, October 1835
John's Story

The war began with the cannon, and it continued with the cannon.

Come morning, after the Mexican departure, I rose with the birds, just before sunup. I left the dead to their eternal sleep and rode east, toward the dawn of a new day — and, I was sure, a new spirit in Texas.

That spirit turned out to be more war-minded than I had anticipated. The camp had largely broken up but not entirely. There were about thirty men remaining, but in two camps — one pocketed in the north, about twenty in number, the other to the south, only ten. The cannon sat in the middle, the banner wrapped round the barrel.

Jim Bowie and James Fannin were in opposite camps, Bowie in the smaller of the two. A few men on both sides were lying down, but most were huddled in small pockets of discussion. Smoke rose from matching campfires, the odor of meat drifting toward me. I approached Bowie's side; seeing me, he waved me over.

"Any sign of the enemy?" he asked as I dismounted.

It seemed odd to hear him call men who were so recently his countrymen "the enemy." I wondered if he felt the same or if this had been so long simmering it was natural, maybe even a relief.

"I saw no one," I replied. "No one alive."

Bowie nodded, respectful of the dead and my apparent attitude toward them as a former if homegrown preacher. We had talked about that on the ride south. Bowie did not appear to have any particular faith other than land and freedom, but neither did he disdain those who had. One could not live among the deeply practicing Catholics of Mexico and hold their beliefs in contempt.

I accepted a drink of water from his skin — mine was empty — then walked my horse toward a tree. The corral that had been used before was on the other side of the clearing. Bowie met me as I returned to the group.

"Fannin and his people want to bury our

gun so the enemy will never be able to take it back," Bowie said. "We want to keep it with us as a symbol. Like Christ on His Cross," he added, oblivious to his irreverence.

I immediately grasped and embraced both points of view. But only one could be chosen, of course.

"Mightn't the banner suffice?" I asked.

Bowie's frozen face announced that I had uttered something akin to treason.

"Most Texians can't read, and the others will believe 'Come and Take It' is a call to supper. There's no disputing an actual cannon. 'That's what started the war!' is all they'd need be told."

"Slows you down," I pointed out.

"Only if you run," he said, still somewhat aghast at my attitude. "Maybe you should be with Fannin and his people."

"I'm with a man I respect, James," I said. "Doesn't mean I have to agree with every thought he has."

Bowie relaxed a little as he considered that. "You speak from the heart, and what you say is fair. Join me for spit-roast hare?"

We walked to a spot just within the trees. I sat on a rock; Bowie crouched on the other side of the fire, facing his new enemies. A trio of picked-on rabbits were on sticks. I selected the one that had the most meat left and began pulling on the greasy white breakfast.

"It took all of a day to find something to fight about," Bowie lamented. "It was Fannin. He's got a leader whose legend he can build because the man ain't here to muddy it. He thinks he can do the same with the cannon."

"In the telling, it becomes bigger than that little thing," I said.

Bowie seemed to consider that. "You think built-up talk of a gun will move people more than the thing what was *there,* that was fought over?"

"I would say that a unified army is more important than the form of the symbol they unify behind," I told him. "Do you picture a hill or a field when I mention 'Lexington' or 'Concord'? I think of men — men whose faces I don't know, whose names I can't remember — taking a stand against the British."

Bowie considered harder. "Aw, shit. Shit."

He got up from the rock and walked toward the clearing with his long-legged stride. I returned the rabbit to the forks that held the spit and hurried after him. I wasn't sure exactly what he was thinking, but I knew him to be a man with a temper and a

83

knife. There was also home brew on his breath, and he did not appear to have slept much, if at all.

The other side saw him approaching and Fannin went out. They met at the cannon.

"John," Bowie said, "tell him what you just told me."

I repeated what I thought was my reasonable point of view. Fannin listened, then addressed me, not Bowie.

"Do you have a compromise to offer?" he asked.

That was a big, big step for a stiff-necked man like James Fannin. Apparently, he wanted Texas more than he wanted a cannon.

I hadn't thought of a solution, other than cutting the cannon in half like Solomon's baby. And then something occurred to me.

"Deeds," I said. "Let men be known by what they do. When I preached, I only had to speak of the Prophets and the Messiah. I did not, in my little barn, need images. Some people owned crosses, others made signs of crosses, others folded their hands in prayer."

"I'm not moved," Bowie said. "I seen friars out here whip Indians to get them to mass, starve them to leave behind their old religions."

"I can't answer for them any more than you can answer for Mingo," I replied. "What I'm saying is, let the folks decide for themselves how they want to worship."

"John, what you just told us was to bury the damn thing," Bowie said with some annoyance. "That's not a compromise!"

"What I told you was that the day James Bowie needs a cannon is the day that Texas is lost," I replied.

That was an open play for his vanity, but it worked. It was as though a second dawning had occurred.

The frontiersman looked at Fannin. "Do whatever the hell you want with it," he said. "I need a smoke."

Bowie stalked away, reaching for a cigar in his vest pocket. Fannin turned to me.

"Well done," he said. "May I ask what your preference might be?"

I answered, "From the numbers I saw, if not the resolve, you're gonna need all the help you can get. It's a weapon. Use it."

I do not know if that is what they did. Over the months I heard all kinds of stories. I left Fannin to rejoin my friend Bowie, who announced to me that he was going to leave this group.

"To go where?" I asked.

"Back north," he replied. "I got land I

want to sell and others got land I want to buy."

"What of the fight?" I asked.

He drew long on his cigar and blew smoke straight up. "It'll find me," he answered. "I am confident of that."

Bowie did not expressly ask me to go, but I decided to go back with him. My idea to go to the Gulf had been pretty general; with Bowie, I stood to learn more about this new land and its ways. Besides, wherever we ended up, I was certain I could secure at least a little plot of land to do what I liked best: grow things.

My plan for the future got remapped real quick.

We were headed north about the same way we headed south. Coming toward us, late on that first afternoon from a heat-rippled plain, was a Mexican driving a buckboard. Its contents were covered with a canvas that was tied down on two sides.

"They're transporting guns and a man inside, probably armed," Bowie said.

"How do you know that?"

"Tenting on the right side of the canvas, see it?"

I had to look hard, but he was right.

"Ventilation for someone inside," Bowie said. "Guns because the front spring is crying. Hear it?"

I did not, though I continued to listen.

"Nothing else weighs a cart like crates full of rifles," Bowie said. "Question is, bound for who?"

"Don't the Mexicans have enough guns?" I asked innocently.

"Not modern guns," he said. "Ours come from the U.S. Theirs are castoffs from Spain. I'm guessing this man and his partner got themselves what they should not have. Arms that we can use."

Bowie had finished his cigar and took another, struck a match on his saddle. He stopped to light it. I stopped beside him.

"I'm gonna ride past on the right, stopping by the passenger," Bowie said. "You pull up right in front and ask to see what they got."

"The man's wearing a holster," I pointed out.

"I'll cover 'em both," Bowie said. "You just palaver with the man."

"What if he doesn't speak English?"

"Tell him you want guns," Bowie said. "That's a universal lingo here. Anyway, I'll understand him."

It was a dangerously vague plan, I felt, but I had already won one debate with Bowie this day. I was not likely to win another, especially where arms-to-Mexicans was concerned.

We parted a little ways side to side, me halting in front of the wagon and raising a friendly hand, Bowie easing around to the side. The Mexican watched Bowie warily; perhaps he recognized the man or, more likely, his knife

"Buenos dias," I said in perhaps the worst-accented Spanish ever uttered.

The man repeated my greeting. His off-white, wide-brimmed straw hat covered his eyes. It also caused him to sweat, streams running down both cheeks and tracking through the stubble of a beard.

"¿Quién es usted?" the man asked thickly.

"He wants to know who you are," Bowie called over.

"I see," I said. "I'm *Señor* John Apple —"

"Aw, hell," Bowie said, impatiently drawing his knife and gun, leaning to his left, and cutting the line that held the canvas in place. He used the tip of the knife to flick the edge back, exposing a man who held what he was probably selling: the new Springfield .69 caliber flintlock musket. Unfortunately for him, lying on his back with the stock on his chest, the gun was pointed at his toes.

Bowie had his own revolver on the man

before he could move. I drew the one I had been given to fight the Battle of Gonzales and aimed it at the driver.

"Venga aquí," Bowie ordered in an accent that wasn't much better than mine, but Mexican that was. The man put the gun aside and stood with his hands up. Bowie motioned for him to ease down. Gun barrel, I saw, was also a universal language.

I was stupidly watching what was going on and took my eyes off the driver. That was when the man in the buckboard whipped his reins and charged me. I pulled my horse out of the way and the buckboard went wide. My gun simultaneously discharged into the ground, causing my horse to jump a second time.

The man in the back of the cart fell, scrambled for his rifle, and Bowie shot him. He fell on the canvas as Bowie wheeled his horse around to give chase. I felt as helpless as a babe, sitting there as Bowie easily rode the buckboard down. He pulled alongside the rider, fired a shot into the air, and the man stopped. I kicked my horse forward.

As I rode past, I could see that the man in the back was bad-hurt. There was a hole in his neck and blood was shooting up. He was holding it tight, trying to rise, failing. His heels were knocking weakly against the side of the wagon; he would not live much longer. The man in the front had his arms raised.

"Obtenga su amigo," Bowie told him.

The man climbed from the buckboard, went around back, and recoiled when he saw the condition of his amigo.

"¿Por qué tienes que hacer esto?" the man wailed. *"Él es mi hermano."*

"Why? Because you run guns, you pay the price," Bowie said.

Speaking in English, Bowie had let the man known he wasn't interested in having a conversation.

The driver climbed up, shouldered the man, and climbed back down. He lay him carefully on the ground, though the bleeding had mostly stopped. The man was dead.

"Give him your horse," Bowie told me. "We'll take his, and the wagon."

It was a decent thing to do, since we could have just left the man there. Though I did not then think that Bowie or I had endeared myself, and it turned out I was right.

CHAPTER TEN

Fort Gibson, May 1836
Ned's Story

"That," John Apple said with a tone of deep, deep reflection — followed by a pause to rally his thoughts — "That turned out to be the turn of the wind in my sails, the move that sent my own life along a path different from any I could have imagined."

"In what way?" the reporter asked, fascinated. "Not the killing, surely. You had just come from battle."

I motioned for Hulbert to be quiet. In my brief experience with John, he liked not to be pushed. I needn't have bothered; once again, John seemed oblivious to the presence of others.

"All I ever wanted to do was to make things grow," John said. "Gardens . . . souls. Now I was forced to become what I beheld, a killer."

"In self-defense," my journalistic companion doggedly pressed on.

Perhaps it was his nature or the tequila or both, but I found his manner entirely annoying. So much so that I took him by the arm and walked him off his stool and back along the bar.

"Do you have any notion of what this man has endured?" I asked.

"Only what I have heard, and I want to hear more," Hulbert replied, rolling his arm from my grasp. "It is my job — my responsibility — to tell that story to the public. To Texians."

"Why?"

"Because they are forging a new country, Mr. Bundy, carving it off from the ailing body of an old one," Hulbert replied. "That is news." He pointed his pencil at John. "This man is part of their very young history. I will have his firsthand account."

Hulbert returned to his stool but said nothing. John was standing in the same position, with the same expression as we had left him. The reporter waited.

"I heard what you just said," John spoke at last. "I agree with you. The people should hear what happened. But only for one reason."

"What reason is that?"

John replied, "So they learn not just from

our triumphs, but from our mistakes. Those men we accosted — they were not Mexican gunrunners. They traveled under the protection of people who did not appreciate our meddling."

"Mexican officials?" Hulbert hazarded.

"No," John replied. "Washington officials. Men who oppose our independence, their only reason being that President Jackson is for it."

"He tried to buy the territory from Mexico," Hulbert said. "We printed his offer."

"We all knew about that," John said. "Most Texians who were American-born felt charitably toward being American once more. But we heard about folks who were against us just because the president was for us."

"In such soil grows the entirety of Washington's social conscience," Hulbert lamented.

"Do you garden?" John asked the man suddenly.

"My sister has a flower garden," he answered. "They are aromatic but they do attract buzzing pests."

"Pollen collectors," John said, suddenly wistful. " 'And behold, a swarm of bees and honey were in the body of the lion.' "

Hulbert wrote the phrase. "That is from

the Bible?"

"Judges, 14:8," John replied. "Like them, we shall create a paradise in this vast beast."

Though I shared a shrugging look of perplexity with Hulbert, I reminded myself that this man had been a preacher and was like to see things with the light of St. Peter marking the way.

"The guns," Hulbert reminded John. "They were sent by enemies of the president to the enemies of Texas."

"Yes," John said. "We found letters of passage and a map in a leather case in the back. These two had come from —"

John stopped.

"Sir?" Hulbert prodded gently. "The men had come from where?"

The older man's tired eyes turned from the past to the present and then to the man before him. "Bloody treason, they came from Fort Gibson."

The empty room suddenly became a colder, empty room.

"You — you retain this documentation?" Hulbert asked.

"No, the papers . . . the papers remained with Jim Bowie," John replied.

An even greater chill descended with the mention of so recent a martyr. Hulbert and I turned from John to face one another across the bar.

"You'll be staying there," I said to him. "At the garrison."

Hulbert nodded sullenly. "I like the president," he said. "I admire him."

"You are not alone in that," I told him, raising what was left in my glass before draining it.

"The president could not have helped Texas directly," Hulbert went on. "There would have been war. He could not even declare in their favor. And there would be charges of treason brought against anyone who aided foreigners." He looked at John. "Even without those documents, you are in peril. Yet," he moved in closer, in an almost predatory way, "were I to put your story before the public, you would be safe."

John smiled thinly. "How do I know that you are what you say you are?"

Hulbert sat back. "My friend, who would claim to be such a scavenger as I were he not?" He nodded. "I dress it up, true, but — you mentioned a lion's carcass before. That is what I search for. I pick it clean of whatever residue will provide me with information, with a story. That man who came after you, at least, had ideals enough to risk his life. Not I."

"Would you have taken lodgings at the

Alamo for a firsthand account?" I asked.

For the first time, Hulbert did not immediately speak. "I have asked myself that, sir. I cannot say as I would have. There appear," and here he looked at John, "there *appeared* to have been no survivors other than women and children."

"John was out wrangling supplies when the mission fell," I remarked.

"Fortunate," Hulbert said.

I could not be sure he was being serious. His tone had the quality of defamation.

John did not respond. It seemed to me that a part of him perished there, that he was a living ghost. I should have liked to know him before Gonzales, before that confrontation with the gunrunners.

John raised his left hand before his face, the palm facing him. He was looking at the nails, at their underside. "How they clawed furiously," he said. "They needed food. They needed to hurt me. I had sinned against a farmer, striking him down so I could take what he had grown. And my punishment was to arrive too late. It was all for naught."

John's mind was wandering and my other companion was clearly impatient.

"Tell me about the garrison and the guns," he said.

"To tell you that, I must tell you of my parting with Bowie."

CHAPTER ELEVEN

Gonzales, October 1835
John's Story

The Mexican asked for permission to gather his belongings, which Bowie denied. If he did not wish the man further harm, he did not want to make his passage to Mexico faster. Reaching a telegraph office, he could have sent news of the meeting and given troops an opportunity to run us down.

Because we did not immediately look in the back, I did not find the satchel until I went to look for food and water. By that time, the man was well away from there. The news Bowie read in the documents was disturbing, as you can imagine.

"I can get the guns to Caldwell," Bowie said. "You have to take those papers to someone in the north who can relay them to the president. Let him know there are Judases in his midst."

I agreed that the plan made sense. I did

find fruit and a water pouch in the back. We swapped out the horse so Bowie could keep his, and went our separate ways. It had been an unexpected meeting those many days earlier and an unexpected parting. I did not doubt that I would see him again. What I did not expect was to very shortly run into Mexicans who were transporting a second wagonload of guns.

Mexicans who recognized the horse I rode.

I found this out because, spotting them as I came around a mesa, I sought to turn to the west to circle around their route. But the man who was hid in back fired — a shot that passed close enough for me to suspect it was an on-purpose miss.

I waited, hands extended at my sides, while they rolled the wagon over, the rifle on me for the duration. I was facing north-south, they was riding west. I knew that when they looked on that side of the horse, I was a dead man.

"¿Dónde obtuvo el caballo?" the driver asked.

"I do not understand," I replied.

"Horse," he said. "Where find?"

"Behind the mesa," I replied. He didn't seem to understand so I pointed.

"Lie!" the man shouted, and spoke to the

99

man behind him. The gent with the rifle got out and came toward me like he was approaching a coiled snake. For all he knew I was some quick-draw gringo who shot their friend from his mount and stole it. That was a fair assumption, I supposed, given that there were two men and a cart unaccounted for.

I was not in a good spot. Even if I was a fast shot, which I wasn't, the man with the gun was an intimidating, dangerous target. One who now motioned me to dismount with my arms raised.

I followed his instructions and he took my gun. The other man came over now and seized the reins of the horse.

Damnation, I thought. He didn't want it to run when they shot me dead.

And shooting me dead definitely seemed to be the plan as he finally saw, and took, the satchel I'd hooked over the horn on the side facing away from his buckboard. He spit. He slapped me twice.

"Where Esteban?" he demanded.

"On my horse," I replied truthfully.

"Where wagon?"

"Jim Bowie," I answered.

The man laughed. He must have thought I was joking. He learnt I wasn't when the top of his friend's head came off and his body followed it to his right.

"Eh?" the man said, as the sound of the shot reached him. That was *his* last word as his back erupted in red and viscera as a bullet penetrated his chest. He fell back on his companion, twitching as he bled to death.

I looked toward where the shot had originated. Bowie was riding toward me from the direction of the mesa, the army rifle at his side.

"These guns *are* something," he said as he rode up.

"I am very happy to see you," I said. "What made you come back? The shot?"

Bowie shook his head and used the gun to point at the satchel, which lay in a puddle of blood. "Those papers," he answered. "Said there was two wagons of guns. Since there were no tracks in the direction we come from, I figured you'd run into the other, so I tagged along." He smiled with satisfaction. "More arms for the rebels."

I was angry at him not having shared that information, but he later explained that if I knew he was there I might've looked back and spoilt the surprise attack.

All of what Bowie and I had discussed was important: the guns, the tactics, my mission. But what struck me hard when I finally rode off with the satchel wiped dry on the sand was this: in the space of an hour, I had watched three men die sudden, bloody, ugly deaths and it didn't stick with me much more, or much longer, than a bugbite.

What the hell happened? I asked myself.

I decided I had left Ohio a pretty embittered fella and this — well, it took my mind off that stuff. I realized later it did more than that.

I left out one thing. There was a knife in the wagon and, after Bowie had ridden off with the buckboard and its contents, I used it to cut two shallow graves for these men. I put them inside and ate my second apple. Once again, I split the core and interred it with them, watering just that spot to give growth a fighting chance. I also kept the knife. It was wider and a little longer than Bowie's pig-sticker, almost a machete. It didn't have a sheath, so I wet it with drips from my waterskin and dropped dirt all over one side. Last thing I wanted was something shiny giving me away to anyone. I kept it in my belt, left side, so I could draw with my right.

I had been thrust into a war, and there was no avoiding that. But how to survive without become a monster who saw murder as sport? What had happened, I suspected, is that my two angel natures — growing and preaching — had conspired to transform John Apple into someone else.

Bowie had suggested I make for Coles Settlement. Said it would take four or five days and that John P. Coles would give me good advice on where to take our information. The man had settled there in '24 and was a trusted confidant and ally of Bowie's.

The journey was not without event. Comanche and Choctaw were not always reliable inhabitants of their own territory to the north, especially when they went tracking game to the south. Either the red men weren't aware — or more likely, they did not care — that they had crossed into John Cameron's Grant or the Immense Level Prairies. Some, I suspected, were just looking to pick a fight. I didn't have much contact with Indians in Ohio, and none in Pennsylvania, but I could tell by the way they raced each other or charged one another like ancient knights, only these warriors were holding spears and aiming at handsome woven breast coverings with painted images of birds and buffalo. A few there were who saw me from afar and stopped. They did not appear at all fearful of discovery — who would I report them to? — but seemed to be considering whether to approach me; for trade, perhaps, or possibly to do harm. Especially the Comanche. Bowie had tales of their aggression against Whites, and against Choctaw for that matter. I was heading northeast, but if I saw other horses or clouds of dust, I turned either east or north to avoid them.

Except for one time when I came upon three Comanche, one of them on the ground, on his back, the other two huddled around him. It would have been easy to ride on, unseen, but I thought: if he's hurt, I might be able to help. So I continued riding in their direction.

Turned out he wasn't hurt. He was having his heart cut out by the other two. By the time one of the braves held it toward the skies, red and dripping gore, I was in easy smelling distance. They stood and turned and I froze where I was. I could see the dead Indian more clearly now, noticed his loincloth bloodied as well; later, Mr. Coles would explain that he had either stolen the squaw of one of them or defiled the daughter, for which disfigurement then death was the punishment. He would have been brought out here to die so his spirit would wander, lost, away from home.

I didn't figure any of that, only knew it was none of my business. That, and the occupants of the three teepees I could see be-

104

ing set up some distance behind them. The redmen and whoever rode with them were going to make a party of this thing.

They made no immediate move against me so, raising my right hand — not both, like I was surrendering — I slowly turned and got back on course. The Indians did not follow. That was my first real exposure to the culture of Western savages, and though I later learned it had a more peaceable side, that first how-de-do stayed with me vividly for the rest of my ride. I have to confess, though I was revolted by what I had seen, there was something familiar about it — something Old Testament, Abrahamic, the Lord God who smiteth. Life is more memorably vivid than words, of course, but it got me to understand that some kinds of acts is universal.

I did not know it then but that realization would stick to me like skunk.

Another unusual encounter I had along the way was with a light-skinned colored man name of Samuel J. McCulloch. He was a free man, about twenty-five, tall, powerfully built, and as we were both lone travelers, and as I had an open heart to all people — except Comanche — we shared jerky and fruit over a campfire. He told me he was looking to join the fight against Santa Anna, and I informed him he was most certainly on the right heading. I instructed him how to get to Gonzales and, if he needed help with anything, to see Jim Bowie and tell him we met.

"I hear'd of him," McCulloch told me. "The knife-fighter."

"Invented his very own," I said. "Big-un. Also cut a lot of trails in the wilderness."

"Ev'body cuts trails," McCulloch said.

I wasn't sure I took his meaning, though as a Negro who was not enslaved, I suspected he meant that poetically, or some such. I had met Coloreds in the north, laborers and such, but this was the first Southern such man I had encountered. He was born in South Carolina, the belly of the South, to a white father who he moved with to Alabama.

"But light-skin, dark-skin, it don't matter if y'aint white-skin," he said, rubbing a bare arm. "Though I tell ya, I do get looks from the pure Black and the White, as if I wasn't human. So I left the U.S. of America to come here with my wife and daughters and son and sisters. I lef' them all on the Lavaca to come here."

I didn't know what the Lavaca was, and he told me it is well southeast of where we sat, a river that empties into a bay that empties into the gulf. He'd come from where I had been headed. Odd world.

"It's a river, a land, worth owning and fighting for," he added.

"That the only reason you come?" I asked.

He looked indignant by the campfire, as though I was questioning his integrity, then broke open a big smile.

"No suh," he said in a syrupy accept. "No. My boy is little an' I needed to get me around some menfolk for a spell. I was gettin' pecked to death by my women."

Come morning I wished Samuel J. McCulloch God's blessing, told him to watch out for Comanche, and said I expected I'd see him again when I rejoined Bowie.

He laughed. "It's a big country, brother Apple, but folks have a way of running into each other in it."

The rest of the ride was without incident except for a gully washer that poured down like God's own wrath. I never saw nor felt nor heard rain so determined to scar and reshape the land. It hit so hard and heavy I had to pull under a ledge and wait, then hoped the ledge didn't fall because so many pebbles and chips broke off and became little bullets themselves. I had heard tell of winds that tore so hard across the land that they ripped up trees and carried them away.

I did not see such as that, but I heard a roar and I heard thunder that made me afraid in a way that stripped civilization from me and left me feeling as naked and unsheltered as the redskins. When it was over, the ground was mud and my precious papers were soaked around the edges — both requiring a pause to let the hot, welcome sun dry them out.

I arrived at my destination stiff and tired. Stiff from the rain that hardened my clothes, tired because you don't sleep in the open the way you sleep in a camp. At any kind of settlement, there are men who are awake and usually drinking, or sentries. Alone in the open, you are always listening — for hungry cats or bears, for Comanche, for escaped prisoners who parted from jail with just their trousers.

I covered the last few miles on the fifth morning of my trip with the help of smoke rising from a hearth. I smelt it before I saw it. The house it issued from was long and low and built from a mix of cedar timber and stone. The storm must have hit here too, because there were several downed trees that were in the process of being chopped to firewood. It broke my heart to see them uprooted and I resolved, before leaving, to see if there was some way I could help plant new ones. My ma had always said, when I was a boy, to leave a place better than when I arrived. I never really saw how that was possible, lest you were a saint, till now.

John P. Coles and family could not have been more welcoming, once I told them who I was from, and the two workingmen lowered the big tree-chopping axes they'd raised in my direction. The master himself came out to greet me.

"Please forgive the manners of Amos — that's the big fella — and Jacobus," Mr. Coles said. "Even though they're cutting wood for what will be, in a short while, I hope, a rooming house for travelers, the two bears have not learned that we have to welcome our guests, not menace them!"

The last part he said to them, or rather at them; not in a way to make them take offense, since he did it with a twinkle, but to educate them.

I put the gentleman with his white shirt and vest bulging at the belly to be in his middle forties. He walked taller than his middle five-feet height, his balding head aglow in the sun. His wife Mary Eleanor did not walk behind but beside him. She stood a half-head taller and had a welcoming, wide-open face. There was, then, a son and two daughters. From the look of Mary Eleanor, more was on the way. Also milling about were a clutch of servants and folks I later learned were slaves; after my meeting with Samuel J. McCulloch I felt bad to know that these people was "owned," as Mr. Coles later put it. But they seemed healthier, in fact, than McCulloch and I left the right-or-wrong of things to the Lord God to judge.

But I get ahead of my narration.

I was taken by the arm by Mr. Coles and walked inside. He was not only friendly, he was curious. Seeing that I was older, and hearing where I was from before Texas, he had nothing but questions. In what I later learned was a North Carolina accent that I couldn't tell apart from McCulloch's South Carolina one, Mr. Coles asked about Bowie. He did this eagerly, persistently, while I washed my face and chest and arms and feet at an outdoor basin, which had its own pump and plentiful water. He seemed downright euphoric — his wife provided that word later, over griddle cakes and eggs — to learn that the rumors of the cannon and the victory at Gonzales were true.

"You fought in that historic stand?" he asked.

"I was there with a gun," I admitted. "Not

sure what that I hit anything. Jim Bowie and James Fannin and the others — they are the real Texians. I just happened."

He pumped my hand anyway. "A man from outside who takes on the commitment of others," he cheered. "Nothing greater! Nothing!"

I felt a little embarrassed by his "euphoric" enthusiasm. If Jim Bowie had not been drunk on a stoop, I'd be at the Gulf of Mexico, fishing.

"A new nation," my host said. "Andy Jackson wanted us. Santa Anna wants us. But we got us!" He added with a shout: "Independence!"

It wasn't until he walked me inside that I got around to showing him what I came with, the papers of passage. Well, I never saw a man's mood turn so quick and fully. He excused himself to another room, taking the papers with him and shutting the door behind him. Mrs. Coles excused herself, then, to give the young children their schooling, and I sat alone at a lovely-set table with second helpings and no real idea of what was coming next.

Until the housekeeper showed up.

CHAPTER TWELVE

Fort Gibson, May 1836
Ned's Story

Deems Pompey Hulbert had been writing hard, using a thumbnail to scrape away a pencil point when the one he was using broke. I just stood with both hands flat on the bar, listening. For a rare long spell, neither of us had spoken.

There was something about this section of John Apple's narrative that was different from the rest. It had a kind of longing, almost like that storybook hero Ulysses who wanted to get home — and finally got there. I daresay it was the first time John spoke without tension and misty pauses. He was almost, toward the end, like a child.

"She was Mexican," John said.

"Mrs. Coles?" Hulbert asked.

"The housekeeper," John replied. "Maria. I never found out her last name. I guess domestics and slaves didn't use them, much. She brought over a handmade clay bowl, painted with a sunset — pottery made and decorated by Mrs. Coles on a wheel out back, I soon discovered, from Maria, that it was a craft the lady of the house learned back in her native Georgia from Creek Indians. She also did some mighty impressive beadwork, I might add, which Maria was proud to point out on aprons, tapestries, and such."

"You like her," Hulbert said. It was the first human-type question he'd asked.

John nodded but did not elaborate. He did not have to. The Southern girl is a universal treasure. I know men from the fort, from the North, who have been untrue to their loves in Boston, in New York, in Providence. I know of no man from the South who did more than look at another lady.

John broke his narrative there. "Forgive me, but I really must rest. The bed?"

"This way," I said, walking from behind the bar, lighting a lamp, and showing him to the small storage room behind the big mirror. He visited the privy in a second door that opened into the alley. The room was wide and stocked with kegs and crates and he had to sidle by to reach the bed. Then, except for removing his hat and shoes, John

113

remained clothed and simply flopped down. There was no window, save for an overhead skylight that I kept open for ventilation. I took the lantern with me and shut the door. Since the room was only about as long as the cot, I figured he could find his way out in the dark.

"Is there any chance," Hulbert asked as I returned to the bar, "that he is spinning clouds here?"

"He was hurting real bad inside when he got here," I replied. "And that hornet-stung Mexican was real enough."

"John Apple could've stolen that horse from him, could've ravished his daughter — we don't know."

"No, we do not," I agreed. "But his story about the garrison would be easy enough for a dedicated reporter to check."

Hulbert grinned. "I intend to, sir. Or are you inviting me to leave?"

"I would never invite a paying customer to leave," I replied, "especially when the only other one I got is dead to all but his God out back."

The reporter plucked a coin from his pocket and pushed it across the bar while he scanned the chalkboard behind me.

"Stew and soup," Hulbert read. "What's the difference?"

"Stew comes with carrots and onions plus a biscuit," I told him. "Soup only has carrots."

Hulbert looked at me. "How fresh is the biscuit?"

"Depends how long you dip it," I admitted.

The reporter half-smiled. "I'll try that. Fort food may not be much better, with the cook gone."

I set about lighting a fire on the other end of the room, which is where I kept the hanging pot. While that warmed, I scraped two carrots I kept in the pantry and brought out a buttermilk biscuit. I didn't tell Hulbert that I'd got it from the fort the day before. Cook's wife, Emma, made them whether her husband was present or not.

"Where do you think independency will end up?" Hulbert asked me.

"I don't share my politics," I answered.

"I wasn't asking if you were for or against —"

"I don't read palms or peer into crystal balls, either," I said.

"You seem put out by my questions," Hulbert noted, accurately.

"News is news, and opinions is for speeches. As I am not running for public office . . ." I began, letting him figure out the rest.

"Interesting," he remarked. "I have found establishments like yours to be fertile ground for assessing public opinion."

"Most nights, you'd be right," I said. "And on those nights, whatever the topic, I'd lose half my customers if I spoke my mind."

"Freedom of speech is never free," Hulbert remarked.

I tended to his stew while he reviewed his notes. I was curious and more than a little concerned about the connection between the fort and Mexican gunrunners, though, as it pertained to John Apple being in the middle. The reporter, doing what reporters do, would not hesitate to put John in the midst of danger to pursue that story. Clearly, John was already in some jeopardy from one side of that equation.

But those were concerns for another day as I suspected that I had seen the last of John until the morning.

Hulbert left shortly after wiping the last of his stew with a biscuit that crumbled from the effort. He seemed satisfied and was eager to return to the fort to, as he put it, "make inquiries" about those weapons. He promised not to reveal the source of his information. I considered that statement after Hulbert took his leave; I found myself believing him. It would enhance the reporter's image, and power, for others to think he had a network of informants rather than just one randomly met transplant from the North.

Or it might earn him a bullet in his back instead of in John's, I also reflected.

I locked up, after first looking up and down the street and alley to make sure there was no one watching for me to do just that. There was enough of a moon that I could see into most of the few shops and outlying fort structures. Except for Loose Lizzie as we called her, no one was about. She waved when she saw me. She must have been hurting even more than I was. I liked Lizzie personally, though she didn't come into my establishment. No woman did. Men fought over them, and men fought over enough — cards, mostly — without me wanting to add petticoats as ante.

The night passed without incident, except that when I went downstairs not long after dawn, I'd found that John had departed. He left a note on my chalkboard.

Ned: bless you, but I got an overdue
chore — JA

He signed it with that strange-looking

117

cross which, I now suspected, was more likely an apple tree.

I wasn't wholly surprised by his early departure but I was sorry. I wanted to wish him good journeys and I certainly wanted to tell him to come back and let me know how his saga turned out. I also wanted to hear his tale of the Alamo, which he had not gotten to relate.

I went about my housekeeping chores such as sweeping and dusting, and I had taken it in mind to repaint the outside of my white building whiter. No sooner had I set up the ladder to continue with that then Deems Ptolemy Hulbert came by in his buggy.

He was in a hurry.

"You have got to come with me," he said.

"Where and why?" I inquired.

"There's a standoff at the fort," he replied, swinging the buggy around so he was pointed back in the right direction. "You have been asked for."

"By who? John?"

"None other," Hulbert said. "And you may be the only one who can end it without blood being shed."

I left the ladder, left the paint, threw off my apron, and got in beside Hulbert. I'm guessing the man had not been this excited

118

since some childhood birthday.

We charged through the streets of the little town, traveling the short distance between my establishment and the wooden stakes that represented the perimeter of Fort Gibson.

"Whose blood is in danger of being spilt, other than John's?" I asked.

"The one he's holding — the boss."

The man in charge of Fort Gibson was a woman.

Colonel Burton Gearhart had left young Lieutenant Hutton Falconer in command, but if Falconer was too inexperienced for border patrol he was even less able in matters of running the garrison. In addition to the skeleton force left behind, the open-door policy to Negroes and Indians who sought protection in the bosom of American might were many — and many of those were looking for handouts, thievery, or bartering goods they themselves had stolen from elsewhere.

In charge was Mrs. Colonel Burton Gearhart — Meggie to all save the enlisted men and Falconer — who was as iron-fisted as she was pretty. She was one of those Southern belles John had been talking about, the kind who needed neither protection nor fear that their husbands would stray.

The Gearharts were childless, though I knew they had lost a little boy to flu many years before. The fort medic had confided that unhappy scrap when he got lost in a bottle one night. Doc Delaney was not as a rule a drinker, but he had been forced to cut off a Choctaw's leg at the knee following a horse fall and that responsibility never weighed light on the man.

I could not believe that John would cause harm to a woman. Not after what he said about Mrs. Coles. But I reminded myself that he had been ruthless with that Mexican, and who knows what could have transpired there.

The gate of the fort was open because cattle were expected for the stockade. We rolled right in and were met by Lieutenant Falconer — a curly-haired youth with a sand-colored moustache and penetrating blue eyes. He had risen in the cavalry because he could ride like he was half-horse, but his high-pitched voice made it difficult for him to be taken seriously when he was on just two legs. His command options, it seemed to me, would always be as a number two or three man. In bartender terms, at the Hick he'd be silently mopping floors and collecting fallen coins as tips.

"I want to go in but Meggie won't allow

it," the young man squeaked. "She asked me to send for you."

"Why?"

"Because that's what the man barring the door asked for."

"You are to be a peacemaker, it seems," Hulbert stated the obvious — which showed me just how bad he wanted to be a part of this story.

I slid from the buggy, glad I was still wearing my white painter's hat to shield me from the brilliance of the sun. Following the lieutenant and followed by Hulbert, I walked past malingering civilians eating army breakfasts or still asleep on blankets. There were a few Mexicans as well, any one of whom could have been the twin of the man John had ridden out of town on a horsetail.

Any one of them could want him dead.

We stopped at the door of the simple log structure that served as the headquarters for the fort. The shades were drawn and there was no sound coming from within. An armed sentry stood outside, an older sergeant whom I knew from his patronage at the bar. He smiled and announced me with a rap on the door.

"Nedrick Bundy, ma'am."

"Admit him," she replied.

121

He stepped aside and I opened the door.

It was a sharp contrast, the blasting sun outdoors and the dark shade inside.

For a moment, I actually felt as though my eyes were shut, it was so dark. In the brief flash of daylight from outside, I was surprised at the condition of the room. The orderly who would have kept things neat and clean was off with the commander; as much as I liked her, it had to be a challenge for a lady like Meggie to actually do more than a little dusting while also keeping the fort's ledgers. There was dirt on the floor, even scraps of dried leaves under a chair. I couldn't imagine Meggie dropping food and leaving it, but then a woman worried about her husband on a field assignment was like to be distracted.

"Thank you for coming," I heard John's familiar voice say from somewhere in the room. "Please shut the door. With Mr. Hulbert on the outside."

I did so — earning a scowl from the newsman, probably for not arguing on his behalf — after which John turned up a lamp. I realized, then, that he didn't want anyone on the outside to be able to see him or the commander's wife. No one would risk shooting wildly into the dark.

I had met Meggie years earlier at one of

the dances held at the fort. I provided the alcohol, she provided the elegance. Twice each year I was happy just to be around her, she was always so gracious and cast light wherever she turned. She was a tall woman, with red hair worn on top of her head — I don't know what the term for that is, exactly. Her eyes were hazel, her cheekbones were high, and her skin was like milk — smooth and unblemished. She always dressed fine, even out here, with high collars and ruffles, the kind of touches you'd expect from a highborn lady.

She seemed at her ease, despite the gun lying across John's knee. John did not seem relaxed, despite what I hoped was a good sleep; but then, he had been stiff as a totem since the minute I first laid eyes upon him.

"What've we got here?" I asked.

"A man with compelling fingernails and a story in progress," Meggie said in her deep, musical voice. "Mr. Apple said you saw something that might explain."

That could only mean the Mexican, but I said nothing. In fact, I didn't move until John had bid me to do so.

"Please sit with us," John said, motioning to a wooden rocking chair with its back to the dormant fire and a cushion on its seat. There was knitting on the floor beside it. I sat, enveloped by a smell of wet wood, which meant the hearth had been recently doused. John and Meggie were side by side, facing the fireplace, so that left me looking at them both. For a hostage-taker and hostage, they seemed mighty calm. I noticed, then, just on the fringe of the lantern's glow, a table with John's satchel sitting open atop. There was a stool below it and a tray that contained orange rinds and two empty coffee cups.

"This situation is not what it appears," John said.

"I was just noticing," I replied.

"Indeed it isn't," Meggie spoke again in that warm-as-fox-fur voice. "It seemed the best way to keep others away for now."

I had to admit being befuddled, quite utterly.

"You saw a threat leveled against my guest, I'm told," Meggie went on.

"That's so, ma'am," I said.

She smiled. "No need to be formal just because I'm held captive."

"No," I agreed.

"About the attempted assault?"

I explained to her what had happened as best as I could, coaxed to recall every detail. The one that came up — the one that she brightened to hear — was that whip was black leather.

"There it is," she said. "The link."

"How so?" John asked.

"I review the quartermaster's ledgers for my husband. Our last fellow, now dishonorably discharged, enhanced his pay by selling goods to the locals. Boots, for the most part. Blankets. And then there was a missing box of leather ordnance."

"Whips," I clarified.

She nodded, then excused herself. She glided across the Indian-wove rug to a room in the back. From the crossed sabers above the door, I took that to be her husband's office.

"How are ya, John?" I asked in her absence.

"Rested, thank you."

"I mean — apart from that," I said. "This is not what I anticipated today to be."

"Nor I," he admitted. "The first person I saw seemed too itchy, so I came to see Meggie."

I left the conversation there as Meggie returned. She reentered the cone of lamplight and I could see that she carried a ledger. She sat, opened it on her lap, and reached behind her for one of the papers on top of the satchel.

She compared the handwriting.

"The foul, foul man," she uttered. "John, you have in your possession a copy of a receipt. It is for cash received at the Trinidad River Outpost in Burnet's Grant. And it is signed by our former quartermaster, Robert Francis."

"Meaning he continued his illegal trading," John said, "but with help."

The woman nodded. For a moment, she was gravely silent. I did not know what had struck her at that instant. On the one hand, there was the responsibility of flushing rats from the basement. That did not seem like a task that would cow her, even for a moment. Just the opposite. This sudden stillness was something different, and I imagined it had to do with her husband. A plot like this could put her husband at some risk in Washington from either friends of Francis and the Mexicans who might look to stop any investigation, or enemies of the Mexicans who might wish to scapegoat the commander.

"This must be stopped," she said suddenly. She turned to me. "Tell me everything you learned from Mr. Coles."

John relaxed a little and went into that faraway look I had gotten to know the previous night. I was strangely pleased that I had apparently not missed any of his narrative.

"It was both Coles that taught me," he began.

Chapter Thirteen

Coles Settlement, Texas, October 1835
John's Story

Mr. Coles loant me some of his clothes, I had a bath and a shave, I slept in a feather bed, and I found myself gripped by the sin of envy. There were orchards and fields and people in need of prayer, I could have settled in a shack somewhere on the property and been most content.

That had not been my plan or expectation. I hadn't even planned on staying more than the night, but Mrs. Coles was fascinated by my work with fruits and vegetables, Mr. Coles needed time to organize a response to Bowie, and my preaching style of talk — which it was, then, even if you wouldn't know it now — had won the interested ear of the domestics and slave workers.

I want to say that meeting slaves was a first — and I did not like it. No one was in irons or bound in any way or lashed. They had the run of the property, save for the bedrooms where it was simply indiscreet for anyone other than family members to be, lest they were tidying.

Mr. Coles was of the opinion, expressed over our first dinner together, that he was protecting them from a world in which they were otherwise unfit to survive.

I told him about Sam McCulloch of recent familiarity.

"Free and yet bound by very real concerns," Mr. Coles stated. "He must be wary of Indians and Mexicans *and* White men. If there is a crime — theft, assault, murder — he is likely as not to be blamed for it and strung up without a trial. If he is seen on a man's property, he could well be shot before being asked who he is or what he is doing there. If signs were posted, almost certainly he would not have been able to read them. I put it to you, John, that this is not freedom."

I had never heard a man argue that slavery is liberty, but Mr. Coles just had. I had only one resource to draw on, and that was the Bible, Galatians — I forgot the specifics but I remembered the words and spoke them: "For freedom Christ has set us free; stand firm therefore, and do not submit again to a yoke of slavery."

With a disapproving look from Mrs. Coles — who was apparently accustomed to her husband leaping from his seat during a meal — Mr. Coles scurried to his den. Even the scrape of her fork and knife as they cut beef seemed loudly critical in his absence. After an eternal few seconds he returned with a pair of books under his arm.

"My concordance," he said as he paged through the first volume. A finger traced an entry and then he went to the second book — the Bible. He smiled, and from it he read, "You may buy male and female slaves from among the nations that are around you. You may also buy from among the strangers who sojourn with you and their clans that are with you, who have been born in your land, and they may be your property." He slapped the cover shut, releasing dust into the candlelight. "Leviticus, 25:44."

I had been very firmly smacked in the head with my own resource. I put a piece of potato in my mouth to buy myself a moment to formulate a response.

"It is true, sir, that the Bible disagrees with itself, depending on the author," I said after I had swallowed. I was about to venture into quicksand flats in the dark. "It is equally true that Santa Anna and Stephen Austin strongly hold differing views — each convinced of the rightness of those views. I submit, however, that God places in our heart a sense of what is ultimately right or wrong. Otherwise, what chance of salvation has any of us?"

I had been looking down at my plate and looked up now, expecting to see Mr. Coles bound to his feet and roll up the welcome mat. Instead, he was looking at me intensely, as if he was thinking; Mrs. Coles had a look of what appeared to be admiration.

"Bravely spoken," she said.

"Like a true Texian," Mr. Coles nodded. "I don't agree, but we here say what's in our hearts. I will think on what you have said, though I confess there is a practical matter as well: how to keep my farm and heads of cattle functioning should freed slaves choose to leave."

I did not say what was on my tongue, that neither God nor the writers of our Constitution had thought livestock merited the same protection as people. But I had spoken enough. I still had a task to fulfill here and did not want to be run off just yet.

After Mrs. Coles had excused herself, and Mr. Coles had filled his pipe, we talked a little about the Indians I had seen, and after explaining their likely purpose, Mr. Coles suggested that they may also have been on a "horsing" party.

"It's one thing to defeat a foe as you described," he told me. "It's another to prove their courage by stealing horses from the cavalry. They're like children that way. They may not *need* horses at that time, but success gives them status and a swagger at home. The very fact that they come to the white man's territory and set up their wigwams is reason to boast."

"Does their life mean so little that they would risk it in idle buffoonery?"

"Oh, it is neither idle or buffoonery," Mr. Coles assured me. "Displaying bravery for its own sake, even losing your life, can serve your life. I know that's a difficult concept to understand — think of it as a martyr who is sainted and thus becomes revered among the people. In the mind of Valentine or Augustine or any such man, to sit by the side of God with such honor not only immortalizes your name, it makes a legend of your faith. To an Indian, a son of such a man begins his own adulthood trailing clouds of glory." He looked at me with serious eyes. "Do you think Colonel Bowie or Colonel Fannin would do any less?"

"For a cause, no," I agreed. "But for a horse?"

Mr. Coles blew smoke and smiled. "To the Indian, the scope of something is not as important as the action itself."

I guess I understood. I also have to admit I didn't quite agree. Those men in Gonzales who died to seize a cannon had died for nothing. Those men who might have died to hold onto it — they would have been dying for something. The object mattered.

The second day, Mr. Coles left shortly before dawn with one of the slaves, Jethro. I found this out later from Mrs. Coles. Two things impressed me. First, that he trusted me at his home. I suspected my Bible faith rather than my angelic looks was responsible for that. Second, his wife informed me that he had departed with a letter for a man who had become as powerful a force for independence as Stephen Austin, a two-fisted fella named Sam Houston.

"I have not met this gentleman," Mrs. Coles told me over eggs and sausage. "He came here three years ago, after being tried for assaulting a congressman back east. Mr. Houston lives west of here, in Coahuila y Tejas, and my husband feels he will know — how did he put it?" she said, gazing at the ceiling. " 'He will know who and where to choke,' though I'm not entirely sure what dear John meant by that."

I told her I suspected it meant whoever was siphoning the guns from the army of the United States to the army of Mexico, both in Washington and locally. But I had no idea who those people would be.

Later that day, however, we did learn that some folks weren't happy about what me and Bowie had done — though they didn't seem to know it was me and Bowie who done it.

A force of Santa Anna's men, ten strong, came riding up to the fence around the Coles place early in the afternoon. They looked snappy, in their blue and red uniforms; crisper and cleaner, the men were, than Mingo's march-weary troops.

The lieutenant out front swept off his bicorn hat as Mrs. Coles came to the gate. They were at ease; behind him, and behind her, the men were not. I was among them.

"Does the mistress know him?" I quietly asked Nancy, Jethro's wife.

"I never seen 'em," she whispered back.

"Señora," the officer said to Mrs. Coles, "pardon the intrusion."

"Lieutenant, the arrival of neighbors is not an intrusion," she replied.

It was a disarming if somewhat facetious line, since they had not only traveled far but the Mexicans were anything but neighborly.

But the officer was appropriately charmed.

"You are most gracious," he said in impeccable English. "You are the most honorable Señora Coles?"

"Yes."

"Is your husband at home?"

"Why do you ask?" she said.

"He is known to be well-informed, and we are seeking information about the two shipments that were stolen from agents of the government of Mexico, during which three of those agents were murdered. We were on patrol and encountered the only survivor."

"That is ghastly," she remarked.

"It is also criminal," he pointed out — with inflection as facetious as her own had been. "One of the killers was said to be James Bowie. The other was not known to the survivor."

His eyes moved across the menfolk, and I was glad, then, that the master of the house had given me a change of clothes. No doubt my attire had been described along with Jim Bowie.

"You are welcome to come into the house, look the grounds over, but I assure you Mr. — Bowie, is it?"

The lieutenant nodded once.

"Yes, no one by that name is here."

"These men — they are all your hands or slaves?"

"Except for Mr. Apple," she said, indicating myself.

The lieutenant seemed instantly alert. "Apple? How curious."

"Why is that, Lieutenant?"

"Because apple cores were interred in the graves of two of the dead men."

"That *is* curious," Mrs. Coles remarked. She turned to me. "John, did you murder two Mexican agents and bury their remains with those of apples?"

I answered truthfully, "No, ma'am." It was Bowie who kilt them.

She turned back to the soldiers. "I suppose if there had been lumps of coal in the graves of these unfortunates, I would somehow be suspect?"

"Most assuredly not, señora," he replied. "I merely remarked at the coincidence."

"It is that, truly."

"Then I may assume that Mr. Coles is not present?"

"Don't assume, Lieutenant. I will tell you that he is not here. He and the slave Jethro have gone fishing. For trout . . . or catfish. Nancy," she turned, "do you remember which?"

"Pike, Mrs. Coles, is what I believe."

136

"Really — ?"

"Mr. Apple," the lieutenant called over Mrs. Coles, "might I speak with you?"

"Of course," I answered, walking over.

"There were apple cores, and seeds, in the graves of other Mexicans we encountered," he said. "Were you, by any chance, present for the fighting near Gonzales?"

"I was," I said. "I had just arrived from the North, from Ohio. I have no rooster in this quarrel. I witnessed the fighting, prayed over those nine graves — I was a preacher up north, you see — and then decided to wander in this direction. I stopped here to ask where I was. Mr. and Mrs. Coles kindly invited me to stay."

"You do not like to fish?"

"Never tried. And I don't much like fish to eat."

"Your horse is stabled here, I presume."

"It is not," I replied. Again, truthfully.

"Would you like to see the stables?" Mrs. Coles asked. "We are proud of them. Mr. Coles fancies his animals."

If he said yes, he would see the horse we had taken from the first agent. But then, he would not necessarily know it from any other horse.

"Your hands," the lieutenant noticed. "They are not the soft hands of a *padre.*

And you are not dressed like one."

"I said I *was* a preacher, sir," I replied. "I am that no more. I came here looking for something else."

"Perhaps the lieutenant requires new agents in this territory?" Mrs. Coles asked innocently.

Right then and right there I hoped I never ended up on the wrong side of a spat with her. She used words like Bowie used his knife, and even the lieutenant was starting to wince at the cuts.

"Lieutenant," the woman went on, "we are not in the habit of harboring thieves and murderers, so I'm not sure what you expected to find here. Is there something specific I can do for you?"

The lieutenant did not reply. He rode his horse a little way along the fence to the west, then a little way to the east. He looked across the grounds as he did so. He may have suspected he was being stonewalled, but short of ordering his men to enter the grounds there was not much he could do. And even then, what would he find? My old clothes, possibly, but they'd been washed or brushed and weren't even the same dusty color as the Mexican had seen.

The lieutenant bowed slightly and returned his hat to his head.

138

"I thank you for your time, Señora Coles, and I hope our paths may cross again."

"Perhaps for a pig roast, if you can give us time to prepare," she said graciously.

The lieutenant ordered his men around and they rode out with the same fine canter on which they had rode in. I didn't see Mrs. Coles exhale, but I sure did.

"They will be back," she said as they became a wormy line on the plain.

"Why?" I asked.

"Because, guiltless though I am, the lieutenant had to have noticed just now the only apple orchard between here and Gonzales."

CHAPTER FOURTEEN

Fort Gibson, May 1836
Ned's Story

"It was God's joke on me for saying I was no longer a preacher," John said, "like Peter disavowing Jesus, though clearly not as infernal. This woman, who had nothing to do with my plantings, was tied to them by purest chance."

"For all you know the apples did come from her orchard," Meggie said.

"Might be so," John answered. "The Coles was in accord with the mission."

"Did the Mexican unit return?" Meggie asked.

"They did," John replied. "Two days later, with the agent who we had mercifully permitted to survive."

"Was Mr. Coles home by then?" I asked.

John shook his head. He fell into one of his silent moods, then, and Meggie took note.

140

"Ned," the great lady said to me, "this may take a while. Please inform the sentry that we are discussing a way to end this situation — that I am safe and that Mr. Apple is being quite sane and civil."

She lowered the light and I got up, cracked the door wide as my eye, and made my report. I caught sight of Hulbert, eavesdropping by the window, and Lieutenant Falconer, stalwart in the sunny compound; he did not seem pleased to be thwarted, but there wasn't much he could do about it. This was the commander's private residence.

I returned to my seat, eager to know how John got from there — the Coles Settlement — to here, still alive. He was sitting very still, the gun resting limp on his knee, his fingers barely holding it. From where I sat, the light caused those fingernails to glow like iron rust in the rain — cool brilliance, gemlike.

Almost, I thought, *the color of a ripe apple.*

"Would you care for any food?" Meggie asked me — which was a way of creating talk that didn't disturb John but reminded him we were there.

"No, Meggie," I said. "Thank you."

John came back to us then, inflated by a sigh and then back to looking at Meggie.

"The thing about Texas," he said, "is that in certain parts of it you can see to the end of the world. The Coles Settlement was such a place. Without hills or plateaus or woods, just the open field, no one coming from the south could just sneak up on you. Even at night, if you started sneaking from the horizon at sundown, you would not have reached the fence by lunch.

"So we saw the approach of horsemen," John continued. "It was late in the afternoon and we could count them by their sprawled shadows. The same number as the previous visit, plus one. It did not take Napoleon to figure out who that other rider might be."

"Had you not considered leaving immediately after the Mexicans first visited?" Meggie asked.

"I had," John said. "Mrs. Coles forbade it."

"Why?"

"She said that Texians do not run or retreat," John said.

Meggie inflated proudly at that. I do not think it was because she sympathized with Texian stubbornness — though she may have, I didn't know — but because a woman had spoke with courage and conviction.

"Mrs. Coles ordered the men to arm themselves, and she herself put a muzzle-loader in her hands. Somehow, the rifle looked at home across her chest. I didn't know if it was loaded, Nancy had brought it from the house; I do know that it spoke of the same spirit I saw back at the Gonzales campsite. Everyone — man, woman, child — was in this fight for freedom.

"Including me."

That last remark, coming after some reflection, gave me a hint at what was to come. If it was for a woman to stand shoulder to shoulder with the men, it was for a man to make absolutely certain, as best he could, that such wasn't necessary.

What John Apple did next caused me and Meggie both some surprise.

CHAPTER FIFTEEN

Coles Settlement, October 1835
John's Story

Faced with hiding behind a woman's dress, and possibly seeing her molested or killed, I decided there was only one course to take. While the men and mistress of the acreage lined up by the fence, I went to the house and donned my familiar, old clothes, then snuck off to the stables. There, I hurriedly saddled the stolen horse, mounted, and rode out the north side gate. I did not do that to flee. I did it to surrender.

I was thinking, as I rode, that I would be sitting on this horse another few minutes before the Mexicans looped a rope around my neck and strung me from the largest tree outside the grounds — a solitary oak that must have been planted when the world was young. The fence had took a detour around it. I later heard from Mrs. Coles that her husband felt it too proud a thing to be caged; odd from a man who kept humans as slaves.

Anyway, I suspected that that was where my life would end, and I thought of Nathan Hale meeting his fate at a far younger age than I. It had been a full life, and I found myself thinking of two things as I circled round the spread: God and Astoria Laveau, the lady I loved. One I was soon to meet, the other I was never to see again. Not that I expected to; but I don't think you ever quite give up hope. Unless you're about to be hanged.

But I had a plan, one which began to formulate when I mounted the agent's horse.

The only sound was my breathing hard and the dancing of the regimental colors in the wind. Mrs. Coles had been alarmed to see me come round the fence, though she said nothing. She must've figured I was do-ing exactly what I was doing: the only ac-tion I could take short of running or caus-ing needless bloodshed.

I stopped perpendicular to the lieutenant. The agent was near the front of the column, behind the officer, pointing at the horse and jabbering. He spit in my direction, and it landed on the man behind him. The lieuten-ant ordered him to the rear of the line. Then he motioned for two men to ride to either side of me.

"Your name, sir?"

"John Apple," I told him.

"How did you come by the pinto you are riding?"

"Me and Jim Bowie took it from the fella you brought," I said.

"You also took papers," the man said.

"Bowie has those," I said. "And also the guns."

The lieutenant regarded me. "I have the authority to hang you as an admitted horse thief."

"I know," I said. "You also have the power to grant me a pardon if I take you to your papers and your rifles."

"John!" Mrs. Coles screamed.

I saw her hand tense on the rifle. I think she had it in mind to shoot me. She didn't know I was putting on an act; that cry was real and hot, and it hurt me to hear it. But unless I wanted to be buried beside her orchard, with apple trees all around me, I had to buy time. She also knew I had protected the actual whereabouts of the documents in the satchel. That helped stay her hand, trusting that I knew what I was doing.

The lieutenant looked from me to Mrs.

146

Coles to the settlement. "Your husband has not yet returned from fishing," he observed.

"The lieutenant has a keen eye."

"And a patient one," he remarked. He bowed his head but had not removed his hat.

With a little bit of ceremony — overstated movements, searching where they need not have — the two Mexicans seized my weapons. Of course, if I'd had it in mind to use them I would have done so before now. But it was a sensible precaution on their part. They also bound my hands in front of me, which allowed me to hold the reins but not assault anyone with my fists — or my fingernails, which were at that point getting somewhat long. I found, being in the wild, such was useful for debugging, mostly. Everything from pulling worms from apples to mites from the skin or scalp. Then, with me still between them, we lined up beside the lieutenant — the column now resembling a capital L, its foot stomping across the scrub.

My mind was still chewing on the last few days and this one in particular. By going to the settlement I had not only put myself in danger, I had jeopardized the entire family. I began to wonder about the wisdom of having blindly followed Bowie's orders. On the other hand, a revolution was like taking a horse down a steep hill: once you start, you can only pick up speed.

"Where are we headed?" the lieutenant asked.

I assumed, since he knew about the apple cores, there was no sense telling him that we had interred the guns in a grave. I had a better idea.

"Southwest," I said.

"Toward Gonzales?"

"Not precisely," I replied. "Lieutenant — this is the only string I got, my only tether to life, so forgive me if I play it out."

"I promise you, Señor Apple, there are worse things by far than a merciful death, should you mislead us."

I did not have to tell him I had seen such as that. It was my fervent hope he would soon see it himself.

We rode till dusk and then we camped. The horses were tied to a line stretched between two trees. I was pushed to the ground beside one of those trees. My hands were freed only to be tied around the trunk. A sentry stood nearby, watchful and occasionally talking to his horse.

The rough bark was to be my pillow, I figgered. Or maybe it was the plan to keep me tired so I couldn't run away or concoct lies.

Back in Ohio, I thought it was tough to understand the mind of a woman. Out here, I was finding it a challenge to predict the thought process of anyone.

With one happy exception, it turned out.

It was the dark of night, with a campfire stupidly burning and two sentries awake. I say "stupidly" because they obviously weighed the benefit of keeping nighttime carnivores away versus letting any two-legged predator know they were here.

This lieutenant looked like he must have seen a few years on horseback. I put him in his mid-thirties, and he certainly knew how to ride the pitted prairie. His men jumped when he spoke in his softish way. But I reckoned, too, he was naïve as to the ways of the natives who wasn't Texians. Specifically, the Indians. More specifically, the Comanche. Hell, until I had seen their devilish ceremony, until Mr. Coles had spoke of their habits, I didn't know much about them. But I knew enough that if I put horses in their midst, the redskins would know it.

I heard the snoring of the men and the occasional crunch of dry grass and whinny from the corral. I heard the frequent, bored sigh of the sentry, the sound of his boots on pebbles as he walked to and fro now and then, the clop of his military shako when he bumped it into a low-hanging limb. There were occasional overhead scratches from night birds in the tree and field mice burrowing below. All must have felt safe around the fire, since they were occasionally brazen in their movements.

Not so the Comanche, who came not from the corral but from the plain.

I had been expecting them since we entered the territory where I had first seen them. I knew they had arrived when I noticed grasses move in a way that was not the direction of the wind. That was not the route I had expected them to take, but it made sense. Why excite the horses and have to deal with an aroused militia when you could overcome the soldiers first and then just ride off?

I felt poorly for the sleeping Mexicans and their duty-doing leader. But I was more worried about me. I was glad to be bound so the hostiles would know I did not represent danger. On the other hand, if they was of a mind to gut me, there was nothing I could do about it.

I wondered, briefly, if I should alert the lieutenant and hope for clemency. I don't like making fast decisions, especially those my life might depend on. Standing with the

Texians at Gonzales, I was one of many and in the back row. Here, I had to choose between standing with Mexican enemies or Comanche enemies. I wished I could do like the mice and just bury myself somewhere. But I could not.

I elected to play my hand with the Indians. I felt a twinge of sadness at having walked the unit into a kind of trap, but no one told them to come after me. That was their overconfident choice.

The Indians came at the encampment in a crescent moon formation, leaving no area of escape except toward the horses. It was a good tactic: the horses were to the rear, which meant the Mexicans would turn their backs to retreat. Moreover, men who were fussing with ropes and reins were men who weren't shooting or bayoneting.

I once saw a South American bird in a cage. It was bright colored, with a big beak and a loud voice. The moment before they struck, these redskins seemed like that bird — except with the cage door suddenly opened.

The firelight briefly lit faces that were covered with war paint, the bright "beak" of their knives in front. And they flew, too, from a belly-down position to a run in a single leap. And they squawked at the same

151

time, rousing their quarry to confused wakefulness.

The suddenly alerted sentries were the first to respond and the first to die. No sooner had they shouldered their guns at the main force than the edges of the crescent came up behind them and cut their throats in a single, deep slash. The two plunked to their knees and reached for their necks. It was ghastly hearing them drown, a loud gurgle accompanying each wet breath. Their tunics were quickly coated in red and they flopped forward on their faces, moving weakly without particular purpose and still gasping.

The lieutenant died third. He had been spotted and targeted by two Comanche who were seeking to decapitate the force. One took him down around the knees and, as he hit the ground hard, on his spine, the other put a knife in his gut and tore upward. I saw his intestines unfurl through the slit, like a freed snake. He expired whilst trying to push them back in.

There were screams aplenty, as much from the fired-up Indians as from the dying Mexicans. With the dancing red light of the fire it looked like the depiction of Satan's minions at work I'd seen in some religious books. The ferocity of the Comanche was such that not a single one of them was injured, save by their own enthusiasm causing two men to cut themselves and another to run through the campfire, burning his bare heel.

When it was done, three of them gathered near me. One of them touched his heart with one hand, touched his eyes with three middle fingertips on each, placed a palm on his head and pointed to the heavens with the other, then clasped both hands in front of his belly. Because they didn't kill me, but cut me loose, I interpreted that as: I had seen their ceremony involving the other brave, which was sacred, and as such I was an honorary member of the tribe. Or something like that. All I know is that when it was over and they had collected the horses, they gave me back my own and motioned that I should join them. I can't say I was honored or touched, since they was following tradition. But I was grateful to the Lord for sparing me.

"What about these bodies?" I asked, sweeping a hand across the dead soldiers.

Well, it turns out they weren't through. I had expected a repeat of the unhearting I had witnessed the other day but that was not what they had in mind. Using ropes some and whips some of the men carried, they were tied feet-first and on their backs to the tails of the horses. When we set out, they were drug behind their own animals. The Indians did not drive their new horses but walked them slowly, so as not to harm them. I expected there wouldn't be nothing but bloody pulp by the time they returned to their own camp.

CHAPTER SIXTEEN

Fort Gibson, May 1836
Ned's Story
"I am sorry, Meggie, for so vivid a recounting," I said to the woman who was more gracious hostess than submissive prisoner.

"No need, I asked," she said. "My husband has never deigned to tell me of such things despite my desire to know. It is only right that a wife should know more about the dangers and savages faced by her husband."

"I have no opinion on that, ma'am, other than I would have been fine not seeing any of it. Today, I don't see an animal butchered or a tomato sliced without thinking of those slaughtered Mexicans."

"Yet you are not so offended as you say," I remarked.

John looked at me. "Because of the Mexican?" I said.

"What Mexican is that?" Meggie asked.

"One who tried to kill me last night," John said to her but glared at me. "I sent him home as the Comanche would have."

"Why did he want to kill you?" she pressed.

"Because — let me tell you, I did not think there could be any people more brutal than the Comanche. I was wrong. Some so-called civilized folks are worse."

I could see John digging the fingernails of his left hand, the hand away from Meggie, into the cushion of his seat. He finally looked away, and I confess to being glad. There was menace and a touch of madness in those eyes. Maybe I shouldn't've brought the matter up, and Meggie was wise enough to let it go. But I don't like when someone preaches one thing and does another, especially when that preacher is a preacher.

"You rode with the Comanche?" Meggie asked, getting back to the topic at hand.

John nodded. "Not just to their little settlement but north toward a larger group that had come to lower Texas. They were paused on the other side of the Colorado River, in Mr. Stephen F. Austin's grant. And a wise place to stop it was."

"Why?" Meggie asked.

"Because Mr. Austin, as a head of the new revolution, was going to need all the help he could get to fight Mexicans," John said. "And even I knew that might include Indians in general, and the fierce fighting men of the Comanche tribe in particular. That was one of the reasons I decided to stay with them rather than head back to Coles Settlement. Much as I felt bad leaving Mrs. Coles in mystery about my fate, I felt it was better to befriend the red man."

"Which you did?" Meggie asked.

John hesitated. "Certain among them yes, certain among them no."

"The women," I said. "They welcomed you."

"They did, though not because I was like their braves. The opposite. I was more like them. I did not participate in the tossing of the Mexican bodies into the river. I did not join in the victory dance that night. The next morning, I began showing the women how to plant and irrigate. The tribe had roved, mostly, living off the land, and had only a child's basic understanding of agriculture. I also told the women and children stories from the Good Book. Which is to say I acted them out, mostly, since I didn't know their tongue. I cast shadows from fires onto the hides they had racked and stretched. I used the few words I learned, which the young'uns shouted out when I depicted a dove or rainwater or a bearded old man."

"You told them Bible stories," Meggie said approvingly.

"I did indeed," John replied. "Speaking of bearded old men, I was not popular among the aging medicine man, Black Moon, and also the ancient storyteller, Eagle Feather, a man whose job I'd took. The medicine man didn't like me 'cause he understood that I was not just telling stories, I was preaching religion. And I was not popular among the warriors because I had no interest in learning horse or knife skills or how to shoot an arrow or string a bow. They performed little plays of John Apple being a squaw, running from a bear, weeping when he was asked to wrestle."

"You called them children, once," I noted. "Your first impression was correct."

"Yet they had enough adult skills to survive," John pointed out. "As for the squaws, the chief got irate at me too because I did not seem to take to his youngest-of-three daughters. Swift Water, her name was — at least, that's what I gathered when she pointed to the river, wiggled her fingers, and pointed to herself. I thought maybe it mighta been Wild Salmon, though I kinda doubt it. She was pretty, she was kind, and she was also only about fifteen. She was also the glow in the eye of several braves who took unkindly to her open affection for me. When one of those braves — the one who had been at the heart-cutting — took to bumping me in the shoulder whenever we passed, I figured it was time to go."

"You were wise," Meggie said, her tone reflective.

"Was I? I thought it was kind of cowardly, then. But it seemed stupid to fight over a woman I didn't want, even if she wasn't the point. So I took the horse I'd retaken from the Mexicans and departed for the Coles Settlement."

"Why weren't you interested in her?" Meggie asked.

John considered the question for a long moment. "This may sound strange, but when I was in Gonzales I had a sense of being on a winning side. Nothing you could point to exactly, other than a feeling among all present. At the Indian camp, I had the exact opposite reaction. Any child of mine and Swift Water would be a half-breed with no future there or anywhere else. It would have been an outcast among the pureblood Comanche. Even if it had been twice as good at everything, it still would have been only half-a-man."

"Or woman," Meggie pointed out.

"Who no Comanche would ever take as wife," John said.

"What about as a Texian child?" Meggie asked. "There are Mexican and American parents — Mr. Bowie, I've heard."

"That is true," John said. "And maybe that's part of what drove him to want a new republic, one where White and Mexican can live together. But not Indian, far as I've heard. So where does a White Comanche go? Indians don't have a nation with boundaries that can be carved up."

"Is that some of what played into your idea of being — your word — a coward?"

John smiled crookedly. "It was not, Meggie. Not at first. Only when I rode out did I consider what I might've been leaving behind. Turns out it would've been a world of struggle."

I decided not to speak my mind this time, which would have been to call that act something more than cowardice. To run from new life because it is inconvenient or presented a challenge — I would have described that as sinful. And I suspect that in his heart, the preacher would have agreed.

"I'm sorry to have brought all this up," Meggie said.

"Don't give it a thought," John said.

"There are manipulative men, like the medicine man Black Moon, that one should never forget. They are the ones who pretend to do good but act from their own interests and ambitions."

"You say you set out for the Coles Settlement," she said.

"That's right," John answered. "And it's a good thing I did."

CHAPTER SEVENTEEN

Coles Settlement, October 1835
John's Story

Speaking well for their courage, and for Mrs. Coles's iron resolve, the men from the household had all departed in pursuit of the Mexicans. There was seven men: the two big-uns I had seen swinging axes when I first arrived, two house servants, and two slaves. Along the way they had picked up Samuel J. McCulloch, who suspected I was the man in trouble.

They had already found the Mexican camp, the blood, the missing horses, and me not there, and had followed the hoof-prints in the direction of the mighty Colorado. If they'd have kept going another half-a-day, they would have run into the Comanche, and on their side of the river.

The big ax man, Amos Dent — his ax firmly in hand — was riding a big Appaloosa and a grim expression — even as I was found. I had learned he never said much, and didn't, now. The other woodcutter was his cousin Jacobus Peabody, a little shorter but a little wider. He was on a lighter Canadian riding horse — a spirited brown I'd noticed before. The horse seemed happiest of all to see me, except for McCulloch.

"How did you survive?" the Negro asked me, breaking from the pack and coming toward me.

"Comanche took pity, even brought me home to meet the tribe," I said. "Which is why it's good I run into you, since they are gathered west of here in considerable numbers and looking for trouble."

"Were you coming back to the Settlement?" Peabody asked. "Mrs. Coles is sick with worry."

"I am on my way there, and apologize that I was not able to leave my hosts before now."

Amos swung his horse round, a signal for all to follow — save McCulloch. He came closer, flashing teeth.

"Told ya this country's strange small," he said.

"Thanks for joining them, Samuel."

"Men on the same side gotta watch out for each other," he said, riding on.

"Hey, the Indians are out there — you'll

163

run into 'em that way! Cross the river."

"Got to if I mean to hit Gonzales," he said, his voice booming over his shoulder.

I trotted after the others, impressed once again by this unusual black man. It was strange to think that somewhere else in this country, sass like that would've got him whipped bad.

We decided to camp in a cave we discovered in a low, short, dusty valley. Having learned from the Mexicans, we wanted to park in a place that could be defended from horse-minded Comanche. I saw how short-lived their feelings of brotherhood were; I did not think they would spare me a second time.

Even without the Comanche, the night was not a quiet one. My companions, though men of the West, were men of the log-cabin West. They were not men of the plains and they did not sleep in caves. They did not consider the varmints that lived thereabouts.

We heard wolf howls, which didn't set anyone on edge because we had a good fire going in the entrance — a precaution we took because there was a brisk, whistling night breeze rushing by to take the smoke down the valley, spread it out where the Comanche wouldn't see it. The grasses of the valley hid coyotes; they came where the wolves were not, and they came in sneaky packs. Moving low to the ground, you wouldn't see them, couldn't hear them till the grass moved nearby. But them, too, were not willing to come closer than the fire — regardless of the rabbit we were cooking on it.

Bats moved about outside. We could hear them flittering, see them pulling curls of smoke along as they passed low to the ground. There were a lot of those, and that was because there were a lot of what they ate — a lot of what kept us awake.

Bugs.

Moths self-killed themselves all night as they came fluttering around the fire. They died with a sizzle and a rotten smell and dropped more on us in a spiraling descent than on the flames. Big beetles came for the leftover rabbit, and then for the moths, crawling ticklingly across our skin. Cockroaches did the same, emerging from cracks in the walls and ceilings in such numbers that we plugged the rifts with pieces of rabbit fur. But they just found other ways out.

And we got bit repeatedly by ticks, who inflicted pain bigger than their tiny size.

"At least the wasps is in their nests," Jacobus commented. To me, he said, "Back at the settlement, you could step wrong and get stung to death."

"Remember how we thought sure the master was to lose his leg when he stepped on a rotted log?" recalled the stableboy, a teenage slave named Levi.

"Seemed strange to treat bugs with more bugs, them leeches," Jacobus said. "But they worked."

I did not participate in the chatter, which was accompanied by a constant brushing, slapping, or swinging of hands to clear flesh or air.

We got through the dark with at least some sleep, one of us always remaining awake to feed the fire with sticks and branches we had gathered. Our band departed promptly at daybreak — a cool one, with gray clouds robbing the earth of warmth and color. We reached the settlement by early afternoon, greeted by Mrs. Coles and all the ladyfolk with smiles, two buckets of well water for drinking or cleaning, and hunks of just-baked bread for any who was hungry.

Mrs. Coles smiled wide when she saw me, which made me feel good and bad at the same time. I remembered, in my heart, that Astoria Laveau used to smile at me the same way.

I cleaned up a mite and followed Mrs. Coles inside. There was someone else at the homestead, though I did not know that until we went inside. Seated in the parlor was Colonel Fannin. He rose, stately and sure, as we entered. I suspected that was for Mrs. Coles, who entered before me.

"It's good to see you, sir," I smiled, adding the "sir" because he was an officer and I had lately fought in his army, which made me somewhat of a soldier.

"And you," Fannin said — somewhat formally, given the effusiveness of my greeting.

Maybe that's just the way he was around ladies, I thought.

The men sat when the mistress of the house did, Nancy arriving with a tray for me consisting of coffee, eggs, and bacon. As I hadn't had breakfast, eating breakfast for lunch was a fine idea.

"You were saying, Colonel Fannin, that you are on your way to New Orleans?"

The officer started a little, as if state secrets were being divulged. But he recovered quickly. Failing to do so would have been an insult to his hostess and the trust she had evidently put in me.

"Yes, Mrs. Coles," he replied — sitting upright without affording himself the benefit of the chair back. "I will meet with Stephen Austin and plan on how to finance and man the revolt that has now begun."

"You may count on us, of course, for whatever we can provide."

"I thank you, deeply," he replied. "Both resources will need to be found quickly, as Santa Anna is sure to march against us before very long."

"As soon as he puts down the revolts in his own land," Mrs. Coles noted.

"We believe, with respect, ma'am, that he will attempt both."

Fannin was clearly unfamiliar with and made uncomfortable by women not just having political or military opinions but voicing them. To his credit, he flowed with that particular river.

"And he may have to conscript people himself," I offered. "Indians killed all the men I was with."

Both of them turned to me, as one. It was at that point I explained, short as I could, what had passed since my departure from the settlement.

"They did us a service," Fannin observed, "not just in eliminating enemy troops but in allowing the trail of the guns to go unpursued. Do you think, Mr. Apple, that you can approach these Comanche for their assistance?"

I answered frankly, "They don't like outsiders much, but they do like to fight. I'd say it's a coin flip."

"Would you be willing to make the effort," he asked.

"I would make my best effort," I replied. "But I would suggest we wait until they are needed."

"Would it not be better to befriend them now?" Fannin asked.

"They do not seem to pay attention to a single thing for very long," I countered.

Fannin seemed to accept that, or, at least, he did not pursue it.

The colonel had arrived that morning from Gonzales, and talked about preparations being made to defend the border regions from incursions. There was discussion, among Bowie and others, about moving southwest to take up positions in improvised well-built missions which might double as forts.

"The thought is that Santa Anna cannot possibly move north as long as there are guerrillas at his back," Fannin said. "An army that must continually look to the rear cannot fully concentrate on the front."

"There is the Mission San Antonio de Valero," Mrs. Coles suggested.

"Also San José y San Miguel de Aguayo and Mission San Francisco Xavier de Nájera," Fannin said. "Bowie is planning to take a look at the first of those — he has a mission in San Antonio de Bexar."

"How intriguing," Mrs. Coles said. " 'A mission.' Might we know something about it?"

Fannin seemed uneasy. It's possible he did not even realize that Mrs. Coles had mocked his tight lips. She was every stitch a patriot, as he was.

"We are hoping to take ground from Santa Anna," he said. "That is all I am comfortable revealing — no affront intended, ma'am. But this is a military matter."

Sternly but not critically — a neat skill she displayed — Mrs. Coles responded, "Colonel — in this matter of independence, we are, all of us, soldiers."

"It is as you say," he agreed. "My only concern, my only caution, is for those who will be facing bullets directly. But I will tell you that, while there, Colonel Bowie will have to consider not just the fortification itself but sources of water and food. If we are to commit men and resources, they must be able to survive there."

Now he was talking about a topic I knew something about. "Colonel, I would like to be part of that undertaking," I said — more enthusiastically than I had intended. "I have experience in agriculture and it might be prudent to begin cultivation before troops are dispatched."

"I like that," Mrs. Coles said when Fannin took too long to accept.

I don't think the colonel was questioning the wisdom of my suggestion or the sincerity of my offer. Rather, his eyes were working like little machines trying to figure out, I suspect, how to have me tie up with Bowie.

"It's a very good notion," Fannin agreed. "Thank you, Mr. Apple. Colonel Bowie said he would leave in about a week — time enough, I think, for Mr. Coles to return and for you to have information about the gunrunners to bring to Gonzales. Does that suit you?"

"Very much," I said.

CHAPTER EIGHTEEN

Fort Gibson, May 1836
Ned's Story

There were two very hard raps upon the door. They did not come from knuckles.

"Mrs. Gearhart, Mr. Bundy," said the speaker in a high, male voice. "This standoff has breathed its last. To the intruder, I say surrender now or we will be forced to enter."

We all looked at one another. Lieutenant Falconer was sincere, there was no question about that. Even as he spoke, we heard a handful of troops — all that was left to guard and service the fort — take up positions front and back of the commander's residence. And there was no question but that he would carry through his promise. The length of the hostage-holding would have been entered in the log of the watch, and there is no doubt but that even Colonel Gearhart would have done no different at this stage. Maybe sooner, given the affront to his wife.

But I guessed, too, that the young officer was hoping that John would surrender so as to make an assault unnecessary. Far as he knew, he was betting large on the man inside wanting prison instead of a noose.

"You may come in," John spoke, firm and having decided. "Alone, Lieutenant."

There was a moment of silence.

"You may keep your firearm," John added. "And you may keep it on me, if you wish . . . I will not object."

That would make things strange, tense, and not very cozy. John was going somewhere with this, I suspected.

"I do not accept," the lieutenant replied. "You will surrender."

The boy had gumption I'd not known about. Even Meggie seemed surprised.

John looked down. He undid the leather strap that held his knife to his hip. He let it drop. I picked it up and, leaning toward the door, handed it to Falconer.

"It will be all right," Meggie said quietly. Then, louder, "You will treat Mr. Apple in accordance with the Articles of War of 1815?"

"Ma'am, is this felon also a soldier?" Falconer asked.

"He served with Colonel Bowie at Gonzales," she replied. "I believe that qualifies."

That was when we all heard another voice, Hulbert's, say, "He was also at the Alamo, a part of the lawful Texian militia organized and sanctioned by Sam Houston."

Meggie had not been told, yet, that John had participated in that widely famed battle. Her expression hardened — but it turned toward the door, not at John.

"Lieutenant, the articles require a court-martial, and I will insist upon the convening of one," she said. "Promptly."

This was clearly a turn Falconer had not anticipated. Again, silence.

"We will need time to prepare the army's case," he said.

"Mr. Apple will wait," she replied. "But he will not be imprisoned."

"Ma'am?"

"You have my word he will make no effort to leave the fort."

John looked up then, at her, and nodded. She nodded back.

"Mrs. Gearhart, the man has unlawfully detained you at gunpoint," the lieutenant said. "The Articles of War — if memory serves — defines an attack on the family of a serving officer or soldier as cause for detention."

"And detained he will be, in the fort —"

she began.

"Until a tribunal can be convened," Falconer interrupted.

"At which time I will act as a witness on behalf of the defendant," the unflappable woman replied. "Shall we do this now? Your court against my testimony? Or," she moved in on him with buzz saw certainty, "would you prefer to sleep on the matter?"

There was nowhere else for Falconer to take this. He agreed. And I could not help but wonder, looking at John's relaxed features, if this was not the result he had wanted all along. To put the fort on notice that someone had come among them who was aware of grave wrongdoing. More likely than not, whichever man or group was responsible would be forced to lay violent hand upon him — or flee.

Meggie stood, brushed down her dress, and went to the door. The world outside seemed bright white for a moment, and then details emerged: the lieutenant, the sentry, and Hulbert, with a clutch of soldiers behind them.

The woman remained in the doorway until the soldiers had dispersed and the lieutenant had stepped back, his weapon pointed at the ground. Hulbert was his usual prying self, looking around the door, past Meggie, and scribbling as he noted the arrangement of the room.

I rose and then John did, his own gun held barrel-down along his leg. He surrendered it to the lieutenant when we walked outside. Falconer did not seem to want to let this affront to Meggie Gearhart pass, but her proximity and having vouched for John made a pouting statue of the lieutenant.

Deems Pompey Hulbert was a happier man. I wondered if he would cut short his intent to continue to the Alamo to report on this story. As John stepped into the warm sun and clean air, I decided to ask.

"One of the benefits of being known at the fort," Hulbert said, after keeping me waiting while he finished what turned out not to be writing but drawing, "— one of the benefits is that I can use their messenger to send stories back. They have two running between the forward position and the fort each day. The third, who knows all the northward routes, sits around doing nothing because there are no dispatches to send. He carries my reports."

"Do you ever intend," I asked, "to write a piece on civilian abuse of military resources?"

He laughed. "My articles spread their greater glory," Hulbert proclaimed. "They should be paying *me*."

"Mrs. Gearhart is aware of this?"

"Most certainly! She approves, my friend. She has ambitions for her husband, and favorable reporting is a part of that."

So rapt had Hulbert been in his note-making that he had not realized Mrs. Gearhart was but a few paces behind him.

"I can speak for myself, thank you," the woman said critically.

"With greater clarity — and suddenness — than any woman I know," the reporter said, turning. His expression was even more contrite than his words.

It was a lovely moment — for me. John did not appear to have noticed. He was several steps to my right, farther from the building he had recently inhabited. He seemed to be lost in his mind some-where . . . again.

Hulbert turned to him — whether to escape Meggie or get information, I did not know. I stayed where I was, hovering protectively. I don't know why I should feel the need to defend someone who survived the Texas Revolution. But I did, perhaps because I knew Hulbert's prying, insatiable nature.

Once again, he was thwarted — albeit briefly — by Meggie.

"Mr. Apple," she said, over the reporter. "I would love to hear more of your story, but it would be unseemly under the circumstances."

He looked over when he realized she was talking to him. "Of course, ma'am," he said.

"I shall be eager to read it when Mr. Hulbert is finally able to publish it," she said. "I know he will present me with a copy."

"As many as you'd like," he replied.

The woman turned and went back to the residence. Hulbert faced John.

"I . . . I heard most of what you said to Mrs. Gearhart, being right outside the door," Hulbert said. "I have hung on your narrative in hopes of having the first, perhaps only firsthand report from the Alamo and other conflicts you may have been in. But," he said, moving a little closer, "what you just did — holding the wife of the commander hostage — does not seem to fit."

"No," John agreed.

"Would you be kind enough to explain?"

"No," John repeated.

Undaunted, Hulbert continued. "Then perhaps you will explain why you will not explain?"

John regarded him with those penetrating eyes. "Because it is not for the public to read about."

"I see. Then would you tell me — off the record?"

"To me," John replied, "you are the public."

And that was that. John remained where he was, sunning or thinking or remembering or all of those. Hulbert — whose vanity was impregnable, it seemed — simply turned and went to his room, presumably to write what he had overheard.

I finally approached John. "Do you want to talk some more?" I asked.

"I do," he said. "It is necessary that someone understand." He looked at me. "I trust you, Nedrick Bundy. It is important that you know why I do what I do."

I was flattered, if uncertain. Other than show him my customary hospitality I had done nothing extraordinary. But then, it is possible that in his many months in Texas he had seen very little of that, of basic humanity. He also must have guessed, from the very act of my having come to the fort, that I would be an ally in whatever he was planning.

We sat on the wooden sidewalk that fronted the barracks, where there was some shade, and he resumed his tale.

CHAPTER NINETEEN

Coles Settlement, October 1835
John's Story

Mr. Coles returned after a week. It was late in the afternoon, the air cool and threatening a nighttime rain. He was dusty and visibly weary, and Jethro was near asleep when Nancy ran out to hug him. But the master of the house was full of his typical good cheer like every day was Christmas.

He kissed Mrs. Coles on the side of her cheek, then turned to me.

"I am glad you waited, John," he told me. "We have a great deal to talk about."

"After you've bathed and rested and supped," his wife told him.

"We'll talk while I do one of them," he said.

He had meant the bathing, but it didn't happen that way. Mrs. Coles took him inside, told me to stay outside, and I saw him well after dark over a chicken dinner that Nancy had prepared quickly and efficiently. Mr. Coles looked a lot better for having followed his wife's instructions.

"I hear from Mrs. Coles that you have not been here the entire time," the master said as I joined the family at the table. It was the first time I had seen his three young children at dinner, it being a special occasion so an exception was made. Typically, the son and two daughters — the boy 11 and the girls 12 and 13 — ate earlier and were abed before their father had his meal.

"Sam Houston, the Lord bless him," Mr. Coles said after I had quickly updated him, "is someone very special, an ace-high straight-speaker, let me tell you."

"For my husband to say that, Mr. Houston must be special indeed," Mrs. Coles smiled.

"It's true, I don't give praise lightly, or often," Mr. Coles admitted. "My children will tell you that."

They didn't.

"But this man has a vision for this land and he will make it happen. He is busy raising money by selling tracts and parcels of land, water and crop rights, everything you can think of to anyone who will honor the sovereignty of our land. He will make independence happen, even though Satan himself stand in the way — which many say

181

this Santa Anna is. He certainly has his minions, little devils who do dirty work for gold and silver and power. Which brings me to your information."

The children were either daydreaming or listening attentively, possibly both; if the latter, I suspected it was as much to learn what pleased their father, by repeating, as it was to learn for the sake of being educated. That was something I had not seen as much in the East, where most of the children this age were brats or flirts.

"Sam Houston said there has been an operation up north stealing army guns and selling them to both the Indians and the Mexicans," Mr. Coles said. "Oh, not stealing exactly — mis-consigning, if you will. Labeled for places that don't exist. That is the army," he sighed. "If they come up short on something when all is said and done, they'll just order more."

"Who is involved?" I asked, gently trying to get him to the point — and thinking that occasional daydreaming would not, in fact, deprive one of information. Charming and enthusiastic though he was, Mr. Coles *talked.* He very much liked being the master of his table.

"That we do not know," Mr. Coles admitted, deflating somewhat. "And it has not, until now, been a major concern. It has been a crate or two we had heard — and those guns were not being turned against us. Now they are. It must be stopped."

"No doubt," I agreed. "How?"

"Bring one of the guns to Houston," Mr. Coles said. "The paperwork you obtained was signed with fictitious names on authentic bills. Your average soldier or sentry — uneducated, underpaid, far from home — would not have known or even cared to investigate. The documents admitted that the contents were guns, so if he had checked he would have had no reason to doubt the rest of the entries. Houston said that if he had one of the guns it would be possible to track them to their point of origin using the manufacturer's own records."

I frowned. "That will take months."

"To punish the guilty, yes," Mr. Coles admitted. "But we do know this much. They passed through the town, or garrison, of Fort Gibson. There is one of those new dandy roll watermarks hidden in the fibers — something used in the printing to mark the paper as authentic. Illuminated from below by a candle, and under examination with a glass, Houston saw an 'FGO' in the corner." He stopped, said proudly, "That stands for Fort Gibson, Oklahoma."

I was impressed. The children seemed roused to attentiveness. Mrs. Coles offered seconds, almost as if a reward for Mr. Coles finishing his story.

I told him I would set out to find Bowie in the morning.

"I have information about that as well," he said.

"The missions," I said.

Mr. Coles was so surprised he actually, involuntarily pushed himself back from the table — as if he were loath to be seated with a spy.

"Colonel Fannin was here on his way to see Mr. Austin," his wife informed him. "I daresay our information is as up-to-date as your own."

Mr. Coles eased his chair back and resumed his meal. "Very efficient of you," he said to us both. "Very efficient. Bowie goes to Bexar first."

"That would have been my initial destination," I reported.

Mr. Coles grunted with satisfaction. "We have coordination," he said. "I like that. Sharp, smart, effective. We are going to win this thing."

It was a particularly large leap of confidence, but there was need for that in this struggle. Because common sense said —

and said it loud, into my ear — that the fight of under a thousand Texians against a force of Mexicans at least seven or eight thousand in number, armed with cannon and a smattering of new American guns, was not going to be won by confidence or even courage.

Fortunately, the Texians had something the Mexicans did not.

A cause.

I rode out for that cause the next morning. It was strange. A few weeks ago, I did not know the fight even existed or that I would be enlisted. But the valor and spirit were contagious. For the first time in my life I felt as though I belonged to something.

If I had been thinking clearly, instead of with my head and heart in clouds of God-blessed virtue, I would have been thinking about the enemy. By now, the Mexicans under Mingo would have missed their fellows the Indians had slaughtered. They would have followed their route, maybe found them. They might have concluded that Comanche butchered them — or they might have thought that Texians did it to throw blame on the Indians.

In any case, they would have been looking for blood this time, not guns. And when I saw a plume of dirt and dark shadows inside, I knew that mine was the first they would mean to take.

CHAPTER TWENTY

Fort Gibson, May 1836
Ned's Story

The narrator stopped suddenly, as though someone had grabbed him round the mouth from behind.

"John?" I said.

He looked down at his nails.

"Are you all right?"

He chuckled at that. "You asked me, last night, whether Texas had healed my broken heart."

"I assumed it had," I replied.

"In a manner of speaking," John told me. "When I dig in the earth, I feel close to God."

"God — is your one true love?" I asked.

He shook his head. "God is my one true judge. Because tilling soil is not all I have done with these hands. And some of those other deeds — after I did them, it was the devil I felt kinship with, not the Almighty."

"You are too hard on yourself," I suggested. "You fought a war."

"Sometimes," he said. "Only sometimes. Other times, I was killing a blacksmith. During my journey south, I had time, too *much* time to think about Mrs. Laveau." His mouth soured. "And . . . her beau. That man who was younger, stronger, fond of ale and a good time. I imagined all kinds of terrible punishments for the hurt he helped to inflict."

"So the Mexicans that attacked you when you left the settlement —"

"Each one of them paid for that lug's sins," John confessed. "Sure, they wanted to do me harm, as did the Mexican I tied to his horse. But each one was a fresh tax on that wrong committed against me. The War for Texas? I committed to that cause mostly due to my respect for the participants. But that was never the only reason, as I discovered that day."

At that moment, John suddenly became more — human is the word that comes to mind.

"I had been a civil man, more or less — with the Texians, the Indians, and even with the Mexicans Bowie and I had stopped. After all my brooding across the plains, I had resolved, with God's help, to try and

188

start a new life here, a life forgetful of the hurt. The three shapes charging at me from the sun — they hit me, then and there, as three of the four horsemen of the Apocalypse. I couldn't tell you who was War, Famine, or Pestilence. All I can tell you is which one was Death, because that rider was me.

"The change happened sudden, like a dark cloud passing over the sun. I really wish, Nedrick, I understood all about it. I wish I knew if it was God or Satan who charged me with sudden fire."

"Wasn't it the Hand of God that set them loose?" I asked. "Something about seven seals?"

"It was. The Book of Revelation of Jesus Christ. The Lamb of God opened the seals of a holy scroll to set them free. But," John said, emphasizing the word, "the three other horsemen and I were on opposite sides. What, then, to make of God's role in that?"

I had no answer. Theology was not my field of endeavor or interest, other than to show up at mass every now and then to pray for my departed wife and child. They were buried so far from me that it was the only way I could be attached to their remains. Unhappily, I could not help John with his dogmatic struggle.

"I stopped my horse, thinking to let the enemy tire his. I took some water from the skin, cupped it into my eyes to clean away grit. I drew my big machete-like knife. And I waited."

CHAPTER TWENTY-ONE

Cummins Creek, Texas, October 1835
John's Story

I had a color map that Mr. Coles had given me so I could mark my trail by landmarks.

Where I was, at that moment, was just on the western side of a stream called Cummins Creek, after one of Austin's friends who was granted land here a bunch of years previous. I had taken a leisurely wade across, enjoying the trickling calm of the waters and the birds that drank from its shores. The creek was fed by the Colorado, which itself the three Mexicans would've had to cross to get here. They would have crossed it recently, since it was close enough to hear, and their horses would have been tired from the effort.

So they ran at me, rifles pointing up; they could not have fired and struck me except by luck at a gallop. They obviously intended to stop and take aim at any moment. They finally did so when they were about upon my position, just a few horse lengths' distance. When they did I reined hard to the left and kicked my horse forward. That put me on the outside of the trio — but within striking distance of the nearest man to my right. I raised the knife as I rode past and sliced his extended arm *hard*. I felt like a jousting knight in a picture book, turning a half-circle as I rode past in order to meet any new challenge.

While the one man I had cut clasped his badly bloodied arm and continued facing away from me, the others had made their turn. But before they could run at me or raise their rifles or do much of anything, I charged the man on the other side. I did not bother to slash him. Instead, swinging my arm up from the side, I plunged the machete into his chest. The blade punctured flesh and sinew and, as I rode past, it remained stuck there and twisted him to the side. He tumbled from his saddle, still holding the reins, which pulled the horse to the side, him flopping all over, his legs on the dirt and his arms tangled overhead.

The man in the middle had taken the opportunity to raise his rifle, aiming it past the empty saddle.

So had I. I had passed the reins to my

knife hand. My Colt was in my free hand, pointing at his chest. Even with my left hand it was an easy shot. The gun discharged. He flew backward against the dragoon with the cut arm, spraying him with more blood, his rifle firing into the air as he fell. That scared all three horses, who, though trained I was sure to hear such discharges, were already spooked. They whirled and bucked and reared and created a small mob of horse chaos in one small spot — two Mexicans being trampled underfoot, one trying to remain seated.

This is the part that scared me. I did not see him as a man. I saw him as a predatory animal, something to be gotten rid of. Then I saw him as something less: a rabbit, a frog, something that survived by running. Driving shiny silver spurs into the ribs of his horse, he left his dead or endangered fellows and galloped away.

I dismounted swiftly, picked up the rifle from the Mexican who tried to shoot me, and made the easy shot. The fleeing Mexican flew over the head of his horse and got trampled as it passed him over. The frightened animal calmed and stopped a few yards past. I looked to my right. The man tangled in his reins was also still, his horse moving in a sideward step to try and dislodge him. The man with the bullet hole in his heart was bleeding facedown in the dirt. His horse was already grazing, having expended considerable energy reaching this point.

I used my knife to cut the horse free of its former rider. Walking to the horse that was out in the field a bit, I used him to carry his former master back. I stamped down on the ground; the earth was pretty packed here, so I did not inter the men as before. Instead, I lay them side by side and covered them with their saddles and used good-sized rocks to plug up the ends. I didn't know when anyone might find them, or what they'd do when they did.

After freeing the horses of all encumbrances, I left them where they were.

Remember how I was talking of the kind of honor I did the men who died in Gonzales? Praying to sort of clean and sanctify the spot?

Not here. Already, flies buzzed around the bloody dirt. The sun would shrink the leather of the saddles and bake the bodies and they would be carrion for whatever creatures happened by. Buzzards, most likely, would be the first — I could already see them flying from the creek where there were trees to give them a perch.

But at least the bones and the uniforms would remain. There would be something to bury, if their comrades ever found them.

It was funny, really. I looked at the rifle I had fired, then at the others. They were clean and new and most likely came from the stolen shipments. I now had three rifles to give to Sam Houston. I bundled them together with cut reins and lashed them to the side of the horse that was off eating grass. I would bring him along on my journey. I still intended to meet Jim Bowie first, since I wanted to know where he and Fannin might would likely end up before I headed north.

I had to cross a lot of waterways to reach Jim Bowie. There was the Colorado, then the Guadalupe, then smaller ones — the Cuchillo, Gilolo, and I finally made it across the San Antonio on the morning of my third day out. A ferryman at the Guadalupe had seen Bowie just a day before, so I suspected I'd find him in the village of San Antonio de Bexar. I did, with a herald angel to announce his presence. It was a boy selling produce from a cart. I couldn't understand anything but the name and the price, which he spoke to passersby; but the lad was holding a cut melon. Either the famed knife fighter had cut it for him — from the smoothness of the slice, he did it in just a single swing — or else the kid was just huckstering.

I found three men, still mounted, at as sad a holy place as ever I'd laid eyes upon. From the look in Bowie's eyes, he must've thought the same of me as I rode up.

"My friend and *calavera,*" he said, with a look of concern. I learned afterward that that was a sugar skull, a pale confection eaten by children on the celebratory Day of the Dead. "It's good to see you."

"The same," I said, not realizing how dry my mouth was until I tried to use it, other than to talk idly to my horse.

Bowie unhitched his own water pouch and handed it to me. I thanked him.

"You're pale with road dust and there's blood on your neck," he said as I drank. "But I don't think it's yours."

I told him whose it was and, briefly, how it got there.

"I'm impressed, John," he said — but if there was more to that thought he didn't share it, as his companions trotted over.

I was introduced to John Ballard of the new Gonzales Mounted Ranger Company and to Juan Seguín, a Mexican who hated Santa Anna and his tyranny.

"James," Seguín said to Bowie after we'd

exchanged greetings, "I am going to see to the volunteers. There is little time."

"Of course, go," Bowie said. He turned to me as the Mexican rode off. "We have word that a peacock with fancy red plumage on his hat, name of Martín Perfecto de Cos, is prancing north with a force of some thousand men. Should be here by nightfall. Juan brought his own countrymen here, about two hundred. We plan to take the town from the Mexican soldiery that's here and hold the rest off."

I wasn't much for arithmetic, but those numbers didn't sound favorable. I mentioned this to Bowie

"I'm heading back to Gonzales to get as many men as possible for support. If the town falls, John'll let us know before we get here."

I looked over at the structure I had seen upon arriving. It was a crumbling mission, one of the ones Mr. Coles had told me about.

"Yeah," Bowie said. "If they end up falling back, the Alamo will have to do. What about you?" he asked. "How did you fare with John Coles?"

Once again, in as few words as I could, I told him what had happened with Sam Houston.

197

"It's important to get those guns to him," Bowie agreed. "But it may be more important right now to have them in the hands of fighters here."

"That was my thinking," I told him. "And I'm also thinking I want to stay."

My words brought a prideful smile to Bowie's sunburnt features. I didn't have the heart to confess that it was not so much my feeling for Texas that was working on me, though there was some of that. I had spent time contemplating my actions back in the lowlands and had come to the realization that I felt alive for the first time in years. There was fire inside of me; the kind you get when you win at poker and want to keep playing, win or lose.

Bowie rode off at a gallop and, tugging my gun horse, I followed the other two gents to where the main line of resistance was forming.

"When do you make your move?" I asked Ballard who was nearer, on my left.

He pointed a hand down a long, dusty street, which went over the river and off to the north.

"In just a few minutes," he replied, "as soon as we reach Main Street."

I looked around. There were just low-lying brick buildings, most with peeling white paint and unfortunate-looking plants and trees. Mexican peasants and a few modestly dressed Texians walked the streets. Though there were a number of troughs, horses and burros were few. There were stray cattle here and there, bound for the butcher or wherever the Mexicans were garrisoned I figured. Because there were Mexican soldiers in significant numbers, some patrolling casually, others on horseback, a few talking in clusters. I saw no Texian force.

Which, I told myself, *is obviously the point.*

The Mexicans probably assumed, from Gonzales, that any militia they might face would be brash, taunting, shoulder to shoulder. They would never expect a guerrilla attack.

Juan Seguín rode a little ahead of us. He was dressed in a black shirt, a hip-length red coat, white breeches, and polished black boots. His head was bare and his black hair high and carefully combed. The man was clean-shaven and there was a great scar across his forehead.

"He has been in battle?" I asked, assuming a saber wound.

It took a moment for Ballard to figure out what I meant. "No," he said. "That's from a clubbing he received a couple years ago for openly criticizing Santa Anna's tyranny. He

199

swore, then, he would pay the bastard back on the field of revolt."

"And you, sir?" I asked.

"I was at Gonzales," he said. "Noticed you there, in fact. This is my home. No foreign prince is gonna tell me how to live where I've always lived." He grinned. "No strutting ass is gonna tell me how to die, neither. Santa Anna's got a price on Texian heads. I intend to deny each and every Mexican gun this paying target."

Like Bowie, like Fannin, this was a man fully committed. I started to wonder if I could measure up. Fortunately, I didn't have very long to consider the issue.

Everywhere I looked, Mexicans were suddenly not civilians; they were soldiers in the army of Juan Seguín. Empty spaces in the windows of many buildings were suddenly filled with gunmen. And the soldiers who ran toward a large church at the end of the street were cut off by horsemen who thundered in along Soledad Street, both from the north and from the south. The northern half cut the city in two while the southern half made for the church, which was where the soldiers were garrisoned. Juan Seguín galloped ahead to join the men who were racing toward the church.

There was a lot of shouting and running,

but no one said very much, and I wouldn't have understood it in Mexican anyway. No one also got very far, there being nowhere to run for safety but indoors. Beyond just a few blocks the village consisted of river, creek, ditch, springs, and open land.

The Mexican soldiers tried to rally and form a perimeter outside the church, but by then the Texians under Juan Seguín had organized a line of mounted men and foot soldiers, all armed, entirely surrounding the church.

John and myself dismounted. At my suggestion he took one of the captured rifles. He smiled.

"*This* is a gun for a cause!" he cheered, gripping it in both hands.

Turning, he rode his horse into the fray. I watched, listened, as puffs of smoke and slightly delayed pops and bangs speckled the field of combat which, just moments before, had been a quiet village path. The sounds echoed here and there, men began to shout and cry, and a horse-blockade had become a battle.

My two horses were uneasy, backing away and jumping with the sounds and acrid smells of the fracas. I pulled the lead animal to a nearby tree and tied him there. Then, my heart thumping hard, I took one of the rifles in one hand and my knife-machete in the other and walked toward the fray.

From the start, I knew that I would not be shooting anyone unless ordered to. At the outskirts, where I was, men seemed to be looking for soldiers on their own, mostly inside structures, chasing women, children, dogs, and chickens out back doorways. A few people took refuge in suddenly crowded privies — which, I suspect, many who were unaccustomed to battle would have reason to use for more than concealment.

I moved along the fronts of the buildings where I was less likely to be struck by a ball that missed its target. And there were some that came close, chipping paint and clay from walls and flower pots. A woman in a window saw me and ran; I did not realize till then that I was scowling something wicked.

The deeper I went, the more the experience was new and exciting. In Gonzales, the battle had lines: us against them. Here, it was all around. Sounds of battle and injury were everywhere. The hurt was mostly to Mexicans who bravely or stupidly emerged from hiding to try and make a hole in the Texian lines, something a mass of men could run through. The attackers weren't having any of that. Mexican bodies flopped in the dirt, some clawing and crawling back toward the church and being allowed to do so: caring for the wounded eats up supplies and occupies men. It's a stinking way to look at things, but war is not a thing humane or civil.

To which subject, my own mood, the scowling one, did not come from the battle itself or from the gun in my left hand but from the blade in my right. That hand, that arm, that breast had a soul all its own. It was like a dog on a length of rope and that rope was being pulled harder and harder causing your step to quicken.

Suddenly, the Texians retreated. It was so quick that John nearly ran into me, into my knife, which was extended farther than I'd realized.

Juan Seguín was backing from the church, head turned to the rear, and shouting something in Spanish. He was waving a saber overhead, side to side. I didn't need an interpreter to know he was telling his soldiers to retreat, to seek shelter, or get off the street.

As they dispersed, I immediately saw why. Several hundred Mexican soldiers were coming around the structure, half of them on foot, half mounted, all charging and shouting.

It appeared that the intelligence about the arrival of Martín Perfecto de Cos and his men was grievously mistaken. Until now, the ground had been covered with mostly Mexican dead. Now there were Texian fallen, mostly wounded, but we would have to care for them and be burdened as we sought to burden the Mexicans.

Two men were wounded carrying off an injured man; that was wrong, and I noted the Mexicans who had taken those shots. Leaving John, I ducked into a cantina and waited. I did not look like a soldier, might be mistaken for a local if I cowered. That was the plan as I pushed open, slightly, the shutters the owner had closed. I saw one of the killers coming toward me, on foot, loading and firing as he went. I waited for him to pause near enough to the window that I could reach him through the shutters.

With my knife hand still feeling like that eager, now rabid little dog, I reached my hand around his eyes to hold him in place and rammed that big blade sideways between ribs into his left side. I pushed it so hard it tore easily through muscle, through whatever it encountered, and found his heart. Warm blood pumped briefly over my hand, then simply oozed down along his uniform. I withdrew the blade with an angry tug and he corkscrewed to the ground.

It all happened in the course of a second or two. A soldier running behind him stopped, raised his rifle, fired over his fallen comrade-in-arms. I had already jumped back from the window, into the cantina. I kept moving backward, certain the next shot would come at me through the window.

Then I stopped, hard, my boot heels digging in. I had time.

I ran forward, ducked, and as he fired a good foot over my head I drove the knife into the soft spot under his chin — the high, stiff collar practically guided the blade in. He dropped the gun, fell back gurgling, and tripped over the other man I'd killed. I realized, then, I would have left without my rifle and grabbed it from beside the window where I'd propped it.

Now, more cautiously, I backed from the window. Only then did I notice two women, two boys, and an old man behind the bar. The man was sprawled over the children, the women kneeling and praying beside the boys.

I continued to back to the rear of the place. Off to my right was a private room with a door in back. Probably, I thought, it was used by the soldiers for private meetings — about love or war or both. The lingering odor of perfume suggested the former.

The gunshots grew fewer in number as the Texians vacated the town proper and the Mexicans had no one left to target. After checking to make sure no one had thought to cut off anyone's departure from the rear — they hadn't, the Mexicans concentrating their counterattack on retaking the roads and small plaza outside the church — I ran into the sun, the light hazed by the collected smoke from the many shots that had been fired.

And then a cannon bellowed from outside the church. Its goal, I suspected, was to warn the Texians not to return.

In that respect, both the blast and Martín Perfecto de Cos had this in common: their ambition failed.

CHAPTER TWENTY-TWO

Fort Gibson, May 1836
Ned's Story

"It is always easy, as I'm sure you know, to look back on something and declare it a good idea or muddle-headed," John said. "In the case of the Mexican commander, securing Bexar was the main and immediate thing he had to do. To chase Texians in their own land, in terrain his soldiers did not know, could not have seemed like a good idea. And it wouldn't've been. The militia and its Mexican allies had already scattered, like bird from a gunshot."

I did not realize, until John stopped his story, how caught up I was in his telling of it. He had spoken in a manner more lively than his usual monotone, and even acting it out a little here and there, holding out his hand — like Lady Macbeth, it struck me — when he talked about the Mexican soldier's heart blood coating his fingers. Or showing

207

me his sad expression when he spoke of the man who was protecting the children.

It actually concerned me, some, how he would feel when he spoke of the Alamo, where so many people he got to know had perished.

"You feel better talking about this?" I asked. "Does it — does it help to *clean* you?"

"Planting helps to clean me," he replied without hesitation. "The cool, damp dirt cleans me. Even burial. I plant a body, plant a tree on top of it. Dust to dust — it is nature's way of things. I'm telling this to you for a different reason."

"What reason would that be?" I asked. That was the first time he had expressed a purpose, other than the simple fact of telling.

"When I'm done, I will need your help," he said.

"To do what?"

He replied with that rarity, a crooked smile. "To finish the tale."

I eyeballed him with a sudden surge of wariness. "You didn't just come to my place by chance, did you?"

He shook his head once.

"Why, then?" I asked.

"We will get there," he told me.

That wasn't good enough, I thought. "I don't much like being used, Mr. Apple. I came to the fort out of decency for a man who seemed like he could use a friend. Was my trust placed in the wrong hands?"

"As Jim Bowie would have told you, had he survived, I do not desert my friends or those who have showed me kindness, like the Coles."

"Then I truly do not understand," I replied.

"You will," he said.

All through our talk, Lieutenant Falconer had passed us in the course of executing his duties. Never once did he miss an opportunity to scowl. I was surprised that for the last half-hour or so Deems Pompey Hulbert had not made an appearance; I suspected he was writing his story to send to Brazoria. In fact, without the command being present, the afternoon was unusually quiet here. Even the civilian population went about their trading or resting or coming and going with a new kind of quiet.

It was probably just the absence of the soldiers and their horses that made it seem more like a church than a fort. But then, as John had just related, sometimes the two swapped places. My own business was built on the remains of two others. It wasn't the structure itself that made them what they were, but the people inside.

Which was certainly true of the Alamo, from all I'd heard. But I would let John get to that in his own time . . . though his announcement of me having a role stuck in me like a burr on a dog.

"There was a different mood among the Texians when, under the blanket of evening, we found each other individually then in groups and collected at Salado Creek east of the town. We had lost a handful of men, the Mexicans more than that, but each of our fighters took it hard. They didn't even know two of the dead, who were part of Juan Seguín's volunteers. But when you embrace a common struggle it makes you brothers. In many ways, I discovered it was a bond stronger than blood — for them."

"Not for you?"

"Never reached that for me," he frankly admitted. "I liked the people. When they started hollering about Texas, they were no different from a wolf pack." He shook his head. "That wasn't for me. I want to be closer to God than to a beast."

"But the cause of liberty is godly, is it not? The Israelites and their flight from Egypt —"

"They didn't howl, they didn't make war,

they left," John replied.

I grinned. "They had God to do the fighting for them."

John considered that. "I can't argue that. And I ain't judging. All I'm saying is I couldn't hold with them when they became an army and not people, as such. Except for Bowie. He was always his own man, even when he worked with the others."

"So you joined them at Salado Creek. . . ."

CHAPTER TWENTY-THREE

San Antonio de Bexar, Texas, October 1835
John's Story

After the success at Gonzales, I think folks expected we could roll through this like a dust storm. But we got our noses bloodied on that wide road in Bexar.

Bowie hadn't got so far that he failed to hear the commotion, and came running back. Another man went in his place, fella named James Bonham, who was to become our official courier. He was second cousin to someone who was to have a greater impact on our revolt, but I'll get to Travis later.

Bowie announced his arrival by tossing his knife into the ground right by the small campfire the men had allowed themselves. Our men were too tired to jump at the sudden intrusion of the gleaming metal, and before they could rally to do so, they recognized it wasn't a Mexican who had thrown it.

His approach, from the darkness into the dull firelight, was like the arrival — well, you may have had this much right: it was like God had sent an angel. Of course, I even had myself wondering if that might be so. Angels take many forms in the Bible, almost as many as Zeus in Greek myths. Who was I to say that wasn't the case here? Bowie immediately set to listening, not talking — which, in my experience, is what the best officers and politicians do. Once the fight had been recapitulated, he lit a cigar off the fire and considered the situation for a few puffs.

"The fact that de Cos has not come after us tells us his plan," Bowie said. "Fortify the town and charge us dearly trying to get back in." He gazed steadily into the night, toward the not-too-distant lights of Bexar. "It's almost as if they're inviting us," he said more to himself than to us. "We're not gonna disappoint the Peacock. Only we won't be moving on his timetable but on ours."

He moved closer to the fire and drew the commanders around, including John Ballard and Juan Seguín, who was simultaneously listening and translating for his men. They looked sinister around the low blaze, like Satanists who had played out their revelry but wanted more. The men were instantly and in some cases openly unhappy with what he suggested.

Bowie's plan was to do nothing until Bonham returned. That met with widespread disapproval from the Texians, who wanted to redeem their stained honor.

"You do that, stupidly, and the enemy will cut you down," Bowie said. "Look, all the Mexicans who are coming to Bexar are already there. We know that from our southern scouts. What we gotta do is wait until the Peacock sets up his supply lines from Bexar to Mexico, which should be finished in a day — two at the most. When he does that, when we got men from Gonzales, we set up a perimeter around Bexar — not one they can see, only feel — and close them in from all sides. We cut off the supply lines. The occupiers will send out men to get supplies; we'll cut them down. The Peacock sends out marching troops to find us, we don't march, we *run* around them and harass positions in the town."

"Skirmishes," one man said dismissively.

"You say that like it's a dirty word instead of a sensible tactic," Bowie said. "If we fight his fight, if we take on one thousand *fortified* men, we lose. We make him fight us where his big numbers don't help him a bit — we win. We do more than win. When Mexican bodies start adding up in Bexar, the soldiers will either lose heart or charge after us — in which case we retreat and relocate, hacking their numbers from the sides, from the rear."

"You're wanting a siege, not a fight," Ballard said unhappily from the opposite side of the campfire.

Bowie approached him. "Ballard, I'm wanting victory, that's all," Bowie told him, soft enough so that only those nearest heard. "You know I'm no coward, and I hope you wasn't calling me one."

"That wasn't close to what I was saying."

"Good," Bowie replied, clapping a friendly hand on his shoulder. That was for everyone to see, to show there was no dissent among the commanders. "Hell," he said to everyone now, "if I thought it'd end this thing, I'd sneak in there now by myself and try to cut the Peacock's throat. But it wouldn't. And glory?" he said with contempt for the word, "that is something to tell your grandchildren about. I ain't interested in one and won't ever have the other. What I want, all I want, is what I first came to these parts for: Texas for Texians. Anyone

215

who forgets that will find himself dead under Mexican bullets or Mexican boots."

Bowie had moved back to his place and stood there, puffing like a steam locomotive. And in the quiet that followed — as everyone digested what he had said — I saw an opportunity. If we was going to be here for October, November, longer, then I would have a chance to plant. I knew it was not an ideal time and place for that, but I knew I could make food grow to help feed the small and hopefully growing army.

Apart from the members of Juan Seguín's militia who, draped in serapes, went to spy on the enemy, I was the only one busy morning till sunset. I tilled about an acre near the creek, good land, arable soil, and foraged through the compost piles the Mexicans built outside of Bexar. There were pits and seeds aplenty, from peaches to garlic, apples to tomatoes, and I put them in the ground under the nourishing Texas sun. It did not take more than a week for some of the first shoots to grow. Now, I knew that the trees would not produce fruit in the time we had. But they attracted the bees and birds that had seeds clung to them; they drew the varmints that had undigested pits in their patties; and with God's help we had beans of several variety within three weeks. And Bonham, returning, had brought dozens of men, each of whom had food they contributed to our own composting.

By the end of the month, we had, by my count, over three hundred troops scattered along the creek. We'd've had more men, save for Bowie making good his plan to cut the Mexicans' supply lines. Those boys stayed in the south, Bowie among them, at the San Francisco de la Espada Mission. Among our three hundred, groups of ten to twenty drilled together. They were the ones who made sorties against the enemy when the Peacock sent parties out to hunt food. The Mexicans usually lost two men for every one deer they snared or took down with bow and arrow; they stopped shooting at birds because ammunition was also not getting through, either.

I confess to being impressed by the numbers of folks who showed up, men and also women. What I heard of kids, they'd been left with grandparents and such, but the wives wanted to be a part of this effort too, just as they'd been there at Gonzales. Some of the women helped me with my labors, and I helped them, too, as they washed clothes and plates and utensils. Though it was still curious how water didn't make me feel nearly so clean as dirt.

Or maybe not the dirt . . . the creating of something alive.

The big news of the month, apart from the original dustup, was the arrival of three men in particular. Spurred by some instinct about the Mexican army or Texas itself, Stephen Austin had come back from New Orleans with Colonel Fannin. And Sam Houston himself had ridden from the north. The meeting with Mr. Coles had alarmed him. Rather than wait for me to visit with guns — said visit obviously having been delayed by more urgent needs — he came down to Gonzales and followed the trail of men to Bexar.

A little ashamed, a little proud, a little not-sure-what-to-expect, I waited till he had been in camp a few hours before I introduced myself and presented him with one of the waylaid rifles. Now this man was tall, just a little taller than me, and he had a serious expression which remained very, very still whenever he was being told something. I imagined some dutiful secretary at a desk in his head, making careful notes about everything. He not only remembered my name as Mr. Coles had given it, he recalled the itinerary that had brought me to the settlement.

"Texas is grateful for your devotion to

her," he said as he accepted the rifle. "I've been told of your agrarian efforts here — very industrious."

"Thank you, sir," I said.

Houston eyed the weapon carefully. "There are mice in the attic," he said. "Vermin enriching themselves with Texian lives. These are cavalry issue and — see this?"

He held the stock in front of me, the back of it. There were numbers cut in the wood.

"Those indicate the garrison where they were bound," he went on. "I brought a ledger with the listings — we can check them later. That'll tell us where our traitor or traitors are."

I also met Austin, briefly, that first day. He seemed prickly, he seemed tired, and he seemed — he *was* — all consumed with just one thing: getting the enemy soldiers out of Bexar, out of Texas, and back to Mexico. That desire seemed stronger at the setting of the sun when, for the first time, the Mexicans fired that cannon again — twice. They must've knew our two leaders had arrived and were letting us know they weren't impressed.

"Let 'em roar," Austin said from the edge of our encampment. "Let 'em come! They will find us unafraid and no longer willing to retreat. I hear their stores of bread, meat, and drink are dwindling — let 'em come and *we* will feed them! Buckshot! Fists! Clubs! Blades! A stew of Texian resolve!"

Well, that was how Austin spoke, probably lines from speechifying these many years about Texas. New or old, the words were fresh here and the men cheered his full-throated challenge. I only hoped that when he made good his vow — and I did not doubt he would spill every drop of his own blood trying — that I had enough apple seeds to go round. There was, to me, no way this could end without rows and acres of new graves.

Near the end of the month — I did not note the day, as there was little need for that kind of record-keeping — we intercepted a pair of deserters from the village. They were posing as peasants, and just trying to get away from what we learnt was unhappy conditions in the town. Many of the shopkeepers, growers, animal herders, and other laborers had already left, most in the night so the Peacock's men wouldn't try to stop them. We talked to most of them; that was how we got our information about deteriorating conditions in the village.

Still, the Mexican commander did not want to risk leaving the fortifications of the church and the blocked streets and plazas. He must have felt, rightly, that we were too skilled at guerrilla strikes. If the small excursions to obtain food and water had met with death, he had to reason that larger ones would meet with greater misfortune. And now, his spies had to have told him, we had too many men for him to simply try and smash through.

And to where? His orders had been to take the town. He took it. Santa Anna would not appreciate his leaving it.

Finally, one foggy night, something happened that Austin had been waiting for: we caught our first pair of Mexican army deserters. They were dressed as peasants and surrendered, without struggle, the arms they carried. We fed them and they informed us that everything was bad in Bexar. It wasn't so much the lack of food but the inability of the town to accommodate sanitation, cleaning, and even drilling for nearly one thousand men.

After the men finished their story, Austin said just two words: "At last!"

The men were held, lest they have a flourish of courage or guilt and return to tell the Peacock that an assault was finally imminent.

Austin sent his swiftest courier to Bowie

and Fannin and told them to move closer to the town. The two colonels left the mission and closed on Bexar with ninety men. The fog continued, and the sounds of men and horses were loud and confusing. It was assumed that the Mexican commander had no clear idea how many men were closing in and from how many sides. We learned later, from prisoners, that he had dispatched one Colonel Domingo de Ugartechea with a complement of 275 men to meet the men under Bowie's and Fannin's command. Our boys heard them coming and dug in on the banks of the San Antonio River. The Peacock should have stuck to his original instincts.

We heard the battle through the mist. Our men, three hundred strong, had been prepared to join if the Peacock threw more soldiers into the fray — but this the commander did not do. Austin had us start to whooping and making sounds like we were charging forward. It was loud enough and enthusiastic enough to be heard on both ends of the town, from the church to the Alamo.

The attacking Mexican army took more than fifty casualties — fourteen of them fatalities — and lost the cannon they brought with them. Many horses fell not from gunfire but from being unable to see. They would add to the problem for the commander as they had to be shot later and baked under the sun. Many were cut up by townspeople for their meat.

The Battle of Concepción, as it came to be called, gave the Texians what they wanted: revenge for the hightailing-out they did during the previous encounter. And it gave Austin what he wanted as well: the start of a real, killing siege. While the Peacock licked his wounds and refortified their position, a gent named Thomas Rusk arrived from East Texas — where I was once headed, I might remind you — with about two hundred additional volunteers. That freed up a bunch of folks who hadn't been home for several months to go see their families. They also needed new boots and warmer clothes, the chill autumn nights feeling more like winter eves with each passing day.

The good thing for us was that we didn't have to do much foraging. Bowie's men kept pilfering from the Mexican supply wagons that tried to get through. The gentleman I mentioned before, William Barret Travis, was one of the new arrivals and lent Bowie a hand with his captures. When Mexican reinforcements tried to reach Bexar, Travis was particularly good at getting horses and mules away from them — forcing them to travel on foot, where they were easy pickings, or return home. Many chose the latter. That had to infuriate Santa Anna, who could not have liked this reputation he was getting among Texians as the generalissimo who couldn't win a battle.

After we'd been hunkered down a few weeks — sometime in mid-November, as I calculated — we got an added boost when over one hundred troops, three companies in all, joined us from the U.S. of A. Austin's first reaction was that we finally had enough troops to seize rather than siege Bexar — but then he found himself possessed of both a good and bad sense about that, which he confided only to folks he could trust — and I'm proud to count myself among them.

"Washington either wants diplomatic ties or annexation," he said. "I find myself needing to go there to make sure they understand we are fighting for republichood, not statehood."

So Austin departed, leaving another Southerner, the sort of formal but nonetheless two-fisted Edward Burleson, in command. Burleson was of a different mind about attacking. Unlike many, he was content to starve the Peacock out. His reasoning made him a prophet.

"Santa Anna won't sit still for long," he said one afternoon to a group of the more aggression-minded soldiers. "When he decides to move himself off his throne, we are going to want every able man we have to send him home. Losing any Texian life here is vainglory, not sound tactics."

We had been ensconced for a couple of weeks more when we got word from our scout "Deaf" Smith, who had lost his hearing to some illness and was married to a Mexican widow who helped me with my gardening; we heard from Deaf that Mexican cavalry was approaching. We guessed that Santa Anna must've been concerned when he didn't hear from his field commander. I had spent that time growing my vegetable garden and gathering wild apples, which our lady cook baked in a variety of ways — leaving me the cores, always, from which I dutifully removed the seeds which I placed in skins of water to keep them hibernating like tiny bears.

That random thought, by the way, was what gave me the notion to grow my own bear claws. See, we didn't really have proper tools for tilling the soil and I liked to get my hands into Mother Earth, so thinking of grizzlies put the idea in my head to shape my nails like they are. And I used bark, like the bears did, to give them their edge.

So Deaf brought word of the cavalry and Burleson fielded a considerable force to go out and meet them. They collided at Alazán Creek which was to the west, and the Grass Fight was on. It got called that because reports was that the caravan was carrying pay for the unhappy soldiers in Bexar. It wasn't. It was carrying hay for the animals, which was more urgently needed. So people died over horse feed.

Come December, the siege was starting to wear on us as much as it was the Mexicans. Deserters told us how the Peacock had re-arranged his defenses to use things like firewood more efficiently. That bunched the enemy tighter in sections of town and they started getting under each other's skin. About a hundred of our people offered to make a run at the town, try to bust through the barricades. Part of that was courage and part of that was not wanting to be here through Christmas, the new year, and into the unwelcome arms of winter. Once those men offered, three hundred or so others agreed it was a good idea.

Two of our commanders Ben Milam of Kentucky and Bill Cooke of Virginia, two tough acorns, agreed to lead the assault. It wasn't Burleson's favorite plan, but a good leader has to know when to pretend a majority view was his own idea. He had the remaining four hundred men who, in addition to protecting our camp from attack, would be responsible for keeping the Peacock's forces divided by attacking the Alamo — which was on the opposite side of Bexar. Most of that would be done with the cannon we took from the Mexicans, though enemy fire ended up taking that out with a damn lucky shot.

I went with Milam's unit because Bowie did. Both of them being Kentucky boys, there was never any question of things being otherwise. I didn't have a rifle for this engagement — just my big knife. My job was to scout enemy positions and bounce the sun off my machete to point them out.

We started the onslaught on a clear, cold morning, quickly seizing the Veramendi and Garza houses, which were situated on the north of the plaza where a large force of Mexicans was stationed. The Peacock was no dope: he let us have those two places, then blew them, and us, all to hell with cannon fire.

We withdrew, which didn't beat the drum for morale. Our spirits sunk further when a Mexican dead shot put a big hole in Milam's head and he died where he stood. After a few days we was reinvigorated, though. The Mexicans charged our camp and were repulsed. We attacked the town, and this time it got nasty. We went in on foot, just the way we'd retreated from the church, and fought the Mexicans hand to hand. I slashed necks and arms and anything else that came in front of me. I realized I didn't have to kill, just injure, to take a man out. Blood? I was dripping with it. It was in my hair, my eyes, my ears, my mouth. I must've had more than a dozen different varieties on my skin and clothes. As a result of this fighting we got planted in several buildings on our camp-side of Bexar. The big blow for the Peacock came when he ordered more troops into the Alamo there. Four companies rode to that side of town . . . and kept on riding. Our crossfire was hellish, and merciless, and the Mexicans lost a lot of men that day — not just from desertion but from our determination to take the damn village.

We succeeded. After a lot of noise and a lot of blood being soaked up by the dirt; with the wounded of both sides crying into the air or their sleeves or into the earth if they fell facedown, Martín Perfecto de Cos took off his fluffy plumage and surrendered.

It was a win but it had been a bloody one.

It wasn't a picnic like Gonzales, with women making soup while we chased Mingo home. We lost thirty-two men in Bexar — which was unexpected. The only consolation was that it was less than the 150 or thereabouts the Peacock had lost. Most of that was from infantry forces because cavalry could get away faster when things didn't go so well. The commander had misunderstood our resolve but also our weapons and our soldiers. We had better guns — the forwardmost of them from the crates that had been stolen that we stole back. We also had better shooters and a reason to fight. Men like that don't give up. They die, but they never surrender.

But I'll tell ya. Though the Texians now had San Antonio de Bexar, we all of us started to realize that the rest of Texas would come at a larger price. Nobody openly questioned the wisdom of what we were doing. But you could hear that in their silence, see it in their faces as we said words over the graves of our dead.

I went about my planting. Some folks found it objectionable, like I was committing a desecration. I explained to them what I had come deeply to believe, that these honored dead required a living grave marker and that my trees would feed the children of Texas for generations to come. Not everybody agreed. But while I worked the fields, I had plenty of time to think. And it struck me out there that I was upholding tradition. I was challenged around the campfire one night by a still-emotional younger brother of one of the dead. Name was Robert Brown, and he would end up being one of those combat veterans who saw the revolution through from first bullet to last.

While chewing tobacco, and spitting, he accused me of disrespect and being what he called a "ghoul."

"Sir," I said, finally voicing the thoughts that had been growing in my head, "how is this different than I heard from men who have been to sea, that those who died shipboard were interred in the arms of the ocean? Meaning no offense, every one of them souls got ate by fish who themselves got caught and ate by people. It is God's way, not mine."

He looked like he wanted to punch me but someone just out of the circle of light lay an arm on his shoulder. It was Bowie.

"Brown," Bowie said, "if it was my wife and children who lay in that field, I believe their immortal souls would be pleased that their mortal bodies were not just food for worms. We are the new occupiers of Bexar and, come spring, we will need food for ourselves and for the populace whose good-will we desire — who will become citizens, in fact, of this republic we seek to build."

Now, Jim Bowie could've said black was white and most people would nod in agreement, such was his stature. But in this instance his words had nothing to do with his and my history. They was heartfelt and no one ever again complained about my work.

Neither he nor I nor anyone present could have imagined how fateful those words would be.

CHAPTER TWENTY-FOUR

Fort Gibson, May 1836
Ned's Story

We were no longer alone.

A sidewinder had joined us, the estimable Deems Pompey Hulbert. I guess I had always had that sense of him at the Hick, but it had never made itself so clear as when he approached in shadow and stayed there during John's story.

"Send your story off okay?" I asked after acting as if I hadn't felt him lurking there.

"Written, edited, and dispatched," he spoke, sipping from a flask filled, I was guessing, with the commander's rum — the preferred drink of Colonel Gearhart. "I did not mean to hear, but I have a reporter's ears. You spoke of stolen guns?"

"I did," John replied, surprising me with both the strength in his voice and a new-found willingness to engage the reporter. John even turned to the man as he addressed him — also unexpected.

Hulbert stepped into the light. I could see, from his satisfied expression, that he believed he had touched a mushy spot in the peach — something to stick his thumb through and touch the pit.

"You heard of these?" I asked. "You being a newsman, after all," I added, appealing to his professional vanity.

"Everyone knows that army rifles end up in the hands of Comanche and Creek," he said. He nodded toward the open compound of the fort. "These Indians aren't just here for the food and clothes. This is where they swap silver for guns."

John's gaze shifted to the idle red men milling near the gate, which was the only area where the savages were permitted freedom of movement. It was strange how they stayed apart from the Mexican guests; I couldn't tell who was avoiding who, which band felt superior to the other. In my world, only one of those bunches was allowed in a saloon and, even then, Mexicans were not welcome at the bar itself. That wasn't my doing; to me, they were just paying customers. White men, though, were partial about who they drank with. As though, passed out on the floor and having to be carried out the door, men had cause to feel exclusive.

"What about those Mexicans?" John asked.

"Those?" Hulbert said, drawing breath as if he was about to sing. "Those Mexicans are too afraid to move. You see, they did not align themselves with the cause of freedom, so in Texas as well as here they are considered cowards and traitors. If these people and the Mexicans of Texas can reconcile on neutral ground in the United States, it is the belief of Colonel Gearhart and his superiors that they can be valuable allies in establishing future peace between Texas and their brethren in Mexico."

"*Or* they can be used to organize the transfer of American guns to Mexico," I suggested. "That puts Texas square between two potential suitors. I hear talk at the Hick. If Mexico is emboldened, and armed, they may return to Texas. Where, then, would the new republic turn but to Washington for assistance?"

"Which would lead to an American occupation force and then annexation," Hulbert said, nodding. "And if things go right for Washington, they get a wider war and claim more territory formerly under the control of Santa Anna. I have heard this said."

"Do you doubt it?" I asked.

"I have learned never to doubt anything that comes from the swamp on the Potomac," Hulbert replied. "Victory has been achieved by Austin and Houston, and they have their republic. But, politically, and cartographically, Mexico still considers Texas theirs. President Jackson regards it as a future state. Oh, he dare not speak that too loud for fear of alienating the men who fought for their independence. But arming Mexico would suit that plan. Members of Congress have said so openly."

"Which side 're you on?" John asked suddenly.

"I take no sides," Hulbert replied grandly. "I merely report."

John just looked at him. It took a moment before Hulbert realized he'd been snared.

"The writing about Mr. Austin and the revolution was, firstly, not mine; and, secondly, fell under the heading of an editorial commentary. It was set apart from the actual reporting of the news."

"Your reporting is uninfluenced by your publisher?" I asked.

"Entirely uninfluenced. And, proprietor, the day those two bottles are poured into a single drink, the integrity of both are lost."

"I once saw honest reporting," John said. "It was in a cave on the Kentucky-Indiana

border. Pigment paintings showing Chero-
kee braves hunting a wolf that had carried
off one of their papooses. That was clean,
clear reporting. Maybe you should take up
drawing, Mr. Hulbert."

"I don't understand this antagonism
toward me," the reporter said, puffing up a
little. "I don't hear you criticizing the activities of these soldiers, all of whom have
broken Commandments in the name of
lesser laws."

"Their uniforms and weapons announce
their policies," John said. "Your tools give
cover to yours." John put his hands on his
knees and pushed himself erect. "You are
snug with these folks. Do you report their
activities fairly? And if you did, would you
be given the privileges you enjoy here?"

"I do report them fairly," Hulbert huffed.
"As for the rest, you'll have to ask Colonel
Gearhart when he returns. Or go and talk
to Lieutenant Falconer."

"You been coming down here how long?"
John continued.

Hulbert looked down and calculated.
"Nineteen months and two weeks."

"In all that time, in all that reporting, in
all that staying at the fort, did you never
report on smuggling?" He looked at me.
"Tell me, Mr. Bundy. Do you provide the

red men with liquor?"

The question caught me off guard. Maybe because I didn't have time to think, I answered truthfully.

"Among friends, I will admit that I have done so," I replied.

"You gonna report on this infraction of U.S. law and policy?" John asked Hulbert.

"I — I would need evidence," Hulbert stammered. "I would need witnesses."

"You got one here," John said.

The man's actions here and now would have made me angry save for three things. First, I knew he probably didn't care whether I did or did not peddle wares to the natives. Second, he couldn't know whether I did or did not do what he suggested. Third, I knew what he was really getting to with Hulbert. And fourth, this wasn't about me at all but about the man standing across from us.

The reporter looked at me uncomfortably. "Mr. Bundy, do you in fact have such dealings as Mr. Apple suggests?"

"That is not the business of yourself or Mr. Apple," I replied.

"That is an evasion, sir, not an answer."

"It may not be the answer you want, but it's the only answer you'll get from me," I told him. "You are, of course, free to camp in the alley beside the Hick, watching all doors and windows around the clock. Though I forewarn you, I will report you as a vagrant after the first full day. That's the law for the area around saloons. Otherwise, we'd have a sea of drunks begging for charity and offending the ladies with their stench and wretchedness."

John held out a coin. "I would like to become a subscriber to your publication. As a reader, I demand that this story be investigated."

"That . . . that is not up to me," Hulbert said, declining to take the money.

John put the coin back in his pocket. "It is inconvenient to report. Do you carry advertisements?"

"Yes, of course," Hulbert replied. "For goods — public notices about estates, the sale of land, offers to translate foreign documents."

"Shippers of alcoholic beverages? Vendors of same?"

"On occasion," Hulbert admitted.

"Would they be pleased if by your reporting of such practices their business suffered a falloff?"

"I think the point has been made," I interrupted. "Mr. Hulbert, whether he acknowledges it or not, is still part of a moneymaking enterprise. Such factors must be considered when he writes his reports."

John moved toward the man. "Rifles," he said. "What do you know about the illegal transport of rifles through this fort and into Mexican hands?"

Hulbert seemed horrified. By the idea of it or some possible collusion in same I could not be certain. Enough to say: he wasn't happy.

"Like . . . like alcohol being sold the Indians, there are always rumors of . . . of what you describe."

"Why does this topic unnerve you, Mr. Hulbert?"

"Mr. Apple, perhaps it would be . . . better if you started at the beginning," he replied, his voice lowering. He fumbled to turn a page of his pad. "T-tell me what you know?"

"I know that this is not 'news' to you, Mr. Hulbert," John said. He stopped, his nose nearly touching the forehead of the reporter. "No one could have access to this garrison and be ignorant of a program such as I just described."

"Mr. Hulbert, is the prisoner bothering you?"

The high-pitched whip crack of Lieutenant Falconer's voice ended the conversation. Hulbert took an unsteady step back, no longer pursued by John. Little creeks of sweat formed in the ripples of the reporter's brow.

"Not bothering," Hulbert replied, still looking at John — whose fingers were scratching the air beside his hip, where his knife would have been had Falconer not confiscated it. "We . . . we are having a conversation about Protagoras and relativistic ethics."

Whatever he had just said effectively shut down further inquiry. Which, I suspect, was by design. Either he did not want the lieutenant to know what John had asked or he wanted to get away before John asked again, more forcefully. Or both.

Hulbert left our little gathering and, on the crest of his own harsh look toward John, Falconer followed. They went to the mess hall, identifiable because the cook, having not so much to do with the majority of the troops gone, stood lazing in the doorway, smoking.

I sidled up to John.

"Do you suspect Hulbert of having some involvement with the rifles, or do you suspect he may be concealing information?" I asked.

"I am sorry to have brought your business

into this discussion," he said, and that was all he said.

I feared that I had lost the man's trust by appearing to be taking Hulbert's side. That was not the case . . . and I wanted to hear the rest of his story.

"Would you like to eat?" I asked just to re-engage.

"What Meggie provided was sufficient." He looked around. "I would like to see the vegetable garden, though, if they have one."

"They must," I said, and asked him to wait while I inquired.

I headed for the main gate, though what I truly wanted to do was go to the mess hall and see what Hulbert was up to, if anything. There was a bit of an altercation as I neared, an Indian and a Mexican having at one another with the one sentry having to break it up. I knew him from the Hick, a bear of a Swede named Charles Gottorp. He hauled each man from the dirt by his hair. The two squealed as they were hoisted up.

"You'd yell more if I grabbed ya collars and tore up your only shirts," he said, flashing a grin that was missing many teeth and tossing the men in opposite directions.

The men skidded to sudden stops, facedown. Each rubbed his head, got up, dusted themselves off, and sulked off with angry, backward glances at their new enemy.

"Bungholes just have a yen to brawl," said the private. "I wouldn't care excepting it kicks up a lot of dust."

"I haven't seen you in quite a few days, Private," I said. "Now that I think of it, in over a week."

"Ya, end of the day, I'm too tired to come over. Troops gone, the rabble fights. As you see."

"How is it that you managed to stay at the fort?" I asked.

"Commander said I'm big enough to do the job of two, and me being here, not there, would help rations last longer," he said, followed by a single guffaw.

"He's a wise man," I replied. "Private, is there a vegetable garden here?"

"Behind Colonel Gearhart's place, next to Mrs. Meggie's tulips and things." He sniffed. "Sometimes, a good wind blows their smell all the way here. It don't help much with all these slobs, but a Creek showed me how to catch the odor and make it last." Gottorp demonstrated by cupping a hand in front of his face, extending it slightly, and pulling the air toward him several times. "You ought to try flowers at the Hick, ya?" he added.

I told him it might spoil the taste of my

242

prime liquors, which I believed to be true. The last thing a man wants in his Scotch is the scent of rose petal.

I had half-turned, intending to go — then stopped. John had said there was one Mexican driving a cartload of guns, two Mexicans driving another. It would take more than them to make a transfer somewhere out of the way. Someone to steady a total of three, maybe four teams. To lift those crates, which ain't carrying duck feathers. I had it in mind to ask Gottorp if he had ever lifted one, thinking it might help to know if one big man could do it. But I stopped myself.

What if the private was *involved?* I wondered. *What if it was a team of soldiers or profiteers from the town? Did it make sense to let them know they was being investigated?*

Best to stay out of it. I finished making my turn and went to find John, who had left the spot where we had been sitting.

I swore when I heard sounds like arguing coming from the buildings to my right. From the mess hall, in particular.

I quickened my step considerably.

CHAPTER TWENTY-FIVE

Fort Gibson, May 1836
John's Story

Deems Pompey Hulbert was standing amidst a row of wooden tables, shouting. John was facing him, but he was being held by Lieutenant Falconer and the cook I had seen just a few minutes before. Though John's arms were restrained, his fingers, waist-high, were scratching in Hulbert's direction.

". . . make unfounded accusations against my integrity!" Hulbert was shouting.

"You talk about all the wrong things!" John yelled back.

"*Both* of you talk too much with your mouths!" the lieutenant shouted in his high voice. To the cook, he said, "Help me walk this man to the jail."

The cook was Cotton March, a barrel-chested Cajun in a tight-fitting uniform and a woolly pair of mutton-chops. He showed

244

enthusiasm for the assignment, grabbing John's shoulder land arm hard, like he was wrestling a sheep to the chopping block.

John did not resist as they turned him around and marched him past me into the compound. I looked at Hulbert.

"He won't let up," the reporter complained, sitting on the long bench behind his cup of coffee and open notebook. "He accused me of keeping secrets."

I walked toward him. "Are you?"

The man took a sip and regarded me. "Every man keeps secrets."

"You know I don't mean that," I said. "John don't see things in a particularly complex way. Think about it. He has moved with an obliviousness to national loyalty through three countries: America, Mexican Texas, then the Republic of Texas. He don't care about flags. He cares about people. And this action he's been pursuing has helped to murder people, Texians and Mexicans alike. Last night — you saw, his life was endangered by someone who is somehow caught up in this. Can you sit there and say you blame him for wanting to learn more?"

"Yes," Hulbert said without pause. "I blame him for not saying what he knows. I asked him, just now. That was what started

245

this argument. I told him I would listen to his facts and then help if I could. 'Lay out your cards,' were the exact words I said. 'Lay them out and I'll see if I can fill in the deck.' He thought I was treating this as a game."

"Mr. Hulbert, John is not a complex thinker. You have surely seen that."

"I question whether he thinks at all."

"You may be right," I said. "You think. Answer me this. Is it right and proper that a man who has been through so much should be sitting behind bars?"

"That was not my determination," Hulbert said.

"You didn't speak up for him."

"Why should I? He threatened to claw out my tongue! No, not my tongue. He called it my 'serpent's tongue.' "

"I'm not calling it that," I said. "I'm not calling it or you anything. So let me ask you, just between us. *Do* you know anything about those rifles?"

"What's your stake in this war?" Hulbert asked.

"I hate asking a question and getting a question back," I said. I was sad and surprised that he would seek to impugn my motives, now. "All right, Mr. Hulbert. My stake is nothing. I'm just a member of the public asking a reporter what he knows about this particular story. If you know nothing, just look me in the eyes and say so."

He turned back to his coffee. "You're just beating the tall grass," he said. "I don't have to participate in this hunt of yours."

"That's true," I said, and held up a finger. "That's one fact. Are there any others?"

Hulbert drained his cup. He set it down gently, then sat in contemplation for a moment. "What is the particular coin of the realm here, Mr. Bundy?"

Lord, this man could talk and dance like no man I ever met. But I figured I'd play along, since I had the time — and maybe it would go somewhere.

"Specie from the federal government," I said.

"South of here?"

"A Republic of Texas note."

"Farther south?"

"The *real, escudo* — what is the *point* of this, Mr. Hulbert?" I was growing impatient. And it takes a lot to make a barkeep say that.

"You would accept gold or silver, regardless of the mint. But probably not paper money from Pennsylvania or Maryland or even Louisiana unless you were planning to go there to spend it."

"Everything you said is correct," I told him.

He leaned closer. "There is specie, if you will, that is better than all of them. What would it take to bribe your way into a general's quarters? A senator's office? The White House?"

"I have no idea."

"I can educate you with one word," Hulbert said. "Information. My work, my travels, my interviews, my observations put in my hands the keys that unlock any doors. Not only because people desire information to advance their own lives and causes, but because they seek to keep certain facts from the ears of their enemies. In many ways, sir, I am the richest man in the Oklahoma Territory."

I hated every word he just uttered. It had an oily quality, like blackmail.

"What secrets open the door to this garrison, I wonder?" I said.

Hulbert sat back. He was smiling smugly but offered no other answer.

"What you're leading to," I went on, "is why give to John Apple for free something that earns you more in the keeping of it."

"You miss one essential point," Hulbert said. "I do not do this for personal gain.

248

Not as such. I do this to secure news for my publication. I do this to enlighten the public."

"Even if, to do this, you withhold from that public information about corruption in their midst."

"Surely you are not as naïve as Mr. Apple," Hulbert said. "You are an educated man, a businessman. A final question, if I may. Under what conditions would you give free drinks to a customer? A birthday or retirement, perhaps? A boy about to go off to battle for the first time? A scholar upon graduation?"

"Probably all of those. Why?"

"In every story I write, I give as much information as I can for very, very little money," Hulbert said. "I am more charitable than any merchant I have yet encountered. Yet you and John Apple hold me in contempt for information I may not be willing to impart — may not, in fact, even possess!"

"Which brings me back to what I asked before you made like Daniel Webster," I said. "I didn't ask what you know. I asked if you knew anything that fits with what John Apple was asking."

"Mr. Bundy, do you want to know something? I wish I had the courage to answer that question directly. Regrettably, I do not."

I didn't realize I'd been holding my breath until I sighed. I looked at the man who seemed somewhat shrunken from a few minutes previous. "Do you want to know something, Mr. Hulbert? In a strange way, I respect the courage it took to admit that. I also understand everything you said to me. I only wish I could explain it all to John Apple. I fear he's going to get less and less settled as this search goes on."

Hulbert nodded. He absently put his hand on his notepad, which struck me as a poignant thing — because I believed that being a good reporter and writing his stories was important to him.

I left him, alone with his empty cup, to see what I could do about getting John Apple his liberty. Thinking of a moral man under arrest and a corrupted one free to come and go, I thought: this wasn't the way stories went. The innocent and pure of heart like the knights Galahad, Percival, Bors were supposed to *find* the Grail, not go to a dungeon just for searching.

None of which meant that I completely trusted John Apple. I don't mean his purpose, I believed in that. I mean his mind. There were times, as I've related, that I wouldn't've sworn to John's sanity. But I did not question his clarity about the rifles.

The garrison prison was a two-cell affair, with no one but John as a tenant in one jail. The other held one of the two men I'd seen fighting, the Indian; from the way he was pacing, I guessed he had gone after the Mexican again, which is why only one of them was here.

John sat on a stool that was perched beside a fold-down board that, I presumed, served as both supper table and bed. He might just as well have been waiting for a coach; he was outwardly at peace.

There was no turnkey, so I sought out the lieutenant, who was in his own residence, a small room adjacent to the barracks. He was not pleased to see me. However, due to my importance to the men of his command, he limited his displeasure to a scowl.

"If you've come to plead for the prisoner, I won't hear it," he told me. "He is a danger to others."

"He is a military volunteer and the veteran of at least three battles," I said. "Gonzales, Concepción, and the Alamo."

"What's your proof, his say-so? He's mad."

"He carries a knife that was given to him by Jim Bowie," I said. "More important, he carries a story that likewise began with Jim Bowie."

"The stolen guns?" Falconer snickered; it sounded like the sneeze of a lady of quality. "I talked that over with Mrs. Gearhart. She keeps the books. Nothing has gone missing."

"Not from here, perhaps," I said. "But somewhere between the boat and the fort?"

"Those shipments would have been under armed and highly trusted guards," he said. "Even if one — even if *two* of the six men were bad, that's not enough to steal those crates between Beaumont and here."

"And yet, they were stolen."

"So your man says," Falconer replied. "A man who only recently took the mistress of the fort hostage and threatened to dislodge the windpipe of a guest of the commander." The lieutenant shook his head. "I believe this man to be a danger, which is why I have taken Mrs. Gearhart's suggestion to consider the matter. Her testimony notwithstanding, I must consider the broader safety of the community we serve."

It was a sensible approach, and a personally risky one given Meggie's soft spot for John. I let it sit.

"Would you at least, Lieutenant, permit me to take Mr. Apple to the garden," I asked. "He'll be peaceable there, I promise."

"You will stay with him?"

"Constantly."

Doubling as acting commander and jailor, Falconer — with reluctance — unlocked the door and left me with the prisoner.

"There's a garden out back," I told him. "Let's have a look? Better than stone and iron, I should think."

John nodded once and rose, his fingernails still working the air very, very slightly. Like a cat at a scratching post, I thought.

We walked around the structure, ignoring the other prisoner who was shouting after the lieutenant to let him go to the garden, too. The large plot of vegetables, maybe a quarter-acre, had been planted to get the morning sun before the heat became withering. It was a not entirely healthy-looking patch, blighted here and there by rot and by strange, fat, green, leaf-eating worms. With only the cook to give the spot any attention, it had suffered somewhat. John immediately set to work snapping off leaves with insects on them and removing weeds.

"These are higher-elevation grasses," he said. "They blew down from the mesa there."

I looked to the northwest where he was pointing.

"The beans are hardy — and good to plump out a stew," he went on, gently inspecting them as a doctor would a patient's abdomen.

If I had any doubts about his story, the way he treated these vegetables supported his being every inch the planter he said he was.

I let him go about his work in silence for a few minutes.

"Would it distract you to continue your recitation, John?" I asked.

"If you want to hear, I will tell it," he said amiably. The earth had calmed him like I've seen liquor calm the men of the fort.

I told him I did, very much, and he went back to San Antonio de Bexar from which the latter part had been dropped.

"We wanted to show the citizens, and also ourselves, that it was a new day in the village."

CHAPTER TWENTY-SIX

San Antonio, Texas, January 1836
John's Story

Texians were now in command of all of what was once Mexican territory. It was too much to hope that, having been chastened militarily, Santa Anna would let things set. But that was still a ways off. First, our army had to fall to squabbling and give him weak spots to attack.

But that was still to come. Martín Perfecto de Cos, the Peacock, had stood and fell at the Alamo. It wasn't much as a fort, but as a symbol it meant something to Texians — the spot where independence was achieved, whence the Mexican army retreated over the Rio Grande. Some of our folks wondered aloud — always a bad thing to do if you're superstitious, which many was — some folks wondered whether this was the least-costly, least-bloody rebellion in the history of civilization. None of us being especially educated, we couldn't say. But I know Bowie, for one, thought the celebrating was premature.

"The generalissimo will come himself," he warned. "Mark me."

Within a few days of Bowie predicting so, that is exactly what Santa Anna did. And not with hundreds of men but thousands. Many of our soldiers had gone home for Christmas, many had left to seek lands in their new republic, and the army of the United States had gone home — it being too obvious a thing for them to have stayed and "helped" set up a government. But they didn't go far, joining the men from Fort Gibson who, it seemed, were in for a long stay.

That proved to be so, as you know.

Anyway, Santa Anna sent units ahead not to fight but like herald devils, announcing his intention to slaughter all the pirates operating in Texas. And by that he meant anyone who took up arms against the lawful government or gave comfort to those who took up arms against the lawful government or who even treasonously opposed the lawful government . . . which he considered himself to be. He rolled north with an army of six thousand that showed no mercy and took no prisoners. This time, they didn't worry as much about supply lines from Mexico. They took what they wanted from whatever farm or town was in the way. What they didn't take, they burned. For two months you could see and smell the smoke. It poisoned the air of Texas and did just what Santa Anna wanted it to do: it brought the Texian army back together. Now, he could crush it all in one place. He sent for an additional two thousand men to make sure this was achieved.

One of the first major towns to fall was San Patricio, which was defended by just seventy men, most of them Mexican immigrants. We later heard — at a very unfortunate time, which I'll talk about when I get to it — the Mexican General José de Urrea had sent soldiers in civilian dress to the town ahead of time, rallying Mexicans who were still loyal to their native land. They were told to hang lighted lanterns in their windows. Then the army moved in. It took just fifteen minutes to kill all but six of the defenders.

Texian leaders was rightly alarmed. We didn't know it then, but they got together at Washington-on-the-Brazos and named Sam Houston as major general of the armies of Texas. I wasn't there, of course; I was with Bowie in San Antonio. But it was Houston's

257

job to unify them and establish regular lines of communication to avoid what happened in the south. His army basically consisted of two commands. To the northeast was the big one: La Bahía, with Colonel Fannin commanding 500 seasoned fighters. And to the west was San Antonio, where just 150 men were uneasily joined under two leaders who did not get along: Colonel Bowie and the fella I mentioned earlier, Colonel William Barret Travis, formerly of South Carolina. They were billeted at the Alamo.

I did not get all the details of their mutual contrariness, but I believe it had to do with Travis's considered dislike for the president of the United States, who he saw as just another leader with greedy fingers for Texas. Bowie did not share that view, and he also did not seem to warm to the dandy that Travis was. I liked 'em both. And it speaks well of both men that when things got ugly, they was there for each other.

Against all military logic, Santa Anna chose to attack San Antonio first. We didn't know till then that Martín Perfecto de Cos, the Peacock whose feathers we'd plucked there, was married to the big man's daughter. Papa Bear was gonna make us pay for that stain on his family name.

During this time, while all the meetings

258

and organizing were going on, I was with Bowie and his volunteers in San Antonio. We was both glad and worried when we heard that the generalissimo was coming for us. Worried because of the obvious: he and his Mexicans were a swarm, like locusts. But we was glad, too, because those locusts had nothing to feed on. There was not enough hunting, not enough farms, not even enough water to keep them moving without supplies from home. Those supplies, as well as his army, were slowed by continual rains and punished by un-Texas-like cold that killed more of his men by freezing than by all the Texian bullets to date.

When the first lines of Santa Anna's army showed up outside of San Antonio, they were a sluggish and sorry-looking lot. Meantime, we had a boost. Having acrimoniously departed Washington, former Congressman and sharpshooter Davy Crockett of Tennessee went west to find a good spot to relocate his family. This big, rollicking storyteller proudly told us he said to his rivals upon leaving, "You may all go to hell and I will go to Texas."

Crockett did not plan to stay with us in San Antonio. He and his party of Tennesseans was just passing through. But he quickly found a friend and ally in Travis over this issue of hating Andy Jackson. Though I wasn't privy to the private talks with his men, Crockett seems to have figured that helping to make Texas a republic and keeping it from ever being a state was worth sticking around for. Especially since everyone figured that no military man in his right mind would go after a town that even the missionaries didn't figure was worth converting anymore. The Alamo had been left to weed years before. Inside, the wall paintings were all faded; even the saints had abandoned the place.

I gotta say this about the hard-drinking frontiersman. Jim Bowie hated fast and he hated hard. Crockett, bless him, had enough good humor to keep Bowie from butting horns with him over politics. When he was with just-folks, he was serious about just three things: telling stories, having plenty of liquor, and showing off "Pretty Betsy," his .40 caliber flintlock rifle. I have to say, it was a purty thing, the stock bearing sterling silver inlay showing the Goddess of Liberty, a raccoon, and various animal heads. The trigger guard was in the form of a silver alligator. The gun was a gift from admirers, each of who gave fifty cents toward the $250 cost.

Here's the tragedy of Pretty Betsy, though. It wasn't with him that day . . . that hateful, damned day.

CHAPTER TWENTY-SEVEN

Fort Gibson, May 1836
Ned's Story

John had not talked for very long, and he seemed to be okay telling his story while he worked among the vegetables. And then, like a sudden fever had come over him, he entered again that dark cloud place, the one that drained him of color, sunk his eyes into his skull, and stole his voice.

None of that had anything to do with Hulbert coming round the corner of the log compound. I'm not even sure John spotted him. The reporter saw at once the hair in the butter, that something was happening with John: the man was kneeling amidst lettuce, his shoulders drooping, his eyes on the horizon ahead.

"Damn them all," John said quietly.

"Who, John?" I asked.

He did not respond.

Hulbert, moving like an overweight cat,

was doing his best to be unobtrusive but still wanting to get himself near the mouse. I was doing my best to ignore him.

"John — the lettuce," I said, trying to ease him back. I squatted at the edge of the garden, near where he was working. "Work the soil. It's what we're here for."

His eyes dropped to the dark soil. He breathed deeply. I marveled that any man could find the smell of compost and horse manure soul-satisfying, but apparently he did.

He slowly began to move those sharp nails through the big leaves, looking for pests. Whenever he found one, he used the nail to scoop it away. I couldn't stop Hulbert from approaching but I turned and made a sign that he should not speak. The reporter nodded. It was strange, but in that quick look I had at him Hulbert looked almost as sullen as John.

The barkeep cannot avoid his fate, thought I, *which is to be dropped amid the inebriated and those who should be.*

"He did not have her with him," John said quietly. He forgot the leaves again.

"Are you speaking of Crockett? Betsy?"

"It was another rifle he picked up," John continued, apparently watching it like a play. "Out in the street, on the final day of

263

battle. It was one of ours. One from here, from this fort, one that had fallen with its Mexican owner." John looked back down at the leaves. "The saints had left the Alamo but not the martyrs."

John's hand dropped limp at his sides and he stayed where he was, on his knees.

"Christ in His Heaven," I heard softly in my ear.

Hulbert had knelt beside and a little behind me. As if in prayer.

"You think this is fakery, Hulbert?" I asked.

"I do not, sir, and I apologize for ever having suggested such." Hulbert was silent for a moment then blurt, still in a whisper, "I — I have come to help this tortured soul, if I might."

I stood, picking him up by the elbow as I rose. I ushered him away from John. Whatever his dream, or nightmare, it seemed best to leave him in it for the moment. We walked a few steps from the garden where I faced the reporter. He was the same sorry-looking fellow I had left in the mess, more so now that there was sunlight upon him. His cheeks were an uncharacteristic white while his forehead had all the flush. Years at my post told me that such a man was either sick with grippe . . . or burdened with blame for *something.* In a territory where men covered their faces with kerchiefs to keep out wind-whipped sand, one learned to catalog frailty and sins as expressed on the nose, which was inebriation; the cheeks, which was shame or love; and the forehead.

"What can you do to help him?" I asked, starting our previous conversation over but on a more amiable footing.

Hulbert had his pad flat in one hand, tapped the cover with the back of his pencil. He was like an Indian sending drum signals.

"Well?" I pressed.

"There's a reason I didn't tell you anything," he said. "And it's not that I don't trust you. You're a good and honest man." He glanced at the vegetable garden. "John's the one I'm not sure of."

"Why? What do you know about him?"

"Nothing," Hulbert said, leaving me fully at sea now. "Let me tell you what I do know. It's not the fort," the man went on, his voice cracking. He swallowed. "The guns are coming from smugglers on the coast."

"How do you know?"

"There's an operation out of New Orleans, goes right to the Rio Grande."

"The crates are taken from the port?"

"I don't know," he said. "All I know is that Colonel Gearhart sent a unit south to find out about it. No uniforms, forged papers indicating them to be licensed agents of the Army Apothecary Department. As much as guns, medical supplies are needed by the Mexican army."

As an apothecary myself, I could certainly appreciate the truth in that. Substances such as laudanum and nitrous oxide, items like stethoscopes and bandages, all were in great demand.

"They hoped to draw the smugglers out," I said. "Did they?"

"Must've," Hulbert said. "The men sent by the fort were never heard from."

"When was this?" I asked.

"Last time I was down this way, late February," Hulbert said. "Came down to do a crop report, wintertime and all —"

"So the smugglers are still out there?" I interrupted.

"As far as anyone knows," Hulbert said. "I . . . I'm not supposed to know this, but, you know, I listen. Soldiers talk." He looked around, leaned in. "Right now, Meggie thinks John here may be a part of that ring, sent here to find out what the army knows."

I felt a little sick hearing that. I glanced sideways at the man who was limp, there, like one of those heads of lettuce. An act? Lord God — had *I* been the one taken in?

266

Maybe that Mexican he killed was working for the U.S. government. Maybe his entire story was a lie. Those fingernails — they could be real useful prying open bales to get at goods hidden in cotton, or scratching secret codes in wooden crates.

"Thank you for your trust, brother Hulbert," I said. I shook my head once. "By God, that woman was brave!"

"Meggie? Yes. The lieutenant had the same suspicion about John — he was fearful the man would cut her throat and shoot his way out the back."

I frowned. "What did he think when John called me?"

"That you are a part of the ring," Hulbert said. "You do, don't you, receive some shipments from New Orleans?"

"Bloody rum," I said. "The stuff his boys drink."

"I'm not justifying, only explaining," Hulbert told me. "You could be a part of the operation. He thinks you're in a damn enviable position to hear things from drunk solders. He wonders if that isn't why you opened the Hick. The two problems started at about the same time."

"*You* obviously don't believe that," I said.

"No," Hulbert assured me. "No. Because Falconer suspects me, too. That giant Swede at the gate — he told me he's to watch that I don't pass messages to any of the civilians. I'm sure his courier reads every word I send to the newspaper."

This was madness, either on the part of the army or on the part of John Apple. I tried to sift through all that I knew or had heard. That was too confusing, too pointless, so I went with my sense about John. Was he crazy or just acting the part? Could anyone be *that* consistent in his fakery?

What do the two different stories have in common, I asked myself. Knowledge of the guns. Knowledge of the Mexicans having those guns. That was all. The Bowie knife? He could have got that any number of places. Except for the Coles and their people, who were far from here, and the folks in Ohio and Pennsylvania, everyone who could have vouched for this man was dead.

I couldn't decide if I really did believe him or now just really wanted to believe him. Hulbert seemed to come down on his side of the fence. I had the advantage, though, of being able to conduct another interview. The question was, should I report what the lieutenant and Meggie — if not suspected, at least feared?

I suggested to Hulbert that he leave us.

The reporter duly parted, his step a little lighter for having unburdened his soul. I crouched beside John again, who was just as I left him.

"We don't have to talk any more about the Alamo, John," I said. "Do you mind if we talk a little about those rifles? Maybe some thoughts about how they got from American to Mexican hands?"

John blinked several times, inhaled, then regarded me. "I never got to see Sam Houston again," he replied, exhaling. "But I did learn something at the Alamo. Something that pointed me directly to the fort."

"To anyone in particular?" I asked.

He nodded. But that was all he did.

"John, I want to help you. And Mr. Hulbert — I know he has his own reasons, but he also wants to help you. If there's anything you can —"

"I do not trust Mr. Hulbert," John said. "His newspaper supported the territorial rights of Mexico."

"A political view does not make a man himself untrustworthy," I pointed out.

"A man who has the run of a garrison is," John said. "I did not go to Mrs. Gearhart's rooms to see her but to see where the ledgers were stored. They are there, in the open. So are the files of couriered dispatches. Any man can walk in there and see arms sent and received. Only a guest, one who is not bound by military protocol, would linger in a room where such information is out in the open."

John's point was well-taken. Now I was really confused. And he was getting agitated. I couldn't leave him alone with his thoughts.

"What about Mexico's allies in Washington, the anti-Jacksonians?" I asked, suddenly inspired. "They could have sent information to . . . to someone about the guns. Their route, their times of arrival."

I was careful not to mention smugglers. Except for Hulbert, I would not have known such men might have been involved.

"Crockett said that to ascribe any intelligence or forethought to politicians is like calling a hog musical," John replied. "From the way I saw Travis receive goods, I can add to that the old saying is true: 'time and tide wait for no man.' Crockett compared the late arrival of men, weapons, food, and letters to a funeral he attended back in Tennessee. The body got there three days after the ceremony was planned, and that was only coming by land from Virginia. So think of a message going from the capital of the United States to Mexico to get people to meet a shipment by land or sea — it wouldn't be possible, or practical. The guns would already be in the fort, most likely, by the time word arrived to intercept them."

"All right," I said. "So leave Washington out of it. What are we left with?"

"Fort Gibson," John said. "This is where the guns come to be distributed among the western outposts. Mr. Coles found out that much from Sam Houston. It is impossible that *nobody* here knew guns were being stolen. Or bought."

John was on his feet again, reinvigorated by his mission. I reminded him, however, that he was my responsibility and had to behave appropriately.

"There's a lot we don't know, and we'll need allies," I said. "How we find things out is as important as *what* we find out. May I make a suggestion?"

"Of course," he said. "I'm sorry, I keep forgetting just how much I owe you."

"You don't owe me anything," I assured him, though it was good to hear. "What I would like to do, though, is for you to bring me up to date. I want to hear what you did, what you saw from the time you reached San Antonio. There may be clues you missed."

"It's possible," he admitted. "So much happened."

"Tell me about it," I said.

He walked from the garden and sat on the ground. Once again, he looked at *home* there, like he was drawing nourishment from the ground . . . a human plant. It was another one of those feelings I had that made me trust him.

He looked at his fingernails, which he curled just below his face.

"I told you I was in San Antonio," he said. "I was there 'cause of Bowie. Mostly, where he went, I went. It wasn't just the fact of liking and admiring him, I felt he was someone I could learn from. He had a bigger view of things than I did. Like an eagle, he saw things from on high." John smiled warmly. "That's why Crockett made such a good companion for him. The Tennessean was big on the right-here and right-now, being the center of whatever was around him. . . ."

272

CHAPTER TWENTY-EIGHT

San Antonio, March 1836
John's Story
All we had, at first, was rumors.

They started late in February — that Santa Anna was on the move, that he was laying waste to everything in his way, and that he was coming to San Antonio. God or the Devil, I'm not sure which, must've had a laugh when Travis decided to send an observer up to the bell tower of the church — the same one where the Peacock had been holed up — to watch the plains for any sign of an army.

A lot of the locals wasn't taking any chances. They left with whatever they could tote by mule, horse, or sledge. Travis, as a precaution, sent us out to look through their abandoned homes for food, drink, and any jugs or containers that could be used to hold water. When, on that first day, our lookout spotted Mexican soldiers, more men were sent out to round up whatever livestock was left — cattle, goats, chickens, everything. I grabbed a canvas sack and sifted through compost for pits and seeds to plant, in case we were laid siege to.

The first of the Mexicans, about fifteen hundred in number — an easy computation since they walked in neat rows — did not camp outside of town but walked boldly in. Those boys up front of their lines couldn't've been too pleased: that was Santa Anna's way of seeing where we had hid troops. He figured they would pick off the leading men and then retreat. As it happened, we didn't have men on the outside. Fearing a full assault — from an enemy that already outnumbered us ten-to-one — Travis had gotten everyone including the lookout inside the Alamo. So there was no shooting, then. Just an occupying army on one side, and some mighty resolved Texians and guests on the other.

The only engagement we had came when the Mexicans raised a red flag, high for us to see. That signaled their intention to do what they had done since crossing the Rio Grande: to give no quarter to combatants. Travis, who did not care for threats whether they was written on paper or on flags, fired a cannon in the general direction of the rag.

He blew up a lot of dirt, no Mexicans; but at least the first shot had been ours.

The next dozen or so were not.

The Mexicans set up batteries of cannon about a thousand feet from the east wall and the south wall. They fired pretty consistent for a couple of days, landing short of the structure but hitting the plaza in front. We returned fire now and then, especially when they started moving the big guns up farther and farther. As often as possible we sent their own cannonballs whistling back at them. But we did that less and less because we knew we would need those when an attack came.

We still didn't know that would happen; there was still a thought that they would try to starve us out. But then everybody's plans got waylaid when the temperature fell to freezing. Men on both sides got sick, Bowie included. I went out on one of the night-time excursions to get firewood, but the Mexicans were waiting for us wherever we went — woods, gullies, homes, stables. I came back with my left hand full of sticks. They certainly weren't worth the life of Harry Russell, a kid who became our first casualty. Didn't matter that we killed nine of the invaders. We lost a brother, and frankly, we could not afford to trade the enemy even one-for-nine . . . or one for ninety, for that matter.

We were cold, and spirits sunk as Bowie's health deteriorated. Crockett suggested using our manpower to push out of the Alamo, take up guerrilla positions in the surrounding territory. But with Bowie down, Travis was the sole commander, and he not only spurned that idea — he told Crockett to take his Tennesseans and go, but he and his command were staying.

"I will die like a soldier," he said. "At my command, not in retreat."

I don't know if that was a decent thing Travis did, no doubt about it shaming the man into staying. But Crockett stayed and Crockett died.

I mentioned before that weather and a lack of supplies caused Santa Anna's main army to straggle. It was still possible for us to send couriers to Sam Houston and others, requesting supplies and reinforcements — until, after that first week, more Mexican soldiers arrived and Santa Anna was able to cut off the road to Gonzales. Conveying our needs was now more dangerous, and took longer, and was something we could no longer afford.

I was one of the few who managed to get out almost every night. My job was to go out with a big empty grain sack and find edibles growing wild, which was mostly cactus and nuts, some roots. I would mud up and leave the compound at night. The mud not only gave me concealment but helped keep me warm, as did the guts of animals I caught and killed on my sojourns. All I had to do was get a nail in 'em and reel the critters in.

While I was out, I spied on the enemy. It was almost inevitable; they was everywhere. It would've helped if I knew Spanish, but it was useful for me to know exactly where soldiers were stationed, who faced in what direction, and when their replacements arrived so I could travel a little safer the next night. What I found went first to the few wives and children who had come into the mission with their husbands. These were families who had been garrisoned in the town itself, which was no longer possible. Once the ladies and young ones departed — a kindness offered by the Mexican when a final attack was near — it was not as easy for me to get out. That was because an ocean of Mexican soldiers finally arrived, kept arriving, and then were reinforced with even more infantry. It livened up the drab landscape with their blues and reds and yellows, but it did not do the same for our spirits.

There was one last opportunity for those who wanted to go to do so. It was just after all five thousand Mexicans reached San Antonio. We watched from the walls as the last of the army arrived, the generalissimo among them, all puffed and proud and covered with braid on top of his stallion. Mexican soldiers filled every street we could see, every window and doorway; they were on the rooftops — out of range of our best shooters — they were every damn where. There were cheers, thrown flowers, and from that late morning parade until the late evening, there was celebration. Part of that, I'm sure, was relief at having finished a long, unpleasant journey and of brothers-in-arms reunited. Part of it, I reckon, was in expectation of an easy victory. Had to be, looking at us behind stone walls that could barely hold theirselves up, let alone soldiers. And part of that joy was probably news reaching them — as it did us, in our last outside dispatches — that General José de Urrea had been victorious over Colonel Frank W. Johnson at San Patricio. Someone with a horn started playing their death song, *el Degüello,* its bold notes cutting through the night and through the soul of every Texian who heard it. It was like having a funeral before there was anyone to bury.

Spirits were low and worry was high. Every man who spoke, spoke of not being sure that staying was the wisest thing to do. If they was afraid to die, no one showed it. But to die like a swatted fly . . . that didn't sit well. Some men argued that every wound inflicted on Santa Anna's men, every minute they were delayed, bought our fellow Texians time to strengthen at La Bahía.

That was a pretty will-o'-the-wisp idea for the men to grasp. For one thing, it was a guess. No one knew how many men had been added, if any, to the five hundred Fannin had there — and, looking at the army spread before us, we wondered if even twice that would be enough. Even some of Travis's 150 were starting to openly question the idea of staying put.

Travis heard the noise and called everyone, save the still-ailing Bowie, to the plaza outside the mission and told everyone that an assault was clearly coming . . . and reinforcements weren't. The last communication, the one that told us about San Patricio, included a private communication from Sam Houston to Travis. The colonel said that his orders were to hold the Alamo if it was humanly possible. Travis told us that he planned to do so, for as long as it was humanly possible.

There was a lot of quiet after he spoke. Even Crockett had nothing to say, which was pretty surprising.

The colonel broke the silence by drawing his saber and cutting a line in the dirt. He asked those who were willing to stay — what he said was, "Those who are willing to die for Texas" — to stand on his side of the mark. Only one man, fella named Moses Rose, declined to do so. He left that night, promising to continue the fight elsewhere. With him went another man, one of our couriers by the name of James Allen. He didn't want to go but he had in his pouch newly writ letters from Travis and others.

"It is more important that our words live out there than you die in here," the colonel told him.

To a well-bred man like Travis, that was a good and noble sentiment. To most of us, we'd've rather burned the papers and joined Colonel Fannin. But Travis would not leave his command and the men would not leave Travis.

Because of my familiarity with the nighttime terrain, it fell upon me to get the men out of the Alamo and into the open. Before I left, the fort medic, Amos Pollard, came

280

to me with a gift.

"From Jim," he said.

The man handed me Bowie's own knife. I was humbled . . . and suddenly very afraid for my friend.

"He'll need it," I said.

"It is important to him that this not fall into the hands of the enemy."

"But I'm coming back," I said.

"I'm only repeating what my patient told me," Pollard replied.

The doctor turned to go but I halted him with a hand on his shoulder. I drew my machete-knife and gave it to him. "I will honor Bowie's request but I will not leave him without a blade. You tell him — you tell my friend that we will exchange them in the morning."

The doctor accepted the knife without comment. His expression, though, concerned me. It seemed strangely whimsical, as though the idea of seeing morning was somehow comical.

I left with the others and, while I was outside the compound, I planned to do my usual foraging. That was when the world seemed to catch fire.

I was just on the lip of my favorite long, deep gulley when the ground was lighted beneath me — a sharp, clear moment of light. It was followed by another and then another. I froze like a mouse when the cannons discharged and guns started firing, lighting the night with white and red flashes and balls of gray smoke. I couldn't see the Alamo from where I was — in a copse, with a wide gully running through, one we'd used for a trail. But I saw the road and the Mexicans shooting their way forward — stopping only when Davy Crockett and three other Tennesseans opened fire at them from behind bales of hay sitting innocently in the street.

Crockett's aim was deadly, and when his bullets ran out he leapt over his bale, scooped up the rifle of a dead Mexican, one he had killed, and began swinging it at the others like he was some Viking warrior with an ax. He fell in a volley that near tore his chest in half. The Tennesseans had stood to follow him but they got cut down first. I saw men run from the mission to take their places but they got drove back by fire. One of them managed to toss a torch into the hay, creating a wall of fire that sent the Mexicans back — right into a volley fired where the Tennesseans knew they would be retreating. To men just coming to the top of the wall to replace fallen comrades, it had to look like a massacre — by Crockett. I counted thirteen dead Mexicans with one man in their midst.

But that was just an opening skirmish, an attempt by Santa Anna to take the plaza and drive everyone from positions in the streets. It quickly became clear that the Texians were going to concentrate their fire in a way to keep the Mexican army on the east from linking up with the army on the south. Travis must've figured if he could break the one on the east they could concentrate all their defenses on the main force.

But Santa Anna and his generals would've figured that, too. Instead of attacking the Alamo, they attacked the barracks where men was still getting ready to join the fight. The fight came to them as — at a great loss of blood on the Mexican side — the invaders shot and stabbed and shouldered their bully way into that long structure. At the same time, Mexicans turned the back door into a graveyard by discharging bullets so fast and deep that the howl of gunpowder was near-continuous. I couldn't see that side of things, but I could hear the cries of those who fell. Funny how, among the dying, I couldn't tell who was friend and who was enemy. In the wild, you know an eagle from a mouse, a coyote from a hare. When I thought of men killing men, the concept suddenly became sinful.

Yet, I was a practitioner and I would continue to be. I figured it would have to be up to God to sort it all out. After all, He was the one who made us.

It had only been, I guessed, a few minutes and yet already the smell of blood was mixed with the powerful odor of gunpowder from cannon and rifle and the mixed stink of burning hay, burning clothes, and flaming bodies. I realized the roar was growing more and more like faraway thunder — my ears were getting clogged with sound, plugged-up. The only things that came through clear were different sounds: now the cackling laugh of fire, now the throaty collapse of stone, now the cries — different cries from the dying — of men who I could dimly see throwing up ladders to try and scale the walls of the Alamo, only to have them thrown back by powerful, Texian hands or pushed back by rifle stocks rammed against the top rung or the body of a Mexican. Santa Anna's men was so thick on each ladder that, in the firelight and cannon glow, it looked like a centipede falling backward, wriggling and writhing as it dropped. Then the naked skeleton of the ladder went right back up, pushed by a new supply of Mexicans, who then climbed back up. Before very long, the ladders stopped falling . . . but the Mexicans didn't stop climbing.

The fighting was hand to hand, then. I say that not having actually seen much of it. The war had shifted from the barracks to the walls of the Alamo itself and I saw shapes on the top there, moving against the dawning sky, struggling, shifting, reaching, pulling, slashing, clubbing . . . if there was a way to fight, the Texians was doing it. I heard shouts, not cries, of a bearlike quality. Men roaring at those trying to get into their den, bellowing . . . snarling . . . then falling silent.

There were fires lighting everything now. Angry orange and red in front, on the wall, and delicate rose from behind. The churning smoke had been grayish-white in the darkness; now it was grayish-black, an ugly reflection of the dead below. And below it, the now visible colors of the Mexican troops as they moved forward like they was demons emerging from hell. Now and then there was gunfire into a Texian body that was still moving on the ground. The remains of Davy Crockett got trampled on by the unawares mob . . . and maybe that was a good thing, I thought, so his corpse could not be identified for certain and toted round in a coffin for all to see.

Thinking of Crockett made me realize, just at that moment, when the battle was starting to quiet, that Jim Bowie was probably also dead. Even in his bed, he would not have let himself be taken, nor would he have stopped trying to kill the enemy. I pictured the infirmary, the cot where he lay. There was only room enough for one man at a time through the narrow door. I could see Mexicans falling till he ran out of bullets, then pausing to take aim and shoot him dead. They would have had to. I have no doubt, running out of ammunition at last, he would have gone for his knife and doubtless perished with it in his hand.

I folded my hands where I lay and prayed to God it was thus. Then I put my cold, wet palms over my ears. I did not do this to block out the muffled sounds but to let myself consider what personal strategy I should pursue. Belly-down in muck, I felt the suction holding me in place . . . but I knew I could not remain there. Come full-daylight, Mexican troops would be looking for people like me, friends of the conquered or escapees from the mission who might still willingly pose a threat.

You may ask why I did not contribute my own fire to the fray. I would have, not from a particular desire to die but from duty and brotherhood, qualities that had grown strong in the time I had spent in Texas. I suddenly missed Bowie hard after it was over and felt shame not having been at his side. I even then thought of going back to see what had become of him and Travis and the others I had gotten to know.

But I would have been gathered up and probably shot, for I did hear a volley against a wall and remembered that red flag: no quarter. Those who surrendered expecting mercy would not and did not receive it.

Still, what stayed me, what got me to moving north before the sun reached my gully, was the thought of those guns and whoever put them in Mexican hands.

I belly-walked like a snake over rocks and through mud and across twigs still wet from the rains. My brain was still working as if I was on a scavenging mission: too wet for a campfire, too small to bother picking up.

You don't need supplies any more, my innards shrieked as I clawed in the direction Moses Rose and the courier had took. I saw the hoofprints and welcomed the smell of the mud that clogged my nostrils because it cleaned out the smell of battle and blocked the stench of horseshit and other man-traps I crawled through. I felt wet fur, the remains

287

of animals that got drowned in their warrens and rose up on the water. There were dead birds that had been dashed against trees and dropped. I didn't realize I was crying till I heard myself gasping for breath. Dead behind me, dead below me, dead, dead, *dead.* And for what use? Here, life had drowned . . . not for food —

"So why, God?" I found myself demanding aloud.

The men I left behind, the Texians: Did they die for a reason? My brain went into a calculating mode. Two, three weeks for Santa Anna to turn to San Antonio. Another two weeks for his army to arrive in full. Add a night, just *one bloody night* for the battle, but cleaning up and rearming and reorganizing and burial would take three, four days, maybe more.

The retaking of San Antonio de Bexar, and the siege of the Alamo, would have added six weeks to the time Fannin and Sam Houston and the rest had to organize.

I later learned I was a little wrong in my thinking. The timing was right: the full Texian army met Santa Anna exactly six weeks later. There were other skirmishes between the Alamo and the fateful encounter at San Jacinto, all of it resulting in Texian retreats. But that emboldened the gay and cocky

Santa Anna to move forward with less than his full force. The wave had become a tidal pool. By the time the armies clashed — and you probably heard this; everyone has — there was seven hundred Mexicans with their Monkey Ward leader . . . and nine hundred Texians under Houston.

I have been told . . . I wish to God I had heard . . . the chant that greeted the Mexican invaders when the armies met.

"Remember the Alamo!" the Texians cried.

Even now, my throat gets choked just saying those words. *Remember the Alamo!* As God is my witness, I would die happy knowing that cry would outlive us, would survive for generations. The strange paths that brought very different people together also united them for a single purpose. When I think of the animal-like combat, what sets the Texians apart is that bond of brotherhood that allowed them to face certain death.

Is that, I asked God — is *that* the reason you did this terrible thing? To reveal a more wonderful thing behind it?

Well, Santa Anna lost the first run-in with Houston's forces. He retreated, then lost the battle with the earth itself. His troops ended up waist-deep in cold mud, got sick from dysentery and influenza or froze to death, lost their weapons, had no food or potable water, their clothes were in tatters —

Santa Anna sued for peace and got it, so long as he retreated with his army to below the Rio Grande, taking all his sympathizers with him. Texians went along with the defeated soldiers to make sure that blessed San Antonio, San Patricio, and other fallen towns were cleansed. Houston's people stayed along the border, fully expecting that Mexican generals who had not been part of the campaign would also not accept this defeat. In particular, I heard that General José de Urrea, the taker of San Patricio, had not been inclined to honor any agreements signed by a leader who remains in Texas as a prisoner of war — not forced to surrender but forced to sign a treaty of peace to prevent the massacre or imprisonment of his sickly troops.

I don't know how any of that will turn out. But I know how that will end. The men of Texas will remember the Alamo and any Mexican who tries to set foot in the new republic will die in the effort.

CHAPTER TWENTY-NINE

Fort Gibson, May 1836
Ned's Story

After listening to John's tale, I would have bet the deed to the Hick that he was telling me about an event he had witnessed and not one he was making up. There was no hesitation, no break, no pause to gather his voice or soul. He was reliving it, talking as if it was happening then.

I've heard men spin tall, tall yarns at the bar. They stop to make sure they remember what they just said before moving on to the next part of their fabulation. Or else they have to think of some development to say next.

Not this man. His eyes moved — left, right, up, down. They narrowed. They opened wide. They teared when he watched Crockett die and again, even more, when he talked about Bowie. If I sat here and told him about my sainted wife, I could summon such tears. They were that kind of real.

So my conclusion was that John Apple was likely not the one making things up. This meant the story told by Hulbert was false; where, then, did that one originate? It had to be with the guilty party, but who was that? If Meggie or the lieutenant told it to him, who told it to them?

Whoever is behind this infernal plot, I told myself.

I had to think more about that, let Hulbert come to me with additional information. For now, the best course of action was no course of action.

"So you ended up in joining with another Texian army, I imagine?" I said to John.

"Not then," he replied. "I never made it as far as Moses and the courier did. I ran full into a unit of Mexican cavalry that had come too late to join the fray. They picked me up shortly after sunrise, attached a lasso under my arms, and pulled me through the San Antonio River. Said it was to clean me off, and maybe it was a little. Mostly, they were having fun dragging me up and down the bank and betting on whether they could smash me into the stones there. I only realized that later when coins changed hands. I was near drowned when they finally hauled me out. I didn't even realize they had took my knife. They kept me tied, and made me walk at a tiring pace behind one of their horses on the way in to San Antonio."

"You had to go back?" I said, horrified.

"Right to where bodies were being stacked and identified, Mexican and Texian alike," John told me. "They didn't make me stay there, though. I was handed off to some sergeant who took me to the small jail. It was already stuffed with Americans and Texians who had been rounded up outside of the town. I was pushed inside, just one more — though wetter than the others and shivering now that I was outta the direct sun."

"The other prisoners couldn't have been from the Alamo," I said. "Not with the no-quarter order."

"They wasn't," John told me. "There was a few shopkeepers who had stayed, a couple of people from other towns who happened to be at the wrong place when the Mexicans arrived, and a bunch of white men who had offered Mexican prostitutes to the soldiery. Of course, none of those ladies had been arrested. Only the middlemen. From what a few of the prisoners was saying, I got the impression this was just to make sure nobody was undercover, sent here to kill the generalissimo while all eyes was on the battle."

"Did you recognize any of the prisoners?"

John shook his head. "All my time outside the Alamo was also spent outside San Antonio, too, looking for food. I was glad they was there, though, since some of them knew Spanish and was able to relate to me what I just related to you."

"How did you feel?" I asked.

"They made room for me to sit on the floor instead of stand, which most of them was doing," John said. "That was a kindness I very much appreciated. I had not slept and — how did I feel? Like everything that had happened had been a dream. Only I knew it had been real. I just couldn't make it fit inside my head. I slumped forward, my arms wrapped round my knees, and now I dreamt a real dream about being on a seacoast where, had Bowie not been passed out on that stoop when I first arrived, I would now have been. I would likely not have gotten swept up in this fight, this cause, but been about some other business."

"Did you regret it?"

John shook his head. "How could I be sorry for having met some of the greatest men of our time? The pain that came with that privilege was a mighty counterweight, but on the whole I counted myself lucky. At least, I did when I woke to everyone being booted out of their cells. At first, I thought I was gonna be lucky. No one there was accused of anything, far as I could tell. They were all being let go and I figured I would be too. Until one of the Mexicans who had caught me spotted me and told the guards to detain me."

"Any reason in particular?"

"Yeah," John told me. "He was the one who had also taken something from me."

"What?"

John answered, "My Bowie knife."

CHAPTER THIRTY

San Antonio, March 1836
John's Story

My captor did not tie me up or anything. He and I just stood outside the jail, in the sunlight, which revived me as if I was an indoor plant. The man's uniform and face were clean, he did not look like he'd been in battle. So many of the Mexicans had not: there were too many of them to fit along the street.

The man did not physically restrain me. There was so many soldiers in front of us, marching one way or the other, dragging supplies or cannon or catafalques or livestock and dogs — including bloodhounds — that there was nowhere for me to maneuver. My jailor even offered me water, which I thought at first was a joke seeing as how I was still wet. But he was soft-spoken and seemed sincere and I accepted the ladle he drew from a cask to his side.

It was a while before the man who captured me returned. Gripping my arm tightly, he took me to a small assayer's office where a small lieutenant sat behind a small desk. The man asked, in English, if I spoke Spanish. I told him I did not. He continued in a decent American tongue, though he made notes in a book in Spanish. I confess admiring his ability to do both. I also confess I had no intention of telling the man the truth. I still had the idea to get out of San Antonio alive.

He asked my name and I told him. He entered it in a column heading in his book.

"Why are you here, John Apple?" he asked.

"I was visiting Mr. John P. Coles northeast of here."

"He is . . . ?"

"A gentlemen who, with his wife, is opening an inn."

"How far away?"

"About . . . let me see . . . maybe three times the distance to Gonzales?"

"You know Gonzales?" he asked, suddenly interested.

"I passed through coming here," I told him.

"Nothing more?"

"I had no time to stay," I said. "I wanted to get here and get back."

"Yes, here," he said, slightly flustered. "Why are you here?"

I had been thinking of how to answer that. I said, "Mr. Coles wanted Mexican objects for his business. Rugs. Blankets. Paintings."

"Is he loyal to the generalissimo?"

"I do not know his political persuasion, sir," I said. "But as he did not send me here to purchase Texian goods, he must hold the empire and its leader in some high regard."

The lieutenant considered this; he seemed satisfied with my answer and wrote it in his book.

"Did you buy these . . . these decorative things?" he asked.

"I did not have a chance. My horses — I had two — were taken from me."

"By?"

"Texians," I replied.

"They stole your horses?"

"Not precisely. They gave me a knife," I said, pleased to have thought of this. "The knife this man has taken from me. I have now lost everything I came with, save the clothes I wear."

The lieutenant frowned at my captor. They spoke in Mexican, after which the man who found me quickly if reluctantly surrendered the knife and sheath to his commander. The lieutenant examined it then set it down.

"Are you aware of the significance of this knife?" the lieutenant asked me.

"I was told I could sell it for whatever my horses cost." I shrugged. "I am not versed in such."

"It is from the rebel James Bowie," the lieutenant said. "You know the name?"

"I have heard it," I admitted.

The man wrote that down, too. "What *are* you versed in?"

I hesitated. If I said I knew about growing, I feared he might keep me there to help plant crops. "I was a preacher up north — in the state of Ohio, near Canada," I said.

"Why did you leave there?"

I answered truthfully, "A woman."

The lieutenant smiled crookedly. This was apparently, happily, something he could relate to.

"You say you came to buy goods," the lieutenant said. "Where is your money?"

"Lost in the river your men dragged me through," I said. I looked at my captor. "Unless you found it?"

He had no idea what I'd said and the officer translated. The man shook his head immediately — and vigorously. My guess, and this is based on nothing but the pillaging and despoiling I'd glimpsed as I was brought into town, is that the spoils of war were to be divided equally among the troops. Apparently, the lieutenant expected his share.

"Why, John Apple, were you moving away from the Alamo when the corporal and his companions found you?" the lieutenant asked.

"Because," I replied, hating myself for the answer I had to give, "only a lunatic would have been moving *toward* the Alamo."

"You were not deserting?"

I laughed. "Your troops, Lieutenant, made it quite impossible for anything but smoke to get over the wall. I realized, after they took me, I should've raised the white handkerchief in my pocket — but I was too scared to think."

The lieutenant noted that as well. Then he used the back of his pencil to push the knife across the desk — toward me, not to the corporal.

"I am sorry for your losses, señor. Take your knife, sell it, buy yourself a horse, and go home. Perhaps the corporal will buy it with any money he may have — found?"

The corporal protested again, in Mexican, and was very unhappy when I claimed the knife and departed. I confess I was not expecting kindness and charity from the Mexican officer, but it reminded me that even in conflict not every enemy has the soul of a devil.

I went out, strapped the sheath back on my hip, and walked sideways along the shopfronts to get by. I headed several dozen steps in the direction of the church; I did not want to go near the Alamo, did not want to see whatever was being done there, did not want to see the bodies of the people I had served with or their pilfered possessions. God help whoever I saw holding Davy's Betsy.

Besides, I had another objective.

When I was about thirty feet from the lieutenant's office, I stopped and turned and watched the doorway. It was not just the church to my back but also the open field where tents had been raised and temporary corrals built. I was still tired, still disoriented from the shock of battle, but a plan had formed and I wanted to see it through. While I waited, I smelled smoke. Bad smoke, the kind that burnt the inside of your nostrils. I craned so I could see a little down the street, past the outside columns of the nearest structure — and saw, to my horror, black smoke rising from the street. It climbed like a pyramid, the point stabbing God's eye: it was a pyre of Texians.

I had no food in my gut or I would've lost

it. Their own Mexican dead were being buried, some four or five or six hundred — I lost count as they were carted past. What contempt, what vile sin, not to put less than two hundred more in the ground? I was more resolved than ever to carry out my new endeavor.

After just a few minutes the corporal came out, headed in my direction. He looked angry. I don't know, of course, how much that had to do with losing the knife or losing me. Didn't care, either. I did not want him to see me and slid myself into an alley between the cantina I had once used to commit murder and the general store beside it. Both were empty of furnishing and goods, our people having raided them for anything they could use, eat, or burn.

I waited until the corporal had passed and then fell in behind him a goodly distance away. I did not want to conduct business with him now. I wanted to see where he and his betting friends were bivouacked. I saw him go to an open area not far from one of the corrals; I guessed that only officers got tents. The regular cavalry had to be ready to mount in case of a surprise attack, hence the proximity. I marked the spot in my head, for I would be returning when it was dark. And there was something I had to do first.

The dead of Mexico were being carted to an area south of the town. They were going to be buried there and a large detail was at work digging graves. I offered to go and help, seeking to make myself known to these boys. There was something else I wanted, though I could not, of course, reveal that.

They didn't speak English, so didn't ask questions. They just handed me a shovel, happy to have a hand. There were about thirty of us in all; the only sound was the wind and the *chuck* of the shovels hitting dirt, as we were otherwise respectfully silent while we dug.

We dug throughout the day — shallow graves, but about four hundred during daylight. The digging continued during dark, by torchlight, which was what I was hoping. My legs and arms — one was locked stiff, the other dangling like vines. The only thing that kept the shovel moving was that my fingers was locked tight around them, like wet leather that had dried. No one blew a bugle to end our labors. Mexican women came with a meager selection of meats and fruit, everything that I had been out securing every night. I managed to get an apple, yellow and tasteless, but I didn't want it for the flavor.

Around about midnight, the third shift

since my arrival began to take shovels from tired soldiers. I offered mine to a man who had to tug to get it from my grip. I staggered back, away from the torchlight. That was an intentional move on my part, though easy to do because my legs didn't want to bend. I flopped on the ground, drawing laughter from the two men nearest me. They said something I didn't understand, then went back to their labors.

I was on the ground, on my seat, my hands behind me flat on the damp earth. Slowly, quietly, I began to move backward. Away from the graves. Away from the men working them. Toward the bodies.

I had eyed one while it was still light. He looked about my size, and his uniform had only one hole, which was in the left breast. It was a knife wound, and I fancied that it had been inflicted by Bowie. The blade had pierced the heart so there was a single streak of brown along the blue; the heart had not continued to pump for very long after being stuck. It was unlikely that anyone would notice the long, dark, caking stripe in the dark.

The soldier's remains was on top of two other bodies. I slunk behind the pile and drew the body toward me from behind. It was already stiffening and had stuck, in back, to the blood that had been spewed by the body below. I had to waggle the corpse from side to side to tear it free. But finally it came loose and I lay it on the ground where I undid the buttons of its jacket and trousers, removed the boots, stripped the poor man to his white army-issue drawers. They was mite-infested, and as soon as I had the uniform I backed away, far away, and shook out the coat, pants, and white shirt. Chances were pretty good I would not be stopping to bathe them away for quite some time.

Once I had pulled the costume on, I make a bundle of my own garments; I did not think it prudent to move through the countryside dressed as a Mexican soldier, where I would be presumed an enemy or a deserter, depending on who I encountered.

My preparations made, I walked a wide path around the gravediggers, around the encampment, through a rain-rutted lowland cut through with deep criss-crossing wagon wheels that made walking a challenge. It was a good thing, though, since I ended up with so much dirt on my uniform it made the blood blend in.

I finally came to the spot I had marked as being where my tormenters had made their bed. There they were, a pack of three, tired from the day's work of riding to a battle they missed, tormenting me, then looting San Antonio. It took all my control not to spit on them as I passed. But, I told myself, there was no need for that, then.

I made my way to the corral. There were not many torches here, they being spaced quite a distance apart due to the scarcity of flammable pitch. I picked up a large tree limb that had come down in the rains. It looked enough like a rifle to hopefully fool whoever was on guard there. I leaned it on my shoulder and began to pace along the far side of the horses. The man who was the real sentry saw me through the deep, slightly restless herd. He did not stop his back-and-forth march but nodded at me, and I nodded back. When he was far enough away, I used my knife to cut a horse free. I walked it away from the rest. There would be no time or opportunity to saddle it. I rigged a kind-of Indian blanket setup using my buckskin jacket and belt. I had no experience riding thus, but I believed that my still-rigid legs would come in useful gripping the ribs of the horse as I made my way out of here.

First, however: I had to do what I came to do. The Bowie knife in my stiff-fingered hand, I dropped my fake rifle, left the horse, and doubled back to where the three soldiers were asleep. The man who had taken my knife, the man I wanted most, was the innermost. He would have to wait. The nearest wakeful soldiers were some distance away, seated around a campfire cleaning guns. I lay down beside the outermost of the three, my head just inches from his. He was on his side, facing the others. When I was sure I couldn't be seen in the dark, I rose on my left elbow. I extended my left hand so it was over his cheek, stretched out my right with the blade facing down, then worked the two hands in concert. I clapped tight with my left over his mouth, stabbed down with my right through his neck, and then leaned my body on top of him to keep him from trying to get up or wriggle too excitedly.

He started with the shock or pain or both, thrashed a little, but I tamped him down until he was still. The man beside him didn't even stir. When the first man had bled out, I rolled over him and repeated the procedure on the second. He died more quietly, I having learned from my first effort.

Think apple, John, I told myself.

This time I plunged the knife hard through his Adam's apple, spilling blood and disabling speech, simultaneous. I felt him give up life with less struggle and greater speed than his comrade-in-torture. Then it was on to the last man. He would not die like his fellows.

There was no one to the right of this devil; just the boots of the three, all in a row, stockings draped atop to dry. Rising on my knees, I simultaneously clamped my left hand on his mouth while I straddled him across the lower ribs. He woke at once, but not in time to stop my right hand from pushing the sharp point of the knife into his godless heart.

I bent low to his ear. "You wanted it?" I hissed in English. "Have it."

Bending caused me to lean my full weight on the hilt, driving the blade farther so that it hit dirt underneath. There was a snarl on my mouth, something animal, a released rage for everything that had been done to the brave patriots of the Alamo. The casual slaughtering, as if they was setting up a town sociable. The picking through their goods and belongings. The heathen disposal of their bodies.

Once more my fist was covered with the warm blood of a dying Mexican. I felt like those Indians I encountered must have felt killing that brave, taking his heart, stealing his power, ending his evil existence. It was all I could do to keep from releasing a war cry of my own.

The man kicked his knees, twisted a little at the waist, and then fell still. I pulled the knife free, feeling it cut rib on the way out. Then I wiped it across his breast, painting a big X. My left knee was already soaking with the middle man's blood — more joy to the animal part of me that had done this.

I rose on legs that were suddenly wobbly. I sheathed the knife, fished the apple core from where I had tucked it earlier, and, bending, pushed it into the bloody gash in the man's chest.

As I hear myself saying all this, it sounds like I was reduced to a creature like the Mexicans I had killed. An observer might think so. But in my mind, I was an avenging angel repaying bloody, soulless acts in kind. Maybe that's too arrogant, to say God was on my side as I broke one of His Commandments. Better to say I was like some mythical being, or like the monster Astoria told me about, the unliving shade created by Dr. Frankenstein in a novel that bears his name.

I don't know. I was only aware of how I felt: as if the world was set right, at least a little. I padded off, my own heart drumming, the Mexican soldier's heart blood dripping from the fingernails that had plugged apple seeds in his dead heart. I reached the horse without incident, walked him to a tree branch so I could swing my leg on his back, held tight to his mane, and walked into a night that felt cleaner from my dirty act.

CHAPTER THIRTY-ONE

Fort Gibson, May 1836
Ned's Story

I was frankly aghast at the story of John's transformation from an observer of horror to its creator. I defy any sane man to feel differently. The Mexican he had punished outside the Hick — it was ghastly but the man had attacked John. He had just confessed to murdering three men in their sleep. Men who had committed some unpleasantness but which no court of law would have sentenced to death, let alone so grotesque a demise.

I don't know if John perceived my discomfort. I don't know as he cared how I felt. I had asked for his story and I got it. I will say it made me trust him even more, however. No man would have owned up to such a deed without having actually committed it. And what was strange, the more I ruminated, was that half the people in this

311

garrison — maybe a greater percentage throughout Texas — would hold him as a hero.

We were still sitting on the ground. My legs were bent and I stretched them out. As I did so, I thought of John's legs having been so stiff from digging he couldn't bend them.

That is not something you think up unless you've done it, I told myself.

Which brought me back to the guns. There were no new clues in his story, that I could tell. But he wasn't finished.

"That was three months ago," I said. "Did you have it in mind then to go to the fort?"

John shook his head. "When it was clear no one was following me — not yet — I stopped and changed back to my clothes. I buried the uniform and moved on very, very slowly as I taught myself bareback riding. By next morning I had a powerful hurt in my thighs, and I'm sure the horse's head didn't feel so good, either, since I used its mane to hold on. I guided him with my heels, which worked pretty good along with a head-tug in that direction.

"My only thought now was to put distance between me and San Antonio. As I said, I figured I had some time before Santa Anna set out, so I decided to head back to Gonzales. Part of that was for safety and part to give a report on the situation westward. If the Mexicans was looking to take back lost property, they might decide to come in force for the cannon."

"You weren't aware of the other defeats the Texian army had suffered after the Alamo?"

"No. I didn't know about our loss at Agua Dulce Creek, or about the Goliad Massacre, where Fannin and his men had surrendered — only to be executed after laying down arms. That was the end of March, and I was already at my destination — where there were surprising developments."

Before John could elaborate, Meggie came from the back door of the commander's residence. Seeing us seated on the grass, she walked over and stood beside John, putting him between us. We both went to stand but she motioned us to remain comfortable. We obliged.

She looked across the large vegetable patch. The gentle wind stirred her dress and the bell sleeves of her blouse, it raised strands of blond hair that made her seem uncustomarily unkempt. I immediately wondered if her presence was the kindly gesture of the Lady of the Fort or a hunting expedition.

"The lettuce is looking a little healthier,"

she observed. "John, is that your doing?"

"I have done a little work, ma'am."

"I wonder if we shouldn't ask you to stay when this other business is behind us."

John smiled politely but made no commitment.

"Has the lieutenant been civil?" Meggie asked.

"Given the circumstances, I would say so," John answered. "You, too, ma'am," he added.

"Yes," she laughed, "we had an uncommon introduction. One that I still don't fully understand. You came searching for information but you seem at peace despite having not succeeded."

"Not succeeded?" John said.

"You wanted to find out more about the guns," she said. "Unless I am mistaken, this has not happened."

"Yet," he replied.

"If the lieutenant puts you on trial, you may not have the opportunity for further investigation," she pointed out.

"My trial will be their trial," he replied.

He said that with an almost religious obscurity, like a prophet speaking doctrine. Meggie and I exchanged puzzled glances.

"How do you figure that?" I asked.

"I will be sworn, before God, to say what

I know," he answered. "I have not yet told you all I know."

"You're referring to events that came after San Antonio," I said. "You haven't said anything about the Mexican who attacked you at the Hick, other than that you knew him briefly. Was he a part of the gun smuggling?"

John nodded.

"Where does he come in?"

"I encountered that . . . renegade in Gonzales — my second visit," John answered.

CHAPTER THIRTY-TWO

San Antonio, April 1836
John's Story

I have to confess I was more ambitious than I was capable when it came to riding bareback. I did not make many miles each day, and when it rained, which it did a lot, I lost ground finding suitable shelter. There would be no need for me to go to the gulf, I thought, not ever; wait long enough and that much water will come to you.

I fell sick during this time, feverish and shaking, but in my lucid moments I did not lament. In fact, I was deeply grateful to God for having guided me to a cave that had drinkable water running down its walls, moss that I found edible if not tasty, and tools left by some previous inhabitant for the making of a fire, a stick with twine. You stuck the pointed end of the stick into a pile of kindling and pulled back and forth with the rope. It took all the energy I had to do

316

that, but said occupant had gathered sticks when the climate was dry, and I did not lack for warmth and light at nighttime. There was even a chimney where bats came and went, and though their droppings wasn't fragrant, there was an owl flew in that opening who got panicked in the cave, broke his neck, and became two days of eating.

A place like this could put Coles Settlement out of business, I thought laughingly; it was like a hotel for men of the wilderness. Before I left a few days later I gathered sticks and dry grasses to leave for the next occupant. I have to add, though, that there was something comforting about the place — so much so that I actually considered returning to make it a home. But when I was well, and the day was dry and bright, I saw no nearby source of water to grow a garden. I did not realize how important that art had become to me until I had to decide whether I could live without it.

I could not, and me and my animal — who I named James in honor of my fallen friend, since I had to call him something other than "horse" when we traveled — me and my animal set out, secure that any tracks we'd've laid down in our flight had been washed away by the rain. If Santa Anna had sent any of those bloodhounds I saw after us, the storms saw to it that they would not recover our scent.

Unfortunately, all of that did not factor in the possibility of a chance encounter, which happened on the fourth day after I'd departed.

It was a warm and bright noon, and there was a scouting party galloping up behind us. James had suddenly grown restless, which is the only reason I risked turning round — I say risked, because it was all I could do to balance on his back, let alone twist and stay seated. But I managed, and I saw four men in uniform riding wide apart but all heading in my direction. There was a fifth man with them, an Indian whose tribe I could not determine. He was at point ahead of the others.

I did not know if they would recognize me or my horse. But if they had come from San Antonio — and that was the direction they was headed from — they might damn well recognize the knife I carried . . . and leap to the conclusion that I had used it to kill their fellows. They would also wonder why a man was riding bareback who couldn't really ride bareback. The only thing in my favor was that the Mexicans had been gathering horses as they moved north, and this one wasn't yet branded with their cavalry marks. It was a slim hope but it was better than none, since there was no way I could outrun them. Then again, not speaking their language, I knew I would have trouble telling them whatever lie I might come up with. The only good thing was, apart from the horse and the knife, my wet, then dry, then wet, now dry clothes were not fit for anyone but the man presently inside of them. I was not sure the stitching would survive another doffing.

I was still turned around, and they would've seen I was turned around, so now I turned the horse around to face them, and waited. There was no time to bury the knife. I was stuck with it. I was also angry that I had not thought to take a rifle from any of the stacked pyramids at the Mexican encampment. I was thinking too much like a marauding wolf then. But now that I belatedly considered it, I realized that I would not have been able to secure ammunition. Even if I had, I probably would've shot game on my journey instead of stopping to trap it. Besides, these fellas all had rifles too, and were probably superior shots.

Dear Lord, I prayed. *You have looked after me this far. All I ask is that these be men not like those I slew for their sins of cruelty and covetousness.*

319

Perhaps, I thought, they would be governed by a more rational man like the officer who came for me at the Coleses'. Of course, I still ended up in captivity so I wasn't sure that wish was helpful. On the other hand, they might not want to be burdened with a man who could only ride slow.

The Indian sped up to see who was up ahead. He was Comanche, I saw by his clothing. If he was a regular with the army, paid a monthly wage, he would've been in uniform.

He stopped and looked at me from several horse lengths' distant. He wore a holster with twin Colt revolvers, and a hat that hid all but his grim-set mouth. From his tight, fit build I put him in his early twenties. The others rode up behind him. They spoke.

I told them I didn't speak their language. It was the Indian who translated, and I had to admit it struck me funny that two so-called civilized men was talking through a savage.

"They ask who you are where horse from," he said.

"I am John from Coles Settlement up north," I replied. "I lost my saddle in the storm. Who are you all?"

"We from Bexar," he replied. "Scouts for

Santa Anna."

One of the Mexicans snapped something at the Indian, who relayed what I had told him and came back with another question.

"They want see horse," the Indian said. "Bring it."

I considered my choices here. I thought of swatting it and letting it run off, but that would leave me stranded — if I survived — though more likely shot dead for being presumed guilty of horse thieving. There was no good outcome that I could see, so I just turned things over to the Lord to do with as He would. And I silently started thinking my way through the Lord's Prayer.

I rode the horse over and stopped by the Mexican who did all the talking. They laughed as I approached, waggling side to side as I held tight to the mane. They was cocky in their saddles, and I wondered how they'd do without 'em. When I arrived and stopped, the man on the farther side dismounted and came over to inspect the animal.

I knew at once I was in grave trouble. The fella removed his nice tan gloves. The first thing he did was check the hooves. He picked up a stick and raised the horse's back left leg and scraped out muck from the horseshoe. Then he chattered earnestly to the others. Damn thing probably had markings that showed it to be one of theirs. Of course a horse they picked up for the cavalry would've been reshod.

He set down the leg and walked over to me. He slapped me hard with his bare hand.

"*¿Dónde buscarlo?*" he demanded.

I looked over at the Indian, who had turned his horse around. "He ask where you get him?"

"I found him wandering," I said.

The Comanche snorted. "They never believe. Try better."

That was unexpected. "I'm tired out. You got any ideas?"

The Indian considered this. The Mexican leader demanded to know what I had said. The brave was looking at me.

"You John Apple?" he asked.

I was caught off my guard, to say the very least, and confessed I was he.

"You friend of chief daughter."

Well thank you, Lord, I thought.

An instant later, the Comanche had drawn both of his guns and put six shots in three Mexicans. All four horses reared. Two shot soldiers got thrown from their saddles and the third, who took just one bullet, cried out and held the reins and sagged slowly against the neck of his animal when it

322

settled, his blood running over its white mane and horseflesh. The man who had been inspecting my horse had tried to run around it for protection before the barrels were turned on him, but the first shots had spooked my animal. It ran him down and continued off to the west. That man had a hoofprint on the right shoulder. It was clear enough that I could've read the marks of the Mexican smith if I could've read Spanish.

"Finish," the Comanche said, pointing to the trampled Mexican who, now that the shock of the gunfire had faded and I could hear again, I heard was moaning.

I don't know. The Mexican meant me harm, but it was in the line of duty and frankly justifiable. I had killed his comrades and stole a horse. Moreover, he could do me no damage now.

"Did he wrong you?" I asked.

The Comanche seemed puzzled. "He enemy of you, my brother."

"But you came willingly? He didn't force you?"

"They buy horses from tribe," he replied. "I help bring."

"What's your name?" I asked.

"Morning Sun," he replied.

"Morning Sun, there is no honor in kill-

323

ing a lame Mexican," I said. "Let us put him on his horse and send him on his way."

"He die anyway," the Comanche replied. "Can only ride one-hand. Not hunt."

"Then it will be God's will," I replied.

The Indian put a bullet in the man's neck, causing the Mexican to hop once like a jumping bean then spout red into the sunlight, like it come from the earth.

"He cause brothers to fight," the Comanche said. "Die for that."

It was not the finish I had hoped for, but I can't say there wasn't a certain predictable logic to the man's actions. In my time with the tribe, I learnt that they had a way of doing things that might not parse with Eastern sensibilities, but I was not in the East anymore.

Rather than continue to argue with my "brother," I let the disagreement go and told him I wanted to bury the men.

"Worms or birds, make no difference," Morning Sun said.

"Perhaps," I replied. "But burying will make the soil richer."

He grunted. "You do. I leave you one horse, take the others back to camp."

"Thank you for saving my life," I said.

"I tell chief you not dead, no matter medicine man see in vision."

"Black Moon saw my end?" I asked.

Morning Sun held his hand toward me, palm out. It was an oath of the truth.

I remembered the witch doctor. He didn't like me. He probably invented that dream to turn the chief's daughter toward some brave. It didn't matter; I did not intend to go back, though I was every bit as grateful to this brave as I had said.

Before departing, my Comanche brother descended, lashed the horses together, and hitched them to his saddle horn. When he was done, he removed the holster and handed it over to me.

"You need before I need," he said.

I accepted the offer gratefully because he was right. "Keep one," I said. "Please."

He waved that palm in front of him. "Not need. Have three rifles now — I smell an enemy, he die from a distance."

I have to remark that in that moment, with that gesture of openhearted truthfulness, and the gift of the guns, Morning Sun made himself a man I trusted more and felt closer to than anyone since I left my family. He *was* family. I did a lot of thinking over that feeling whilst I buried the men . . . and beyond.

My muscles had just stopped being sore from the last round of digging and here I was at it again. This time I was on my hands and knees, using the knife like after Gonzales. It still struck me as sad and strange that so much killing did not affect me as it should. I guess when it's you or them, or when it's payment for evil acts, your conscience makes exceptions.

I hoped earnestly that God did.

I let the horse rest a bit while I trapped a hare with a rope from the saddle. After my meal, and after giving the horse water from the Mexican's canteen, I resumed my journey — blessedly happy to have leather under me instead of horsehide.

I crossed rivers with water for drink and fish for food as I made my way east. I avoided a path that would take me through the place where we had fought and killed the Mexican soldiers. I didn't know but that more advance parties of Santa Anna's men had gone there. It wouldn't do for me to try and be innocent and casual when I was seated in one of their saddles astride one of their horses. Instead, I came at Gonzales from the northwest. I did so cautiously, not knowing whether there would be Mexicans there or just fidgety Texians who might shoot me without waiting for me to identify myself.

There was no guard. There were no Mexicans.

There was no Gonzales.

There was, however, the smell of rotten, burnt wood in the air. I did not know it then but while I was laying sick, Mrs. Susanna Dickinson, wife of one of the ill-fated defenders, and Travis's slave Joe had got to Gonzales ahead of me. They was allowed to leave by Santa Anna just an hour after the Alamo fell. They took horses and came here directly. Not only did they have the sorry task of informing all what had transpired, their hearts carried the burden of telling the family of the thirty-two volunteers of the Gonzales Mounted Ranger Company that their kin had all perished.

Believing that Santa Anna might turn on the "Come And Take It" town next, Houston ordered it set afire, end to end. Like the children of Moses, the populace left with what they could and were relocated as well as the army closer to the U.S. border. That was good thinking on his part: troops were still stationed there to prevent a Mexican land grab, and Santa Anna would approach very, very carefully.

Though Gonzales and its people were gone, the ruins were not empty. That was

where and how my feet was set on the path
that brought me here.

CHAPTER THIRTY-THREE

Fort Gibson, May 1836
Ned's Story

"The Mexicans," I said.

"They were there unearthing what they had delivered before the burning," John replied. "Bad timing for them. Bad timing for me."

Meggie had stepped behind us and now bent a little closer. "Would you both like to come inside for coffee and biscuits? They're left over from morning mess, but they're quite good."

It was getting onto late afternoon, and as I hadn't eaten since my early morning breakfast, I gladly accepted.

"John?" she asked when he did not reply.

"Yes, of course," he said graciously. "Thank you."

We rose and followed her, John excusing himself to wash his hands by the well. I remained with him.

"You didn't seem eager to accept the invitation," I suggested.

"Why be inside surrounded by dead wood when I can be outside surrounded by life?"

There was a certain sense to that, given his interests, though I wondered if that was all.

"You said, John, that you learned something in Gonzales. No, how did you put it? Your feet were set on a path."

"That is true."

"May I inquire what happened? I assume the crates that the Mexicans were unearthing were more guns . . . our guns."

"That is also true," John said. "It was under the ruins of a toolshed, one that stood behind the blacksmith's foundry. Though blackened, his brick building and most of its fixings were intact, save for the roof having caved in."

"Do you think he knew what was there?" I asked.

"There is nothing that was not known to Señor Esteban Gonzáles, son of Rafael Gonzáles, the Tejano military leader and governor of Coahuila and Texas whose name the town bore."

"A blacksmith, the son of so august a figure?" I said.

"One of the stories someone told me and

330

Bowie that first day was how the elder Gonzáles was a courageous and outspoken advocate for independence from Spain. That made him well-liked at home and also in Texas. He was a great military commander, and his efforts resulted in the end of Spanish rule."

"That was 1821, yes?"

"That's right," John said. "Three years before many of the Texas towns were founded. What worried Mexico was that his next move might be to try and liberate Texas. They was especially concerned after he granted to every Shawnee family in Mexico a square mile of land along the Red River if they settled in Texas. A lot of folks in Mexico felt he was manning the territory for war, and feared his skill and resolve if he decided to join that cause. In 1826, after just two years, Rafael was replaced. Esteban saw his own future political prospects turn to ash — which, fittingly, is where his life ended up. He went to work at the blacksmith's shop and inherited it when the owner died."

"But he was always bitter," I said.

"Bitter and contrary," John said. "He was not among the men fighting for independence. But until I reached the charred acres of Gonzales that April day, I didn't realize that he was working against it."

"He was there?"

"He, along with his fellow smugglers or murderers or whatever you want to call them," John said.

Meggie came to the door then to see where we were. I saw her, waved, and apologized. I scooted over, told her I was asking John questions. John followed after drying his hands on a cloth slung over a pump handle. He also, thoughtfully, swatted off his seat and I paused to do the same. We had been sitting on the ground, after all. He looked like a wild man, but I could see he had been inside the home of civilized folk — most likely a lady, possibly one who chastised him about bringing in dirt on his clothes. Another bit of evidence supporting the story he had told of his life.

Back inside, I saw that the modest kitchen area was actually a little less clean than the sitting room had been. Part of that was due to the fire burning in a brick oven in the corner, warming the coffee; but part of it was due to scuffing on the old wood.

"You'll help yourselves," Meggie said, pointing to the round oak table where she'd placed the tray of biscuits and honey. "The dining room is through that door."

We did as she'd instructed, then went into

a room bright with sunlight from both sides. There was a long oak table with six places, three already set. John and I sat opposite one another. Meggie came in with the coffeepot and took the head of the table.

"You were telling us about Gonzáles," she said. "It must have been heartbreaking for the people not just to leave their homes but destroy them."

"I wondered," John said, "if it was not like the temptation of Lot's wife to look back on burning Sodom."

"Yes," Meggie said. She sat and seemed both pleased and challenged by the remark. "But would you be seeking the evidence of your eyes to know, for certain, that you would not be returning . . . or would you be saying farewell to an old life? Perhaps both?"

"I imagined the men would not have time for such sentiment," John said, adding, "no knock down intended. Sam Houston, for one, would've been looking to see which way the smoke was blowing and how high. He had to know that if Santa Anna saw it he'd've figured out just what had happened. He had to be concerned whether the army would figure whether they head north toward the United States rather than south toward Mexico."

"Of course," Meggie said. "His concern

was for the people he had committed to this course."

"And the future of Texas, ma'am," he said. "He had an army with him but out in the open, with women and the young — that was not where any militia would want to make its stand."

"But Santa Anna did not come."

"He was still snaking east from San Antonio, stopping to crush settlements and towns and any Texians who he believed would not offer fealty. From his saddle, Texas was its land and not its people. He could do what the older Gonzales had done, offer land to Indians and Mexicans who wanted to come north and kiss his ring."

"Like clearing farmland of chaff," I said unhappily.

"For a despot like Santa Anna, it was more personal. Like Fannin and his people, he liked to have them beggared and corralled and then executed."

Meggie looked down.

"Sorry, ma'am," John said. "I — I am not accustomed to gentler company."

"No, it isn't that," she said. "I have had this conversation with Burton — my husband — about the Comanche and their ways. I don't like to think of civilized people behaving in such a manner."

334

John's head tilted curiously. "Ma'am, one thing I have learned is that fine clothes and hammered trappings do not a cultured or kindly man make. The savage who saved me from the Mexicans acted in a way that was spiritual and fraternal beyond the ways of Sunday churchgoers. Foreign as he was, foreign though his ways, I felt closer to him at that moment than to any man I have ever met." He broke a piece of biscuit and poured a drop of honey from a spouted brass container. "I have been talking, for instance, to Mr. Bundy here for near a full day. He knows a lot about me. He can suppose qualities about my soul and nature but that Comanche — we *knew* each other in that moment. I was very moved."

"Are you saying that white men cannot know each other, lest they share blood?" I asked.

"I'm not even sure that's a good measure," John replied. "The Bible that begins with Cain and Abel warns of betrayal. I saw that in Ohio, where families broke up over wills and coveted brides and all manner of pettiness."

"The eye of the beholder, Mr. Apple," Meggie said with an edge of chastisement in her tone. "You yourself are on a mission of vengeance."

"And you spoke of Esteban Gonzáles being a corrupt man," I said. "Yet by the law of the land, the laws of Mexico, he was a patriot."

Meggie hadn't been part of that conversation, so I made her current while John ate the piece of biscuit. He did so almost reverently, like it was manna from God. Perhaps all food was, to him. Another thing a lying man would not think to add to his webspinning.

"This Esteban, then," Meggie said. "He was behind the stealing of the guns?"

"He was a part of it," John said after pouring coffee. "He had the meanness but not the cleverness to plan. I got to experience that firsthand."

CHAPTER THIRTY-FOUR

Gonzales, Texas, April 1836
John's Story

Esteban Gonzáles had an evil face.

His eyes were dark and deep set and far apart — he looked like pictures I seen of sharks. A thick, drooping moustache helped create that image by forming a big, wide top to his mouth — which was always hanging slightly open, showing blackened teeth that only got cleaned when he liquored up. Between the eyes and the mouth was a nose that had a high, fat ridge from where it got broke several times. That, in itself, was a testament to his fast temper and foul nature overall.

If such as he be a patriot, I am for treason.

There were four men pulling charred wood from the site of the shed, fine particles of ash flying along with larger leaves of the stuff. Now and then a live ember floated through the air, winking out on the dirt or shriveled, black grasses. When the wood was removed — which is when I arrived — they started hauling out random metal objects like tongs and scythes. I suspected, from the diversity of these things, that Esteban charged townsfolk fees for storing them. While that didn't seem quite neighborly to me, I reminded myself that I used to charge for the produce I grew. One has to earn an income. I supposed, thinking on it later, that intention has more to do with a thing than the actual fee charged.

The men did not stop when they saw me. I did not stop when I saw them. Maybe I should have, because there was obviously nothing here for me. But I had to consider where to go instead; I spotted ruts from wagons and carts on the other side of the shell of a town and realized the population had likely gone north. Maybe if I'd bolted I could have avoided knowing that foul crew. Yet while it stained my soul to be around them, it was not a bad thing. God always knows best.

While I was thinking all this, strategizing, one of the team cut across the yard between the ruined shed and the collapsed black-smith shop to intercept me as I rode by the latter. He noticed my saddle and the rifle hung from its side and grabbed the reins to stop me.

He asked me a question in Spanish.

"English," I said, not as a command but an explanation.

Nonetheless, he took it as a chastisement and snarled up at me. He had an evil face too. Or maybe it was the white soot in his hair or dark smears of black that made this impression. Regardless, I did not expect charitable treatment from the fella.

"Esteban!" he yelled, looking up at me, his fist tightening around the reins in case I tried to bust free.

The previously described man emerged from the wreckage of his former place of business. I didn't see his face, then, just his form — which maybe gave me my first sense of his being like a shark. He was long and round with massive arms that made him walk with a kind of swimming motion. He had on an apron which bulged with the shape of a small mallet, a sack of what was probably iron penny nails . . . and a hand-gun. Each swing of those arms brought his hand in front of that weapon which was centrally located in his pouch.

He took me in at a glance, then shooed the other away. His eyes rolled from the horse to its rider.

"Murderer," he did not ask, but said.

I remained silent, though I twisted slightly to show the knife which was on the side he was coming at. His eyes fastened on it and that became his target, like the fish I had thought of.

"Where did you get this," he said, touching the sheath with his fingertips when he arrived.

"Same place I got the horse," I said, the lie coming easily, as if Satan hisself was whispering in my ear. "From the paymaster in San Antonio."

Esteban pulled the knife, held it blade down, and admired it. "Which side?" he asked.

"The winning side," I said, seeking to endear myself to the man — and, hopefully, survive this encounter.

"You were there for the battle?"

"No way other that Jim Bowie would have parted with that," I said. I boldly held out my hand. "I was here with him."

"Eh?"

" 'Come And Take It,' " I said. "The battle. We broke company over that. If you was here — and I take it you was, being the town smithy, yes?"

He grunted and nodded — now like a hog.

"Well, I didn't approve of this rebellion and I left to the east. Fell in with the generalissimo on his way to San Antonio. I actually saw him, spoke to an aide in his company."

Esteban seemed doubtful. "Why did you leave, then? It is dangerous for a lone rider."

"I didn't leave," I told him. "I'm scouting."

I said this as I noticed, off to my right, the men still working and drawing, from a shallow hole, like a grave, a crate, like a coffin — one remindful of those I'd seen before. The fiends, as I probably knew in my heart — the fiends were the gun traders. Esteban was their boss, or at least their taskmaster. It didn't seem like he could be higher than that. There was not, in those eyes, in that voice, the intelligence to craft such a scheme.

"What are you scouting for, Señor — ?"

He had drawn out that word questioningly, and I told him who I was.

"John Apple," Esteban considered. "I never heard you mentioned."

"I'm from the North. Accompanied Bowie after I found him passed out in the street."

Esteban guffawed. "Yes, that is — was — James Bowie."

The bluntness with which he uttered that one word made me want to trample him dead with my horse. Instead, I sat still and extended my hand. "The knife *was* his, too," I said. "Now it is mine."

Esteban hefted it, as though considering whether he could use it. I shifted a little so the light hit my side. Right where one of my two Colts rested beneath my buckskin. The toothy shark grin returned and, having done his consideration, he handed the blade to me hilt-first. I felt, based on nothing but his ornery soul, that he had contemplated ways he might use it — stabbing my horse or my leg. He decided against that for reasons he spoke next.

"You planning to rejoin Santa Anna's men?" he asked.

"I am," I said.

He shifted a little, the glint still striking his eyes. "Is he paying more than knives and a saddled horse?"

"Not much," I confessed.

"Do you wish to earn . . . 'much'?" he asked.

"That has some appeal," I replied. "How?"

He said, "These men of mine have deliveries to make to your friends. Would you take them to him? The trail has proved dangerous for my men and goods."

He was referring, of course, to the two wagons Bowie and I had waylaid.

"What are your goods?" I asked, to make

this seem like it was a real transaction.

"Rifles," he replied. "To help put down the rebellion. Santa Anna loses too many men to Texian sharpshooters. His marksmen need to be equal."

On the surface, again, this was the speech of a Mexican patriot. I would never actually help him, of course, but however many guns there were I could see they never reached the foul hands of a tyrant.

"What are the wages?" I asked.

He looked at the other men who were working real slow . . . trying to hear, I was sure. I didn't know if any of the others spoke English, but they surely spoke numbers.

"If I give my boys less than they're gettin', you will die on the road," he said thoughtfully. "I will give you ten percent of my take: eighty *reales*, fresh struck at the Zacatecas mint. The paymaster with the generalissimo will pay you himself with a note you'll carry, from me."

"You make it sound like you won't be riding with us."

"That is true," he said. "I will be arranging the next delivery of arms. I can only secure so many each month. A little bit for the United States Army . . . unnoticed so long as it stays a little bit. My men return with my share so they can earn their next share. It is a good business arrangement." He laughed. "We all trust each other because we have to."

I had been holding the knife and noticed that my fingers was white around the hilt. I could've plunged it into his neck right there and then. But then I wouldn't know how he obtained the weapons. I sheathed it and dismounted.

"I'm hungry," I said. "Time to eat and maybe have a siesta before we go?"

"There is time," he said. "The hours are not wasted, after all, if Santa Anna is moving closer."

This man was a shark and a swine and a number of other beasts of the Lord's creation that He must not have felt too good about having created. But again, God has his reasons for all He does. Especially when it comes to directing me places where I can be of use. I wanted to do this right, lest I be exposed as a well-baked liar and end up dropped in one of those holes. I had heard, at the Alamo, that some of these *banditos* enjoyed burying folks alive after stuffing their mouths with dirt so they couldn't be heard and cutting off their fingers so they couldn't dig.

I wondered, honestly, whether I would do

344

that to Esteban if I could.

To the man who helped supply the Mexicans with guns that fired at Davy Crockett? I thought.

Yeah. I could.

To keep from seeming earnest, I took some bacon and eggs that was offered, enjoyed the nap I had said I needed — which I did, still weak as I was from my illness — and woke when it was late afternoon. I stayed abed after waking, trying to listen to whatever they were saying . . . but they spoke only Mexican. And not quietly, as if they had something to hide in case I *did* understand. Maybe they was just what they appeared to be — a bunch of stupid, greedy gunrunners.

I got up with about six hours of light left in the day. Three carts, this time, was loaded up. I left the corner where I was lying on burnt hay; I'd selected the spot knowing that no field mouse would have cause to disturb me here.

"I was coming to wake you, John Apple," Esteban said. "We are ready to leave."

I rose, washed my face in a covered basin of clean water, and saddled my horse. Esteban swam behind me.

"You have the rifles, provisions, and my

men watching you as well as each other," he said.

" 'The thief cometh not, but for to steal, and to kill, and to destroy,' " I said.

"Eh?"

"It's from John," I informed him. "Once you cross a boundary, there may be no line you do not cross."

Esteban shook his head. "I have not read the Bible since my father was here, and he has not been here for ten years. Be careful of my guns, not your psalms."

I didn't reply. What was there to say?"

The thing that preyed on my mind was what to do. Six men, in wagons that would probably have some distance between them, presented a problem. Even if I chose to attack them, to kill them, I was not that fine a shot — and all it took was one of them to be so and my lights would be out. I needed another approach to keep the guns from the Mexicans . . . and me alive.

It came to me as we started out and I saw, again, the rutted trails to the north. Travel with a whole bunch of civilians could not be a simple thing. Or a swift one. There might be a way I could use that. But the only way I could would require some daring — and I was not averse to that. Not after what I saw Davy Crockett do.

346

What I had to do was formulate the particulars of my plan and, fortunately, I had some hours of daylight left to do that.

CHAPTER THIRTY-FIVE

Fort Gibson, May 1836
Ned's Story

There was a knock at the front door and Meggie went to answer it. John had finished two biscuits during his talk, and an equal number of cups of coffee. I hadn't eaten a thing, and did now.

"I am seeing where you sharpened the pencil to a finer point," I remarked, "though I am eager to hear of the connection to the fort."

John said nothing as the voice of Deems Pompey Hulbert resounded our way. He preceded Meggie into the kitchen, obviously pleased to have been invited to join our circle. Meggie handed him a cup and saucer and a plate and indicated a seat beside mine.

"I had come to invite the Lady of the Fort to supper in town — only to find that she has guests," he said.

"There will be time, later," John said

348

without looking over.

"Perhaps you will both join us as guests of my newspaper," Hulbert said. "We may even have reason to celebrate."

"Oh?" Meggie exclaimed as she resumed her seat.

"I believe the lieutenant will not be preferring charges against Mr. Apple," Hulbert said. "At least, that is the feeling I got when we just spoke. I assume you are pleased with that information, John?"

"After these weeks of bloodshed and carnage, Mr. Hulbert, and with the purveyor of illegal guns not yet brought to justice, it is tough for me to be pleased about very much," John answered.

That was quite a mouthful of justifiable grievances, delivered straight into Hulbert. I had never before seen the reporter wear an expression like the one he had on now, that of a man who had tasted whiskey when he was expecting tea.

"I did not, with my report, intend to diminish the other afflictions in your life," he said contritely. "My apologies."

"It is not easy to know the burdens of others," Meggie said. "I am often guilty of troubling my husband with some matter about fabrics or broken pottery without considering that he may be thinking of a

349

fellow lost in the field."

The uncomfortable silence that would have followed Hulbert's statement now followed Meggie's. It is a gracious hostess who accepts the embarrassment of another as her own. Though I do fault Hulbert for taking a biscuit and pouring coffee just then. The clattering seemed unusually loud and asking anyone if they cared for a refill, while polite, only heightened the wooden ear this man possessed. I wondered if a coldhearted man becomes a reporter or the profession transforms him.

Ignoring the other, I turned to John as if we were still in the yard, alone.

"Is Esteban Gonzáles still at liberty?" I asked.

Hulbert seemed surprised to hear the name and made a move as if to speak. Meggie raised a hand slightly in his direction and shushed him.

Realizing I had jumped a fence John was not yet at, I asked, instead, "Did you feel safe with his men?"

"I did not," John replied very, very softly. "I did not believe, for one thing, that some headman would willingly give me a portion of his income, though both modest and reasonable that sum was. I did not believe he would do so to pay for a guide that was not needed. I did believe that any of his men would have killed a stranger like me just for his horse. I had seen just one other in Gonzales, a fit enough mount belonging to Esteban. Mine was fitter, less load-weary, not as gaunt and hard-rid than any of their own. It would do to replace any of theirs."

"Which meant they could not have allowed you to ride with them to Santa Anna's position, since they would reclaim the riderless horse," I said.

John cracked a little grin. "You're gettin' the knack of these fellas."

It was intended as a compliment, I think. I smiled.

"Based on nothing but what you just said, and having met a fair share of scoundrels in that territory, in that struggle, I believed a likely plan was to get me a short distance from Gonzales, kill me, and ride back with the horse to swap with Esteban's."

"Why wouldn't they have killed you in Gonzales?" Hulbert asked, vaulting back into the discussion.

"Because, Mr. Hulbert, that charred hay I slept on? The floor was covered with it and it crunched something awful. Had they tried to creep up on me, I'd've likely woke and shot 'em. The same is true when I was on horseback and they was on foot." He smiled.

"They couldn't know I was only a modest shot who had never yet fired either of those Colts."

"And you were riding behind the train?"

"More and more behind," John said. "But they didn't have a spare horse to run back and ask me why. And it would've wasted time for one of 'em to get off, run back, and find out why."

"Your plan," I said, "was already formed."

"Enough so that I knew I would break from them wherever I was bound," John said. "All I needed was nightfall."

"Isn't it dangerous to ride unfamiliar territory at night?" Meggie asked.

"Even familiar territory is a danger in the dark, ma'am," Hulbert replied, inflating his manhood like one of those hot-air balloons a customer had talked about seeing in France. He even drew a picture of it, which hung on my wall. The stitched fabric of that thing was filled with the same thing as this man: heated air.

"From a story, Deems?" I could not help myself asking.

"From experience," he huffed back. "One of the hazards of going from story to story to make a press deadline."

"You have lavished a great deal of time on this story," I noted. "Will you not be missed?"

I tried to sound sincere, like it was an earnest question and not an accusation; I was surprised at how annoyed I suddenly was with this man. He had repeated gossip and briefly turned me against John. However, as I looked at his wounded, then indignant face, I realized it was me I was mad at for having believed that tale of smugglers and John protecting their secrets. But the question was out there and Hulbert answered. He actually seemed pleased to have the conversation suddenly about him and not John.

"It is the desire of my publisher, Mr. Wharton, to see our stories circulated in the press of other cities," Hulbert replied. "The revolution and in particular the death of so many noted citizens in the Alamo are stories few are in the position to report. That is why he sent his most experienced reporter. One who can, in fact, journey in darkness and inclement weather if necessary."

Well, I had been rapped across the knuckles with a hickory stick and I accepted the punishment.

"Now that that has been resolved — whatever it was; I'm sure I don't know — I would like to hear again from our other guest," Meggie said. Her face turned toward

John. "But before we do, there is something I wish to say to all."

A deep hush fell on the table. Even John, who had been staring at his reflection in the coffeepot, looked up.

"I have heard, since this morning, the story of the growth of a man," she said. "A gardener and a preacher who was compelled to become a nomad living off the land, a prisoner, a Comanche, a revolutionary, a soldier. He has shown compassion to the fallen and for the earth, and for the fruit of the earth. He has freely admitted his own failings, his own crimes, his own mission. If all men were as honest, we should have a better world. Now, gentlemen, if we can resume the story without interruption, there is still something that this man will, I hope, reveal. And that is why he has come to Fort Gibson."

I speak for Hulbert and John when I say that no one present expected such an impassioned speech, so clearly laid out. Meggie — bless her, years of living around mostly men, men of all stripes from soldier to slave, from Indian to Mexican, had developed a talent for *reading* men. I had wondered why, from the start, she had tolerated and then forgave being held captive in her own home by this man. Now I understood. My Lidyann had that same keen sense of things, though I had not realized until this moment how much I missed that.

My new respect for Meggie, for my late wife, was like a blanket that spread to all such women I had not yet had the pleasure to meet.

"I am honored and grateful for your words," John said, surprising me by holding his hand up chest high, palm out, in the manner of a Comanche. Whether she knew it or not, John now considered her his sister. "I hope, more than anything, that I continue to prove worthy of them, for some of the least pleasant deeds were as yet before me. The next, in particular, is one that has caused me much suffering." He turned the open palm to his chest, to his heart, and waited a reverent moment before continuing.

CHAPTER THIRTY-SIX

Gonzales, April 1836
John's Story

The decision of my destination was surprisingly simple, when I faced the future honestly. I had been on my current path twice. First time with Bowie and Fannin when we went to the field of battle outside Gonzales. Second time going to the burned-out town. I had some sense of the lay of things, which was more than I had about any other direction.

Also, the burnt bones of Gonzales offered me something I wanted and had to get to swiftly, lest I miss it. That was Esteban Gonzáles. He was likely the only one who had the information I sought. Certainly he would not likely have shared his connections with his men, who would then have been in a position to kill him and take his share.

It happened as natural as if I was merely

an observer and not a participant. My horse slowed and slowed some more. Twilight settled and deepened. I dropped back — and when the caravan was just a small dark shape getting smaller and darker, I pulled the horse around and picked up speed before the light completely failed and rode hard back toward Gonzales. I slowed when I could no longer see the terrain, for to fall now would be disastrous to my intent. I took comfort knowing that Esteban would not likely be traveling now and, having rested, I did not have to stop. I was pleased that my heroic steed, like his namesake, was a natural-born frontiersman, picking his way back more or less the way we'd come. I felt a little like that schoolteacher in the tale Astoria had me read about Sleepy Hollow. My horse was padding through the night toward a sanctuary and away from a great evil — not a Headless Horseman but a multi-headed monster from Greek myth somewhere behind us. But, I reminded myself, it was no haven to which I was headed. If Esteban saw me first, he would know my intention and kill me if he could. I began to consider how I might prevent that.

I had been out on the road headed west, I reckoned, some five hours. I would be back in Gonzales by dawn. Chances were good that Esteban had set out to the east, south-east or northeast, not wanting to waste the hours of light that had remained. I would be in a fair position to pick up his trail in Gonzales — there was enough soot adhered to the ground to mark hoofprints — and would figure out then what to do.

The sad part about pursuit, if such came to pass, is that I would not be able to then ride to Sam Houston and pull off some of his men to capture the guns. The thought of all those arms in the hands of the Mexicans troubled me. I began to wonder whether I should have done that first rather than try to close the man who was the bottleneck.

It was a big thought for me. Death of Texians resulted in either case.

I stopped and swore.

"You made the wrong choice," I told myself. "Get the guns in the field and stop Esteban when he comes back to Gonzales."

But what if he didn't return to Gonzales? I thought. It was only because the guns was buried there that he had come.

"Shit," I said again. "James — we gotta go north."

I knew from what I saw in Gonzales what direction Houston's exodus had gone. Risking my horse's legs and my own neck, I turned north at a faster pace than I should've. James protested, but I spoke to him soothingly but urgently, explaining the need for such risk. We paused to rest when we found a creek, and I let him drink and feed. Of course, all the provisions Esteban had provided for me were with his men, so I had to content myself with just water. I could have had a frog, since there were plenty along the muddy banks, but I was not inclined to spend the time making a fire.

With less complaint, my horse carried me onward until sunrise — when, by blessed miracle, I found myself within eyesight of a trail of bent women and struggling children, with a wide line of seven horsemen protectively behind. I did not wish to alarm them and risk being shot by galloping up, so I fired a bullet upward and then waved my hands. The women turned. The horsemen all stopped and looked back, several already raising their guns.

"I need Sam Houston!" I cried.

They couldn't hear me but they didn't shoot me, neither. It occurred to me, then, to pull my white hanky from my pocket and wave it. When I did so, one of the men — covered by the rifles of the others — came breakneck in my direction. We both recognized each other at the same time: it was Willie Miller, the aide of Captain "Old

Paint" Caldwell from the Battle of Gonzales. "I need a handful of men," I said when he was within earshot.

"What's on?" he asked.

I briefly explained as we rode toward the rear guard of the party. He listened intently, and when we arrived he sent one man ahead to inform Sam Houston — then told the others they were taking a ride.

"You trust this man?" one of them said as we organized the party.

"Can I trust you?" the black-bearded Miller asked flatly.

In response, I showed him the sheath on my hip. "Bowie gave this to me the night the Alamo fell," I said. "Colonel Travis bade me lead two men out, one a courier with letters for families. I would cut my own throat with this before dishonoring his memory."

"The Mexican horse?" one of the mistrustful men pressed.

"Comanche brother gave it to me after killing the soldier who was on it."

Even as I said it, I know that story was so unlikely it could only be taken as true. We were off and riding southwest in just a few minutes, the man who had gone to inform Houston catching up with us after putting several other men in the back of the exodus.

We rode the best part of the day, making better time surely than those men in the wagons. I was pleased with the change of decision I'd made, and more pleased than that with the conviction that overcame me to make it. I had always let events more or less move me along, like life was a river. This was the biggest thing I ever did against the tide of events.

Me and my horse James. And having made it through the night, I think we was probably proud of each other.

Speaking of the night, I didn't converse much with my fellows when we finally made camp. There was still a somberness that lingered over the burning of Gonzales, the lost battles, the fall of the Alamo and San Patricio. They was all trying to keep from despairing which, I have to say, was pretty difficult. This mission was, in a way, redemption. If we could stop the guns from reaching Mexico and put them in the hands of Texians, it would go a long way toward boosting spirits. Especially because, as these men informed me, they did not like the idea that Sam Houston had his army moving north and babysitting instead of attacking Santa Anna wherever he was. The truth of things was, when we rode out the next morning — with a very good chance of catching up to our quarry that day — we carried with us more than just a mission. We had an invisible banner flying over our heads, one that we decided would say, "Rise Up Texas!" if we'd had the materials to make it. It was a call not so much for action but resurrection. I did not think Jesus would have been offended by our sentiment.

We rode harder than we probably realized, caught up in a kind of frenzy to do this thing. When, at just after noon, with a blazing sun upon us, we spotted the wagons, it was a moment of high fever for us all. Even I caught it, I who was not to the soldiery born. The men had their rifles and I had my Colts. The plan we shouted from man to man as we rode was for the Texians to attack the wagons separate, from back to front. The idea was to concentrate fire on the man who wasn't the driver, disable him, then shoot the driver.

It didn't go as well as we had hoped, since the men we was pursuing had one advantage: a steady platform to shoot from. Turning round, the man riding shotgun was able to shoot without the wagon stopping. The first shot, the very first shot from the rear wagon, put a bullet in the neck of Miller's horse. The animal fell at a gallop, spilling its rider hard and leaving him inert — but we couldn't stop to see to him then. That wagon was the target.

Two men poured on the horsepower, but not to shoot: they was raising a dust cloud to cover the movements of the others, who went wide of the wagon train. When the dusters stopped and three men emerged from the cloud, firing, the gunman went down in the crossfire. The driver followed. The horses, uncontrolled, turned to one side and I had to ride after them to keep them from getting too far. The remaining riders broke off into two groups of three, one on each side, and performed the same tactic — though the remaining Mexicans were not sitting still. They veered in opposite directions, forcing a smaller force to follow each. It was three men on horseback for each wagon with two horses and two men . . . all of them, now, thundering westward. It was like I have seen when coyotes run after a deer or pig or dog — a frantic burst of speed from all, with both skill and fate deciding the victor.

There were gunshots from both sides, shrinking from bangs to pops as they rode away. Just as I reached and restrained the runaway cart, I saw another of our men go down, though this time it was the man and not the horse that got struck. Then another wagon turned sharply when a Texian bullet struck a horse. The horse fell and the wagon went over with it, pulling down the other horse and throwing the occupants. The men tried to get up from the dirt and find the rifle and shoot back — but they wasn't able, being trampled by the Texian horses who were racing after the last wagon. The concentrated fire of five guns from both sides killed the men in the front and that wagon coasted to a stop.

Switching onto the back of one of the cart horses, I rode to where Willie Milller had gone down. He was on one hand and both knees, his left arm having been broke in the tumble. I helped him sit and we waited for the others to arrive. One of them had peeled off to check the other fallen member. He had taken a bullet in the shoulder and it required waiting for a wagon before bringing him over. That took some time, as the other four men had to load the crates from the upended cart. That weighed it down considerable in the loose, dry earth.

While I broke a board from my collection of crates to make a splint for Miller, the other men finally arrived. I took a look at the wounded man while the others put some of the extra boxes on the wagon I had recovered. The bullet wound, in the right shoulder, was bleeding hard, and I patched it best I could with my white truce handkerchief and a ribbon from the hat of one of the other men.

I later learned he bled out before they reached the Houston party. I tried not to feel guilty about that . . . or about the rest of us leaving the Mexicans in the sun to rot. The guns had to get to the Texian militia and I had to get to Esteban Gonzáles.

We parted, the men having a little less bonhomie, I think they call it, than we had riding in. I made my way east along this increasingly familiar terrain, once again having a bout of indecision as I rode. I had a sense I should go back and bury the Mexicans since Esteban wouldn't be going anywhere anyway until they arrived.

I decided against it, however. And, as you know, that nigh cost me my life.

CHAPTER THIRTY-SEVEN

Fort Gibson, May 1836
Ned's Story
"The Mexican — last night," I said to John, making the connection.

"Not all were deceased, it seemed," John said.

"What a selfless and heroic tale," Meggie enthused.

"But incomplete," Hulbert declared.

"How so?" Meggie inquired.

Hulbert took the floor from John, sipped coffee, touched a napkin to his lips, then replied, "Without meaning to in any way wishing to contradict our hostess or impugn the brave acts of these men, Mr. Apple included, I am obligated to point out that the Texians were not all selfless and heroic. I mention this only because, when first we met, Mr. Apple condemned my newspaper's disapproval of Stephen Austin and his crusade. Now that victory has been achieved, I think it only fair to point out that the paper may have been on the losing side — but not without cause."

"What has that to do with anything we are discussing?" I asked.

"You hit the point exactly, Mr. Bundy," Hulbert said. "We are not discussing this but *should* be. Like the rights for which the Texians fought, the honor of *The Brazoria Advocate of the People's Rights* is very much something worth defending anytime and anywhere," he said. He regarded John. "Would Mr. Apple object to a footnote or two being inserted to his narrative?"

"It is not my table," John replied.

Hulbert bowed his head deferringly and turned to Meggie.

"If you think there is need to speak, do so, please," she said.

"I believe there is need, because myths grow fast and cling hard," he said. He drew his notepad from his pocket. "Over the past few weeks, I have been recording information from stragglers I have met on the road and soldiers who fought on behalf of Texas. Mr. Apple, you rode east, not north, is that correct?"

He nodded once.

"Then this may be news to you," Hulbert went on. "As Mr. Houston pressed north to the Brazos River he and his group went by way of San Felipe de Austin, which Sam Houston unilaterally burned to ash as he had Gonzales. Leave nothing for the enemy was his explanation. The locals had a different view, feeling it was a punitive action for their refusal to join his cause. He next achieved the plantation of one Jared Groce. The resources and shelter of that estate were confiscated. And with good reason: Houston was losing men to disease and defection — some two hundred in number, leaving him with a force of eight hundred men. Many in his command urged him to stop the shilly-shally and attack the enemy. He disagreed. He felt they needed to drill . . . and wait for reinforcements, which he said he had information would be forthcoming. Some came, it is true, but seeking land — not war. Many had not even heard of the scale of the rebellion. Texas was large, they had heard, and they sought to own a piece of it. There were even a few Shawnee still responding to the offer of Governor Rafael Gonzáles unaware that his offer was older than some of their grown children, and far less active."

"I suppose, Deems, there is a reason you are telling us all this," I said. "I am slow. Can you share with me that reason?"

In truth, I was angered by his recitation. This seemed nothing more than an attempt, by him, to discredit John by association.

"There is a reason, Ned," he said, leaning forward. "Every rebellion, every war has its heroes and villains — on both sides. Let me repeat: on *both* sides. There is a new republic to our south. We must form commercial and political alliances with that state. We must be charitable toward our neighbor. But we must be realistic, too. Do they want to govern us? Will your husband, Meggie, be defending our border not from Mexicans but from Texians?" He sat back. "All I am saying, friends, is that we must not be blinded by occasional flourishes of men like Mr. Apple, Mr. Miller, and the revered Mr. Bowie."

There was another silence, different from before. This was thoughtful — or, more accurately, searching. Like you feel when you wake from a nap and wonder how long you slept.

"Perhaps you raise valid points, Mr. Hulbert," Meggie said, ever the gracious hostess, "although I believe that the actions of men may be separate from the actions of nations."

"I meant to tar no one —"

"Except Sam Houston," I pointed out.

"I was about to say, Ned, I meant to tar no one who did not hand me a bucket of pitch." He regarded John. "Sir, if I have offended you or I seemed to criticize your brave deeds, I apologize. Sincerely."

John considered this then said, "Mr. Hulbert, I hope you will forgive me for saying that I put no stock in your opinions or tales. I only talk about what I know from having been there — and I spent considerable time in and around eastern Texas. I have never met Mr. Sam Houston. But I know this. Before I would criticize him or Stephen Austin for their actions, I would point out that like General Washington, these pulled together an army from men who had only hunted rabbits, men who attended university, men who came from Tennessee and Kentucky, Mexico and Ohio, men who were under twenty and over sixty, men who missed their families and men who brung them, men who were asked to defend crumbling missions and men who crawled through gullies to find roots to eat. They took on odds greater than any newspaperman, publisher or writer, ever faced at his desk."

"Every man chooses his own battleground," Hulbert replied.

"I wasn't insulting desks, sir, or the people

who work at them," John said. "Andy Jackson uses one too. And me? Before Texas, my place was in soil or behind a pulpit. But that is an important distinction: 'Before Texas.' That land and its people are God-touched special. The leaders and the volunteers all had a prophet's vision of something big and new and good. If you're saying they made mistakes, only a fool would disagree. If you're saying that politics is a part of war, I would have to agree with that, too. If you're saying anything else, then — well, all I can say is for your personal safety you'd best not continue the journey you spoke of last night, to Texas and the Alamo."

Those were the words of a John Apple I had not yet met — a man with a larger view of things, a worldlier view, than his provincial life and reliance on scriptural wisdom had suggested. He had not insulted Hulbert or left the table, both of which I felt inclined to do. And he had even managed to insert a touch of humor that caused Meggie to smile behind her own napkin.

Hulbert was obviously surprised, too, since he sat quietly, nodding thoughtfully.

Which is when John, with a preacher's sense of his congregation, resumed his story.

CHAPTER THIRTY-EIGHT

Gonzales, April 1836
John's Story

We stopped by our little creek and, this time, I did make time to cook a pair of frogs. Their meat was stringy but tasty. It felt good to talk to James without being on his back. I'd come lately to horses — spending this much time with them, I mean — but I'd learned that they did hear you and they did react to you. I think he appreciated the talk because I wasn't asking him to do something.

The next day was clear and unusually warm, and I bathed before leaving, just to cool myself. By the time I was making for Gonzales, I was rested, refreshed, and most of all clearheaded. And there was something else. A sense that this was like no war ever fought, at least to my limited knowledge, one in which every man made a difference and was expected to shoulder the most he could bear . . . and then some. Willie Miller had taken independent action, with Houston's blessing, and had gotten a dozen crates of guns for the Texian cause. That could turn a battle. Which meant that what *I* had done, getting to his attention, could turn a war.

The rational side of me said, "John: you've done enough. Esteban has no men to haul his guns. Let it be."

But there was a stronger part of me that disagreed. The part that was a stew of a gift from Jim Bowie, Morning Sun, others — a sense of honor that dictated that I pit myself against the cause of all of that activity, Esteban Gonzáles

I saw his shark face in my mind as I rode. I pictured his walk, his arms, the rough sound of his voice, reminded myself of the *deaths he had caused.* That part of me rose like a cauldron in my gut, sending hot fumes everywhere . . . just like it had when I killed the Mexican cavalrymen who tried to take me, knifed the soldiers in the retreat from San Antonio, cut out the lives of my tormenters as they slept.

It was clear that John Apple had grown to quite a different man than he had been. I wondered just who this person was . . . and who he would become. I confess being afraid of that thought; imagine suddenly not knowing yourself. Who do you talk to? Who do you ask for guidance when events ain't finished with you?

And, God help me, they wasn't.

Esteban was not in Gonzales. I considered whether I should wait for him or try and track him — and risk missing him, because while I may have been blessed by Morning Sun I was no Comanche scout. But that's when I heard a voice say to me, inside my head:

You came to Texas to see the coast, the thought spoke loud. *Go.*

I can't say whether it was God or too much sun that spoke, but I was glad it did. Sitting around in this acrid ruin was not something I cared to do.

I headed out the east end of the village, saw the frozen-mud tracks of a single horse and rider headed in that direction, and followed them. Realizing that I could very well meet Esteban coming back from that direction, with a cartload of guns, I was attentive to every sound, every movement that wasn't caused by the wind, ever —

"Shit."

There are times you get caught up in a thing and forget something so basic, so large, that you don't understand how you could have overlooked some large aspect of it. I did that back in Mansfield, when I used to plant for the season. I would go to the plot of land with my spade and seeds and twine to build little fences the rabbits couldn't get through — and forget the bucket of water I'd need.

I had done that with Esteban Gonzáles. Not once while I was with him did I see a cart for hauling guns. He was bringing them in regular, if the shipments I encountered was any indication. That meant, wherever he was coming from, one or more drivers with one or more carts would be coming with him. I would be facing more than Esteban.

I quickened my pace and prayed to the good Lord that wherever he had gone he had not started the return trip. I hoped he had a woman somewhere, or drank with fellow conspirators.

I had to get to him before he came west with a trained and able team like the one we had stopped.

I was lucky, in a way. Talking to stray folks I met along the way — long after Esteban had stopped leaving a trail that I could detect — I learned that the only place where shipping took place was the newly established port of Beaumont on the west bank of the Neches River. Like so many of the towns I had come through since arriving, Beaumont had been settled in 1824 as a farm run by Noah and Nancy Tevis. Other settlers came to what was then called Tevis Bluff and then, just a year ago, all fifty acres comprising Tevis Bluff and neighboring Santa Anna was bought by speculators from the north who merged them into a town named after Jefferson Beaumont, kin to one of the buyers. The main thing the townsfolk did, then, was ship what they grew or manufactured to other towns along the river.

What made this information lucky was two things. First, it gave me a destination; and second, it was over two hundred miles from Gonzales. Esteban would just be reaching there by now. He would still have to pay off whoever had transported his goods — by barge, I reckoned, since I was told that was what fit best with what had been built there — and rest a spell. He would also have to come back along the only decent dirt road, which was the one I was on.

That still left the puzzle of who got him the information. I knew from what I heard at the Alamo that a lot of weapons for Oklahoma, Missouri, and Arkansas came by boat from the north, down the coast and around Florida into the gulf — usually through New Orleans, which was one of the reasons Stephen Austin had went there, hoping to secure arms for our cause. The army ordered guns in too great a number for a new port like Beaumont to handle. They would have to be taken off a larger ship and brought along the gulf coast.

I hoped that I would get that information from Esteban. I wondered, if I did, whether that would cause me to spare his life.

The trip to Beaumont took five days. I arrived shortly after the rising of a full moon, probably after midnight as it had been dark for several hours. I could smell the fresh water before I could see it; I could also feel the presence of the Gulf. The air had a motion, a scent, a power that I had never felt before having spent my life far from any sea. It was like the fluttering you feel, holding a moth by one wing and it buzzing the other to try to escape. Only that batting sensation hummed all over my body.

I had read that God was everywhere. If so, He had a concentration of angels here, their wings aflutter.

The moon cast the water and the structures beside it in a kind of plum shade. There was an inn, which suggested to me the kind of establishment the Coles was trying to establish inland. There was light in just one window, which I took to be a dining area since there were shapes seated inside. I was too far to make them out, which meant I was too far for them to make me out. That was fine; I intended to do some exploring first along the river.

I walked James down a gentle grass slope to the banks. A stone wall had been erected for quite some distance, roughly four feet high, suggesting that the Neches had a habit of sometimes overflowing. There was a mooring post atop the wall, a canoe banging lightly on the other side. I left James tethered there and moved low along the levee. There were three sturdy-built docks that did not go far into the river, telling me it was pretty deep along the bank. Each was guarded by a gate comprised of a waist-high horizontal log. And each was occupied by a vessel. The nearest wharf held a barge with a pair of large poles proudly upright in holders astern. It would take powerful arms to shove off from shore and move against the current. The second vessel was a dory with a single sail furled about a central mast. It was big, about two horse-lengths long, though the lazy-moving waters lifted and lowered it without effort. The third vessel, which I could not see until I had maneuvered back to the slope to see past the dory, was a large raft with no pole. Or, rather, someone took the pole with them when the raft came ashore. Because there were still contents onboard. Four crates that I knew well from having handled their brothers. They were lashed by heavy rope to iron hooks in the raft. The cargo must have arrived too late for them to be loaded onto a cart — a cart which would not have been protected. So they would rest here until morning.

I felt fire rise in my belly, reaching my throat as if I was a dragon. The guns made me mad, for sure, but so did the realization that no one here apparently questioned their legality or their destination. Is that how the new republic would operate, the one we had fought and bled and died to create?

That must not be, I told myself. I was in the core of wickedness, the place where death was distributed. It *had* to be stopped.

But I could not let that feeling take charge of my actions. I had to think, and with good reason: just beyond the raft, built on a stone foundation, was a shed with a small cupola. As I came closer I saw that it was not a shed but a guardhouse with a guard inside. The angle of the moonlight etched a white line about him, showed him leaning against a wall, sleeping. I crept closer, saw a cowbell on each gate. The clapper seemed to be weighted just so; though the wind gently moved the bell it did not sing out. The gate being moved would cause it to ring. Someone putting a hand on the log to jump over would shake it enough to cause it to ring. And the gate being moved was the only way to get on the wharf without going over the wall and hitting the river with a loud splash.

I wondered what the pay was for a man to sleep unless wakened by a hollow clang.

I drew my Colts, not intending to use them but to keep them from making the holsters squeak. From the first time I heard that canoe hitting the wall, *thuk, thuk, thuk,* I realized that out here, with that magical air, I noticed that sound carried. Still bent low, I crept around the shack like a big cat, on my toes. My ears was turning like I was a cat or a dog, listening for any sound from the inn which was receding to my left. I reached the waist-high log gate and saw fish net hanging from the bottom. Was that to keep critters in or out, I wondered — too late. I suddenly picked up an odor I had not smelled since Pennsylvania; unfortunately, the sleeping goat *baaaa*ed at my presence, jumped to its feet, and ran off.

"What?" the guard sputtered.

I didn't have time to swear, let alone think. I was nearly opposite the raft with the crates of rifles. Shoving one of my guns back in its holster, I vaulted the log barricade with the help of my free hand, causing the bell to sound. I landed like a dropped piglet, lost my gun, and didn't have time to look for it. Two ropes, fore and aft, held the raft to the wharf. The crates was stacked in the center, two and two, with about three feet on either side for whoever was steering. I drew my Bowie knife and ran onto the south side of the raft. I prayed that I had enough of a head start.

"Hey!" the guard said, more alert now. "Who's out there?"

The wakened sentry rang his own bell, located in the cupola, which caused James to whinny and roused the inn. Lights ignited in several windows. I heard shouts through an open door.

I cut one of the restraining ropes, which freed the tail end of the raft. It got caught in the flow, turned the raft sideways, and I lost my balance, landing in the water. Well, that was stupid. But as I said previously, I was a babe when it came to water. I had now been properly baptized.

I'd've swore but there was water in my

mouth. Coughing it out, I slogged to the shore, where there was barely room to stand on account of the stone wall. I was grateful that my fingers had not panicked like the rest of me and had dutifully remained locked around the knife. I had no idea whether my guns would still function after their soaking, and I wasn't sure what to do next. The guard was out of his booth and holding a rifle; luckily, the moon created the narrowest shadow where I stood frozen.

If I ran to James, I might get away — but I would never again have a chance to take the rifles or their owner.

There was something I had learned from Colonel Travis back at the Alamo, when he had answered that cannon shot from the Mexicans with one of his own. Show no fear. Attack. Otherwise, you will be fighting on the enemy's terms.

The guard reached the wall, looked out at the river, then looked down. He knew this terrain, would discern enough of me in a moment to shoot me where I crouched. The gun barrel was over the wall, on my side. I did not think, I acted. I sheathed the knife, vaulted toward that barrel about two feet up, and grabbed it. My falling pulled it down, not free of his hands but causing it to discharge into the river. It was useless for the moment and, releasing it, I ran back to the wharf.

"He's here!" the sentry shouted. "Esteban's raft!"

The man ran to the gate, obviously intending to engage me. We arrived simultaneously — he had obviously done a share of poling and had arms like the log which he moved by his own self. I drew a wet gun. He hesitated. I did not know if it would fire, but he obviously had the same concern.

"You shoot me, you get hanged tonight," the guard warned.

I switched gun hands and drew the knife. I started to cut the other rope. "Get back on shore," I told him.

"They will follow you."

"Get off," I repeated. I could only entertain one worry at a time. Right now, my worry was getting the raft free.

The man looked at my moonlit gun. I had an answer, sort of, to my previous question: he was not being paid enough to risk that my gunpowder was still dry. He returned to the dock and backed through the gate as other men came running toward us — with more rifles.

I did not have but one course of action open to me. I cut the rope and ran behind the crates and lay flat down as the raft spun into the river — in my haste nearly stabbing myself in the chest with my own knife. That wasn't my only near-calamity. The key word I just imparted is "spun," because in about two seconds, though I was lying down, I was facing the shore, vividly exposed by moonlight — a near and easy target. I scrambled around the raft just a heartbeat before the first volley struck wood, causing crate and raft to spit splinters into the air. I did not lay down now but crept around the long wooden boxes as the long wooden raft turned lazy circles. They happened to impede my view of the shore for a moment — the moment when Esteban set out in the canoe. That wasn't good for me, since the raft was drifting back toward where I had hitched James — near the canoe. He proved to be an able paddler, and we were destined for a collision. The only good thing was, far as I could tell as I twisted toward the center of the river, my hated adversary was not armed. Thinking ahead, I considered our certain confrontation and the fact that even if I survived, I would be a target for any allies he had ashore.

But, as I said, one worry at a time.

Esteban was shouting at me, almost baying like a wolf. It was in Mexican, so it was as incomprehensible to me, but there was no mistaking his rage. This was a good time to find out if my gun fired; I aimed, the hammer clacked, and nothing else happened. Once, twice, three times.

I holstered it and realized I would have to rely on the knife. As I spun at the mercy of the river, I found myself talking to Bowie as though he was there. Not to God but to someone who I had seen use the knife. I pictured how he held it, how he moved. I prayed some of that would find its way to my right arm.

The canoe speared toward me, reached me, and Esteban went from a sitting position to being in the air with a powerful leap.

"Bastard!" he cried as he flew toward me.

My nemesis carried one of the two paddles with him, high over his head like a big shark fin hovering over his shark body. It came down at me as he landed, and only rolling tight against the crate protected my skull. The oar shattered, but now he had a jagged stick to use as bludgeon or knife.

Or harpoon. He raised his arm high and jabbed down at me. All that stopped him from impaling me was the heavy rope around the crates, which I had used my heels to scoot under. Problem was, now I was trapped. I could not roll overboard if I so chose. It would take time I did not have to wriggle to the end of the raft. I was in pain from one of those iron hooks in my back. And the movement of my right arm, the one with the knife, was limited by the rope that was now above it. Esteban screamed like a demon, grabbed that rope with one hand and leaped over it to where my head lay, my face exposed.

I was not so much afraid of dying but of failing at this last, important moment. I looked away, not wanting that to be the last thing I saw. I'm not sure an iron hook was much better, but — it saved my life.

The hook was to my right. Of course. That was where the crate-holding rope was tied. Dear blessed God, what was under my back was not that.

With a cry of my own, I pressed my body against the rope, at the same time worming my left arm under me. Esteban landed between me and the water, facing my trapped self. I was staring up at him, at that wood stake, at his wide, dark maw. I was able to see his narrow eyes grow big and bright as my left hand emerged with the gun I had dropped, the one that had not gone in the water, the one that put a bullet square in his dull shark's forehead. Like a skunk, his malodorous blood spewed from him as his body went the other way. This time I had the devil's own baptism as his gore painted my face while he was flung into the river, first bouncing off the side of the canoe. He bobbed facedown in the moonlight, a brownish grease forming around him as his foul essence poured forth.

I squirmed from under the ropes, knelt on the raft, looked back toward the shore. Men were at the wall, near the guardhouse. They had rifles but didn't use them; I was too far to make a good target, and I was still spinning. One thing at a time: I had to deal with the guns first. The solution actually solved two problems.

I holstered my dry gun, thanking Mr. Colt and God, then reached for the canoe and felt inside for a mooring rope. Finding it, I tied that to the nearest iron ring. I did not have the strength or leverage to shove the crates overboard, but I had another idea. I proceeded to use my knife to cut the ropes that held the raft together. The twisting became more like a serpentine movement as the thing came apart fore, center, aft. I couldn't get to the bindings under the crates but the current worked the ends of the raft, side to side, up and down, and soon the whole structure was like a sheaf of wheat in a strong wind, working against its central bond.

I got in the canoe and untied it just moments before the raft came apart, dumping its contents into the Neches with a dull, deep, sustained splash. My own vessel rolled a little from the waves — a most blessed sensation, I must say.

Retrieving the surviving paddle, I rowed Indian-style, switching from one side to the other, to return to shore. The men had begun to gather behind the wall, rifles pointed at the canoe, aligned like the picket stakes we had at the Alamo.

They hadn't shot me yet, and I didn't know if they would, but I took a chance and said to them that which summed up what I had done and why.

"Remember the Alamo!"

No gun was discharged as I closed on the shore and stepped from the canoe.

Chapter Thirty-Nine

Beaumont, Texas, April 1836
John's Story

What was more miraculous than not being shot — and mind you, through all of this I never felt that the Lord or Jim Bowie was far from me, protecting me — was what I learned after my horse was stabled and I went with the owners and their guests back to the inn.

I gave them a quick summary of my Texas history, which seemed to persuade at least my hosts that I was a solid citizen. After that, there was a general discussion among the folks there-gathered, whose sleep I had disrupted beyond repair. To begin with, there was no threat of legal action. For one thing, there was no lawman anywhere near Beaumont — nor any written laws to uphold, other than a legal charter that did not address the killing of a traitor who was trying to stab me. And I was not stealing legal goods so, technically, even if a law did exist, I would not have broken it. This, mind you, was all decided in an improvised hearing by six folks, none of whom had any legal knowledge and two of whom could not read or write.

Dorcas and Dick Harris, the proprietors, had been fooled into believing that Esteban Gonzáles was, like his father, devoted to the free state of Texas. The owner of the raft, Jack Howard, a former New England whaler, was angry at the loss of his conveyance but angrier still that he had been used by the Mexican to help Santa Anna. It was he who had been sitting watch, not an employee of the inn, safeguarding the goods.

"Every time he came, Esteban had letters from the garrison of Fort Gibson, on their own printed paper, signed by their own commander, authorizing this transfer," the big man said.

"May I see those?" I asked.

He produced the most recent document that Esteban had presented. It was indeed on the printed letter paper of Fort Gibson, and signed by Colonel Burton Gearhart, Commander. I asked if I might retain the letter. Permission was granted.

"I arrived to drive the cargo in my cart," said another man, who went by the name of

Pedro — just that. He shrugged. "I got no politics. I just carry goods."

"You just went back and forth to Gonzales," I said.

"That's right. Just back and forth and back and forth." He held up his thumb and index finger. "Two days a week — I go home to my family along the Neches." He shrugged again. "Who run Texas, no matter to me."

The other two occupants of the inn were a young married couple bound for their honeymoon in New Orleans. When they got back, they planned to work on the Tevis spread. I envied them. The angels of this country called to me.

But I could not stay, not more than the night. I had to get back to the fort to make certain this kind of blasphemous behavior never occurred again. The Harrises gave me some of Mr. Harris's clothes, and mine were set out to dry a little. My soggy belongings were put on the dresser in my room. And their kindness did not stop there. I would not have been able to pay for the room, the few coins I carried having been lost in the river. Happily, my hosts wanted no money.

"You gave me a story to tell travelers for years to come," Dick Harris told me, showing me to a room after making sure the other vessels were still secure. They belonged to local men who ferried goods from Louisiana.

"Your guests may not believe you," I pointed out. "This land — the West — is famed for its tall tales."

The man smiled. "This land is famed for stories, as you say, but I suspect it will be more for the real heroes who lived here. Of which I count you as one, John Apple."

I was flattered and thanked him.

"Besides," he went on, "the remains of the raft have washed against the seawall, and I believe I can use the barge to salvage the crates. The water will have ruint them, but what a display they will make." He eyed the knife that had been wiped dry and set on the furniture with my guns and holster. "I don't suppose I could buy the knife."

"You recognize it?" I said.

"More than anything, that is what made me trust you," he said. "No man could've taken that from Jim Bowie so you *must* have been a friend."

"Bowie was here?" I asked.

"Before the inn was built, when we was just running the single wharf we had put up," he replied. "It was 1832. Bowie had sent to New Orleans for some clothes for his wife, came to pick it up himself. I heard, later, what had happened to them, and my heart busted for him. And now . . . now we've lost him."

He asked me to talk about the Alamo; I was too tired to talk but too tired to resist, and the words just came out. So did the feelings I had about what we had won and also what we had lost. I wept, and Dick Harris wept as we knew all of this great new republic wept.

Which is why, finally, I had to get rest so I could help make sure our loss had not been for nothing. My host graciously accepted my decision to retain the keepsake and bid me a good night.

I slept deep, trusting that if anyone here had deceived me and came for me in slumber, the same guardians would watch over me as had done so on the river.

It was the smell of eggs and griddle cakes and strong coffee that woke me the next morning. There was still something I didn't understand, and I was wondering if anyone there had any ideas.

When we had gathered around the table and said our prayers — me leading grace, which honored me powerfully — I asked the diners for their indulgence.

"I will leave here and go to Fort Gibson directly," I said. "It is my intention to expose the one who sent the letter, whether it is the man who signed it or someone who stole his good name. But — Mr. Howard," I turned to the owner of the late raft, "is there a printed document that announces the schedule of these shipments? How would Esteban Gonzáles have known to come here now?"

"I had been wondering that myself," Dick Harris said. "I would have thought such shipments, like payroll, are not publicly known in order to prevent just such theft."

"I do not know the answer to that," Howard boomed. "But I can tell you that when the army arrives to collect their goods for distribution, they do not come just for them."

"Do you know what else?" I asked eagerly.

Howard said that he did. He told me what it was. And with that information I had narrowed to a very few the number of sinners who could have done this thing.

It was with gratitude I departed after a good meal and even better fellowship. I left also with food and drink enough for several days. It would take, I knew, the better part of two or three weeks to make the journey to Fort Gibson; a dangerous trek, for it would bring me through territory with a Mexican army closing from the southwest and Sam Houston's men doing who-knew-what to the northeast. For all I knew, they might have orders to shoot to kill.

I decided it was probably safer to head for where the Texians might be — which was how, by yet another miracle, I found myself on the outskirts of San Jacinto as the terrible reign of Santa Anna came to an end in Texas. My heart felt like it was being twisted by big hands when I heard the sound of warfare — the same as it sounded at the Alamo, big and loud and near. I was drawn toward it, for it was large enough to sound like the end of someone's dream.

It happened not to be our hopes that were being blasted by cannon and gunfire. From the time I heard it until the time I arrived — less than a half-hour by my reckoning — the war was ended. The republic was achieved. The tyrant was thrashed and returned to his homeland, accepting the terms of surrender as dictated to the dictator.

I did not stay for the celebration that followed. There could be no joy in my heart until the felon who had aided in the death of my friend had been brought to justice. I did not go out of my way to stop at the Coleses' place, though I resolved to journey there after my trip to the fort. However, I did detour through Comanche country to visit with my brother Morning Sun and to see, again, the squaw who had been so enamored with me. I knew it might cause Swift Water some ache to see me again but — well, I was feeling alone and there was something inside that compelled me to go.

I reached the settlement in time to see her joined with Morning Sun. First, San Jacinto — now this. I had to ask myself if God was conducting all of this, the timing, wanting me to close doors so that I could open new ones. Sweet Swift Water seemed very happy, as did Morning Sun, not just to be bound but to see me. The braves taunted me with their light dances, but only for a moment — only until Morning Sun called their attention to my Mexican saddle and Bowie knife, all won in battle. I feared that someone would take that as a sign to challenge me, but none did. I did not understand the words of Morning Sun, but his tone was respectful rather than mocking. To attack me, they would be attacking him. None was prepared to cause such a rift.

I moved on, just me and James . . . and that important paper I carried in my breast pocket. As much as it was a journey across the land, it was also a journey through my insides. I reflected on everything I had experienced, everyone I had met, every scrape I had survived. I thought about all of those who had not, all of it for an idea — one they did not even survive to enjoy. What a quality of man to make such a sacrifice as that. Fate and circumstance had forced me to take some of those risks, perhaps less willingly than a Bowie or a Fannin, and I wondered how, when this was finally ended, I could dedicate my remaining years to that level of charity and goodness.

The answer, I decided, was roam the land with one great purpose in mind: to help the oppressed by killing those who needed it, and to plant the seeds of the future in their otherwise unworthy carcasses.

CHAPTER FORTY

Fort Gibson, May 1836
Ned's Story

The kitchen was very, very quiet when John finished his tale. He seemed spent, though no more than his audience. Hulbert and I were looking at each other as if assessing our own lives in light of those John had shared with us. Meggie, though, was the most affected of all. She did not cry but seemed at the very edge of doing so — though perhaps for more than just the values and ideals that had come with the tale, like fine and precious cargo.

With a slight clearing of the throat, Meggie said, "You have this letter with you, yes?"

"I do, ma'am."

"May I?" she asked, extending a hand.

John reached into his jacket and removed a document that was folded in three parts, slightly soiled with perspiration and inclement weather and perhaps a bit of whatever someone had at some point eaten while reading it. He stood and walked around the table, almost like I have seen a cat do with prey. I was somewhat alarmed by his approach; I was not sure if Meggie or someone she was close to was the intended victim.

He stopped between my left shoulder and the end of the table where Meggie sat. He put the document down and spread it with splayed fingers.

"You have seen all the fort pay vouchers," he said.

"I have."

Only now did he remove his hand to reveal the bottom of the letter. "Whose writing is this?"

Meggie regarded it intently.

"Mr. Apple," she said. "What were the other goods that came on that vessel to New Orleans?"

He raised an arm to his side, indicating the rest of the room. "They are here, in this kitchen."

Showing sudden great composure, Meggie rose. She took the letter and went to the room where we had been seated earlier. I was concerned with this liberty she had taken, but John seemed untroubled. Hulbert had returned to life and looked from me to John and then around the kitchen.

There were utensils, a sampler, furniture — a great many things.

"What was on the boat?" Hulbert asked with quiet urgency. He was not a man who did not like *not* knowing things.

John did not answer. He did not move, in fact, for the several minutes it took for Meggie to return. She did not come directly; we heard the rustling of papers, then her tread upon the floorboards, then her voice at the front door. We heard the voice, but not the precise words, uttered by Lieutenant Falconer in response.

Only then did she return. In addition to the letter John had brought, Meggie carried with her ink, a pen, and fresh paper. She sat, spread all of them before her, but refolded the letter.

There was no sound other than our breathing, Meggie's the loudest. It was not fear that moved her bosom thus, but fury. I could see it in her eyes as well. She had found the likely author of the letter among the vouchers. Now she intended to prove it.

A few minutes later, the front door opened. There was no knock, just the sound of boots on the floor. The lieutenant entered the kitchen, stepped aside, and ushered in the fort's Cajun cook, Cotton March. He came in with his usual lope — only stopped when he saw us arrayed around the table with a cross-looking Meggie at its head.

Lieutenant Falconer stepped within the doorway to prevent any thought of exit. The back door was far enough so that if March made for it, John or the lieutenant would intercept him.

"Mrs. Gearhart?" March said. "You wanted to see me?"

"Not especially," she replied bluntly, "but it is necessary for me to obtain a specimen of your handwriting."

"Mine? Why?" he asked. "You have plenty of samples —"

"I don't want your name," she interrupted. "I want you to write what I dictate. Mr. Bundy, would you kindly surrender your seat?"

"Of course," I said softly, and rose.

March was not yet sunk, only leaking grievously, and he saw no path forward other than to take the chair that was offered. His hands were shaking slightly, and he placed them flat on the table, then restlessly moved them to his knees.

Meggie separately pushed the inkwell, the pen, and the blank paper in front of him, watching his expression all the while.

"Please write for me the following," she said, nodding for him to pick up the pen.

401

March did so and waited. Lieutenant Falconer, who did not seem to be aware of what was going on, came forward. He was not watching the table but March, clearly aware that something was not right.

"Yes, m-ma'am?" March said.

"Write, 'Colonel Burton Gearhart, Commander,' " she said.

March hesitated, which was damning enough. Then he put the metal nib in ink and started to write, stopped, and started over. He had begun writing in a cursive hand then switched to block-style letters.

"No, in script, as you began," Meggie ordered.

March held the pen which was now shaking as well. He redipped the nib, held it in the ink, then let the pen go. It clattered against the squat bottle and came to rest.

Meggie opened the letter but held it up; it took me a moment to realize why. It would have been too easy to spill the ink and obliterate the evidence.

"Yours?" she asked.

"N-no," he replied. "I've never — what is it?"

"I think you know very well," she said. "The rifles sent to this fort and others arrive under the same shipments as kitchen supplies from the east. Canned goods, utensils, plates, cups, pots — you know when these are coming."

"Of course, that is my job," he said. "I — I don't have access to such as this!" he added, indicating the letterhead.

The index finger of John's right hand uncurled, the nail extended toward the sitting room like the Sword of Judgment itself.

"Out there," John said, then pointed down. "On the floor here. I have seen dirt and dried leaves from the garden."

"I bring food items to Mrs. Gearhart —"

"Do you bring them to the commander's desk?" John asked.

"That area is not for enlisted men!" Lieutenant Falconer snapped, openly horrified by these developments.

"Did you, Mr. March, steal this paper from the commander's desk?"

The cook did not answer in words, merely lowered his chin.

"Did you profit, Mr. March, from the sale of American rifles to the government of Mexico — an act strictly prohibited by both army regulations and federal mandate?"

"My family in Louisiana — they are poor," he said. "I cannot support them on the earnings of an army cook."

"A hardship, to be sure, but you chose a remedy that will land you in a penitentiary."

March looked over at Meggie. "Please, ma'am. Is there no way I can fix this? Anything?"

"One of your rifles was in the hands of a dead Mexican when Davy Crockett took it from him at the Alamo," I said. "How will you fix that?"

Lieutenant Falconer did not wait to slap a hand on the man's shoulder and pull him from the seat. He wrested him up with such force that the table shook; I dove for the inkwell to keep it from emptying on our hostess. She did not appear to notice, her gaze set on the man who had abused the good name of her husband in a criminal undertaking.

"Wait!" John shouted.

Falconer stopped and March just hung there; everyone else fell still. John went over to the cook. His left hand opened and came up under the prisoner's throat, five sharp, long nails digging into the flesh. At once, trickles of blood began to run over them. John's face turned feral.

"Hold it, there," Lieutenant Falconer said uneasily.

The lieutenant pulled on March to draw him away but not only did John hold fast, he placed his right hand on the back of Falconer's — the claws wrapping round.

404

"Hutton, no," Meggie ordered.

That caught the attention of Hulbert and myself. Meggie had no legal authority here; that was a personal command. Something from the heart. For John? To protect Falconer?

The young officer relaxed without quite surrendering his authority over March. While the cook squirmed and bled, John released Falconer's hand and pointed the index finger of his right hand directly between March's eyes. It was a vivid depiction of wolf and hare, eagle and mouse. It was like I've seen at the Hick when a drunk suddenly turns very, very hotly sober over some affront or challenge.

I could hear Meggie breathing heavily behind me. I tried to ignore her; there was something more happening. Something that had nothing to do with the risk to March or Falconer. Five streams of blood continued to run into the blue tunic the cook wore.

John's face moved to within just inches of his captive.

"I wondered, these many weeks, whether I would kill you when I found you out," he said — no, he hissed. It was now snake and chipmunk.

"I'm . . . s-so sorry," March stammered.

"You are not sorry, you are afraid of facing your final Judgment," John replied. "I hardly blame you. Your greed spilled noble blood into the soil as I now spill worthless blood into your shirt."

"I will d-do anything."

John did not appear to believe the man or care about what he was feeling. This fight was John against John. I could see the struggle in his twisted mouth, narrowed eyes, the breath flaring his nostrils.

"Anything," John said. "Will you stand here with me until you have shed as much blood as there is in your body? And even then, not enough to repay the debit in your account."

"See here, John, this is enough," Falconer said.

The lieutenant tightened his grip on March and made to pull him free, only this time John did not slap a hand on his. Meggie gasped when she, and I, and then the lieutenant, saw the Bowie knife move around the cook's side to point straight at the belly of the lieutenant.

"I have little enough reason to spare you, either, Lieutenant," John said. "This garrison was your responsibility. You should have known."

"I keep the books and *I* did not know!"

Meggie said urgently. "Will you kill me, too?"

That female voice was frightened and pleading, and somewhere in John's head he may have connected it to another time in his life, a time when a lady — refined and capable with letters and concerned for others, perhaps like Meggie — when Astoria Laveau dominated his thoughts and feelings.

Like a swordsman who had delivered a not-quite-fatal wound to end a duel, John withdrew both knife and then the fingernails, with a suddenness that caused March's head to flop forward. Falconer had to grip the cook's shoulder to keep him from slumping to the ground. Sheathing the knife, John grabbed the cook's lapel and showed him the blood-covered fingertips.

"I grew these for two reasons," John said. "One was to till soil, to care for a hungry population. The other? When I found the responsible party, it was to remove their tongue from below when I found them. You, pig, may thank the mortal voice of Mother Earth that I did not do so."

Feeling the matter somewhat concluded, Meggie fetched the napkin from her lap, inserted herself between the men, and tucked it around March's wound. The cook held it there himself, his blood staining the cloth so that it was soaking red before he turned.

'We'll be in the infirmary," Lieutenant Falconer said as he hurriedly escorted the cook from the kitchen. Once again, no one moved. Not until Hulbert inserted his own movement into the stillness.

"You know," he said, "I don't think the lieutenant was terribly upset by March's misery."

Meggie exhaled, a reminder for me to do the same. But not John. Dripping blood on the carpet, he just glided back to his seat at the other end of the table and collapsed there, his long mission finally complete.

"I am sorry about that display," he said, then noticed the floor. "And about your rug."

"The commander, my husband, has bled pugilistic blood on this floor many times," she said. "He and the lieutenant — it is sport, to them."

Once again, Hulbert and I exchanged looks. This was increasingly a separate and intriguing tale.

"I . . . I lost myself for a moment," John said.

Meggie's eyes softened.

"Your conduct was understandable, John,"

she said. "You have been under great strain and without respite at great risk. The people of Beaumont called you heroic, and I quite agree. To which I add that you acted selflessly and, unlike the men of this fort, you were under no legal obligation to do so. Your honor is not only unblemished, it is — well," she smiled, her eyes on his bloody hand, "practically beyond rebuke."

"I have very little that is my own," John said. "All that I am I owe to the Lord God, to the soil, and to the great men who came before me. Were I to fail any of them, my grief would be boundless."

If John had been a predator and March prey, Hulbert now looked like the hyena who had to feast on offal. He cleared his throat to announce a coming speech.

"I doubted you, John Apple, for which I apologize most profoundly. The story I write, with your permission, will reflect that change of attitude."

"You do not need my permission to write this story," John replied.

"But I do," Hulbert said. "For it has occurred to me, just now, that 'this' story is not all that I intend to write."

I looked at the reporter with puzzlement. The others did not look at him at all.

Meggie gathered up the writing implements, asking to keep the letter for March's court-martial. John gave her his permission, with gratitude. Then, as an afterthought, he took a biscuit and slowly consumed it as if it were holy manna from God.

I went over and took Hulbert by the arm, walked him to the back door, and gave John his well-earned moment of private thanksgiving.

CHAPTER FORTY-ONE

Fort Gibson, May 1836
Ned's Story
John was not taken back to a jail cell to answer previous allegations or answer for the assault on March, which was described to the doctor, I was told, as "a freakish accident with a serving fork and a stumble on the rug in the too-eager service of Mrs. Gearhart."

He was escorted to the guest quarters that were reserved for army and political dignitaries. I left in the early evening to open the Hick, and Hulbert — without Meggie, who was understandably not in a mood to have a sociable dinner out — came to my tavern after a meal at the Cornucopia in the hotel.

"They didn't have much of a selection," he admitted.

"Owner gets his beef from the garrison," I told him. "They ain't butcherin', he ain't servin'," I added.

"Even fish, though," I said.

"No beef, no money for staff, no one to catch the fish," I pointed out.

"I do not think I much care for the West anymore," he admitted. "I think I may move East. Though I must say, I have a fresh respect for Lieutenant Falconer and Meggie."

"You're uncouth."

"And you're a hypocrite," Hulbert charged. "The commander in the field, the commander on patrol, the manly, bloody bouts between the two men — it all suggests something big and lurid and . . . ah, if only I could write those kinds of tales. I would retire to a great metropolis and live the good life."

"What's stopping you?" I asked.

He grinned. "I think I have an idea that may make even more money and not force me to use a pseudonym or risk losing my friends."

I gave him a tequila. He nursed it.

"That's right," I said. "What did you mean before, when you said that this wasn't the only story you wanted to write?"

"That is part of my thinking — about moving East, I mean, to Chicago or New York."

"I'm not following."

412

"The story of this revolution is going to fire the hearts and souls of American readers," he said. "And the people who were a part of that will be made legend."

"That's a lot of people," I observed

Hulbert waved a hand like he was wiping a chalkboard. "No, not everyone. The ones who have something special. Jim Bowie with his knife — he will be remembered. Davy Crockett with Betsy — he will be remembered. Santa Anna? A loathsome villain who sought to crush liberty and was forced to race through scrub to avoid capture."

"And John?" I asked.

Hulbert wagged a finger. "He will be remembered perhaps best of all."

I frowned. "You know that my quick affection for John is second to none. Indeed, I plan to invite him, along with the lieutenant, yourself, and Meggie, to a party in his honor tomorrow evening."

Hulbert returned my frown. "John . . . does not seem the partying type."

"Then it will be celebration, a commemoration — whatever you want to call it. Something to honor everyone he has shared with us."

"I like it," Hulbert said, "and I accept the invitation most graciously."

"But returning to his fame," I said, "you

know John well enough, I think, to know that he would be mortified to be placed beside Bowie and Crockett or any of the others in a pantheon of heroes."

"I didn't say hero," Hulbert replied, again shaking that dog's-tail of a finger. "The word I used was 'legend.' "

"I'm all eager ears," I said. "But I don't see how that report gets written."

"My idea, sir, is that it will not be a report but a story. Fiction."

"You're saying you write the report you came to do, for your paper, and you write John's story like he's Rip Van Winkle or Natty Bumppo?"

"Exactly like that," Hulbert said excitedly. "Only with a few changes."

"Such as?"

"Such as him not killing people and stuffing apple cores in their corpses," Hulbert replied. "Such as . . ."

CHAPTER 1

July 1836 — San Antonio, Texas
It was another hot summer day in the oldest town in Oklahoma, the settlement that had grown up outside proud, mighty-timbered Fort Gibson.

The families that lived here were buzzing like bees as they moved through the wide streets, decorating the storefronts with bunting, cleaning drowned bugs from the troughs, and polishing windows so they shined in the sun.

At the red schoolhouse, children — save one, who was elsewhere — were gaily learning songs and dances under the stern but proud hand of their teacher, Miss Victoria, while at the stable, parade animals were being groomed and at the assayer's office portraits of Davy Crockett and Jim Bowie were being removed from storage, the canvas wraps carefully removed so as not to scuff the paintings. These would be hung from the walls outside the Alamo by the peaceful Comanche, who lived on the plains outside of town. Throughout the day the red men would beat on their drums — not loud enough to frighten the older residents that an attack was underway, for those days were now bygone; but firm enough to be heard in Heaven above by the spirits of the great men.

On the other end of town, in the plaza outside the church, a feast was being prepared with roast pork and lamb, the animals already turning on open fires while corn and carrots cooked in pans above the flames. Some of the corn was popping, causing the littlest children to shriek with glee while it set their dogs to barking.

Perhaps most important of all, however, was what was taking place at the cantina. Señora Lupita Villarías's famed roses grew in large ceramic pots outside the window but inside — inside was where magic was being crafted. In her large ovens, apple pies were baking and sending their fragrance out into the street. Men and women passing by were instantly made more cheerful just by inhaling the scent of those glorious desserts.

Outside of town, where an army once gathered to fight for the freedom of this village, of this republic, a young boy of seven, a straw hat on his head to protect it from the sun, stood watching the field that lead to rolling country in the north. His name was John-John — named twice in honor of the town's beloved former resident — and he could barely contain his heart within his chest, so great was his excitement at meeting his hero, at the honor he had been given to watch for his arrival.

When, finally, a man on his burro finally appeared over a nearby rise —

"Oh, gosh," John-John said gloomily. "It's only the padre."

Padre Álvarez smiled as he passed, blessing the boy for being so vigilant. John-John bowed out of respect, though he did not take his eyes from the hill.

John-John carried a pair of apples in the deep pockets of his trousers and he took one out now. He polished it on the cloth, revealing a fine, red glow, and bit down greedily. The juice was sweet and the meat sweeter. He went to take a second bite, but stopped and stared.

This time it was not Padre Álvarez. It was a tall, lean figure astride a great white stallion, its long mane moving gracefully in the wind. The rider sat upright, his face turning this way and that as he whistled. Atop his head was a straw hat like John-John's, but frayed at the edges from the elements, from the spray of rivers, from being used to collect seeds in the wild.

A hand went up from the man on the horse. He waved and the boy waved back, not quite believing that the greeting was for him.

"Sir! Sir! I have to go and tell the townspeople that you are here!" the young boy shouted.

"Nonsense!" the mounted figure shouted back. "Come, ride noble James behind me, and we shall tell them together!"

"But sir — Mayor Gearhart and will want to be there to greet you!"

"No need for such formalities!" the man said. "We will greet all the people at once!"

Almost beyond his ability to contain himself, John-John ran ahead, to the hand that was stretched down to meet his, to the long arm that pulled him into the golden saddle from which hung sacks of apple seeds — canvas bag upon canvas bag that John-John believed could hold a dozen children on top.

The boy turned his face upward, to the face that was in shadow as the sun was behind it — yet John-John could still make out the blue eyes and gracious smile of the man to whom they belonged.

The great man who planted the first apple trees in San Antonio . . . in Beaumont . . . in Gonzales . . . planted them with seeds he had nurtured in the blessed grove of Coles Settlement, where he briefly lived after the war for independence.

The wondrous man who went from Texas to the North and to the South, from Vermont to Florida, planting apple trees so the nation should be fruitful.

The hardworking man who slept but an hour or two a night because he needed not rest but was nourished by the sun and by the apples he ate.

The glorious man known as Johnny Appleseed.

ABOUT THE AUTHOR

Lancaster Hill is the pseudonym of *New York Times* bestselling author Jeff Rovin. Rovin has worked as an assistant editor for DC Comics and as the editor in chief of the *Weekly World News.* He has also authored multiple titles in the Tom Clancy: Op-Center series. This is his first western novel.

The employees of Thorndike Press hope you have enjoyed this Large Print book. All our Thorndike, Wheeler, and Kennebec Large Print titles are designed for easy reading, and all our books are made to last. Other Thorndike Press Large Print books are available at your library, through selected bookstores, or directly from us.

For information about titles, please call:
(800) 223-1244

or visit our website at:
gale.com/thorndike

To share your comments, please write:
Publisher
Thorndike Press
10 Water St., Suite 310
Waterville, ME 04901